Dew on Ginkgo Leaves

The Tigress and The General

A NOVEL BY

Todd L. Shuler

Tora Press
Macon, Georgia

Todd L. Shuler
Tora Press
A division of TSO, Inc.
3780 Northside Drive #140, Suite 456
Macon, Georgia 31210
www.toddshuler.com

Publisher's Note: This is a work of fiction. Names, characters, places, and incidents are a product of the author's imagination. Locales and public names are sometimes used for atmospheric purposes. Any resemblance to actual people, living or dead, or to businesses, companies, events, institutions, or locales is completely coincidental.

Ordering Information:

Quantity sales. Special discounts are available on "quantity purchases by corporations, associations, and others. For details, contact the "Special Sales Department" at the address above.

Dew on Ginkgo Leaves: The Tigress and The General / Todd L. Shuler – 1st ed.

ISBN 978-0-9889589-8-2

BY TODD SHULER

The Emperor's Last Arrow (Book 2 of the Dew on Ginkgo Leaves Series) – Coming Summer 2018

Dew on Ginkgo Leaves: The Tigress and The General

The Tiger Tamer

The Well-Watered Life

One Month of The Well-Watered Life Devotional

For previews of upcoming books and more information about Todd Shuler, please visit his website at www.toddshuler.com or find him on Facebook, Twitter or Instagram.

PRAISE FOR DEW ON GINKGO LEAVES: THE TIGRESS AND THE GENERAL

"A ravishing work of historical fiction about devotion and revenge amid the 'bloodstained dust' of war." - **Kirkus Reviews**

"Meet Jade Flower. She's the Tigress—a warrior in the service of the Emperor of China. Meet Yu Luan. He's the General—also an imperial warrior. The Tigress and the General find themselves in a high stakes battle with the Golden Ginkgo Society—a shadowy and mystical organization bent on overthrowing the Empire. Their adventures take them on a wild ride of romance, intrigue and betrayal as they try to save the empire while learning how to be on the same side in a fight ... and in love. A whirlwind page turner!!! "
– **Maya Kaathryn Bohnhoff**, New York Times Bestselling author of *THE MERI* and NYT Bestselling Co-Author of *Star Wars: The Last Jedi*

"An epic ride! A wonderfully, visually, luscious descriptive story...beautifully captures that Eastern sense of heroism and duty... with all the action, politics and intrigue, there's plenty there to satisfy all readers." – **Cate Hogan**, *Romance Writer and Editor*

"A fast-paced, mesmerizing and action packed story!!! It's hard to read *Dew on Ginkgo Leaves: The Tigress and The General* without thinking about the famous Chinese actors like Jet Li or Jackie Chan; and yes, this novel could be great on screen!" – **Christian Sia**, *Readers' Favorite*

"Full of courage, quiet strength and charming romance." – **Kenya Cassell**, *Deloitte*

Acknowledgments

My heartfelt gratitude to the following people:
Mr. and Mrs. Allen J. Shuler, Sr. (my parents)
Kenya Cassell
Lamar Harvey
Artis Johnston
Mary Myles
Michelle Rumph
June Saunders
Charlene Latrell Taylor
Remeka Turk

DEDICATION

To my wife Evetta:
Without you,
this book, as true of so many other wonderful things in my life,
would simply not exist.
Love, Todd

TABLE OF CONTENTS

PROLOGUE

Plumes of thick, bloodstained dust rose like clouds amidst the dull thunder of hooves. The war horses' muscles roped on their haunches; their eyes rolled with fear at the smell of blood all around them, and the air was pierced by the clang of iron and steel and the cries of men. Blades rang, and pointed projectiles found human hearts.

Jade Flower and her husband, Wu Lei, fought side by side. Out of the corner of her eye, the warrior wife saw her husband's blade disappear into the body of an enemy and emerge, bloodstained and triumphant. She saw his grin—Wu Lei was never one to hide his emotions—and grinned with him. Their mutual love of country was fierce—each plunge of the blade into an enemy brought them a keen satisfaction that made them grind their teeth. Each blow was a support that strengthened the throne of the Emperor. Their eyes flashed at one another in mutual exultation.

They fought the personal army of a rebellious official who had been defying Beijing and had set himself up as a warlord. Although the number of men in the army was greater than that of their elite corps of husband and wife warriors, the army was no match for the training and expertise of couples like Jade Flower and Wu Lei.

In a mock dance, Jade Flower took on her next opponent—a burly, armored man—and skillfully poked each seam and opening in his coverings, probing weak and uncovered spots unerringly, then penetrating just deeply enough to bring exquisite pain, all the while distracting him from being able to land his blows. She was quick—quick as the sharp claws of a cat—and she knew Wu Lei watched her appreciatively out of the corner of his eye as he deftly cut the throat of an enemy he had driven down to his knees. Jade Flower shrugged as if to say, "Not bad!" and then she gouged her own opponent more fiercely, maddening him and making him charge her. She danced daintily aside, letting the man's own weight carry him behind her into Wu Lei's path. The thug tripped and fell. Jade Flower gave her husband an insouciant shrug and he plunged his sword into the middle of the man's back.

"Thank you, beloved," she said.

"My pleasure, sweet."

Around them the battle raged on, surging and changing each moment, now bringing her face to face with a new enemy. Jade Flower noticed that her husband had moved a bit further out in the field. No matter. They always found each other. Their special battle cry was their homing call.

The frontline of the battle kept changing—sometimes it was behind her, sometimes to the side, and Jade Flower whirled and whirled, using centrifugal force to make her singing blade more deadly. After a time, she noticed the dust slowly settling, the noise dying down, and the field clearing. The enemy was on the run. She was ready for hot pursuit, her teeth gritting on the dust, enjoying the prospect of cutting her blood-lusting blade across retreating calves and slicing off heads from behind. The signal to stand down sounded from a horn far away in the dimness to her left, and Jade Flower reluctantly lowered her blade and watched as the enemies fled. She was hungry for more of their blood.

As in victorious skirmishes gone by, she roared out her battle cry to signal to her husband Wu Lei that she had vanquished her final combatant. Her cry was that of the tigress. It echoed alarmingly across the battlefield—a combined growl, snarl, and roar. It was so realistic, she had seen men on the battlefield glance feverishly about, as if in fear that a tigress was loose among them.

No leonine battle roar answered her own.

She roared again, using her lungs like a bellows to pump out more sound to carry over more distance. There were men everywhere— where was her husband? They always fought close to one another. How had he gotten separated from her?

In the silence that followed, she heard other members of their elite unit calling to their partners—husbands and wives assuring each other that Death had not claimed them. Eagles cried; hawks shrilled; wolves bayed, but the lion was silent. Jade Flower almost dropped her sword.

Horror and desperation rushed over her. Was he wounded, too weak to make a sound? Jade Flower ran in the direction she had seen him last before they became separated in battle, calling out to her surviving cohorts, begging to know if they had seen him. No one had.

Where is he? Her heart fluttered and raced, as if the battle were beginning rather than ending, pumping with the adrenaline of fear. As she searched through the vast wasteland of dead and maimed bodies, she reflected that only a liar said he or she had no fear going into battle—courage was the conquering of fear, not the absence of it.

Her fear receded when she saw him lying on the ground a short distance away. He was alive, just wounded.

"Wu Lei!" she said in relief, kneeling next to him and pulling his head and shoulders into her lap. He was barely conscious and extremely pale, as if he were succumbing to a wound—a wound that was not even bleeding. She could see no blood anywhere on her husband.

"Fight!" she told him, almost angry with him. "Fight! Don't leave me! Why are you leaving me?"

She raised her eyes to the heavens, silently pleading, but the skies did not answer.

Blood gurgled from his lips as he struggled awake and said, "Tell—me—you—love—me—one—more—time—"

"I do love you, now and for all eternity!" Jade Flower nestled him closer to her bosom and rocked back and forth. "Please, don't go. There is no need to go."

He must have sustained a mortal wound—one she could not see—but she feared to search for it lest she kill him faster in the process.

He flashed a smile as he reached upward to stroke a lock of hair from her brow. His hand fell back to his side.

"Please … don't leave me," she begged.

His eyes rolled back, staring into nothingness.

Jade Flower pleaded, "Dear God, not like this…"

He exhaled once more and died.

Time stopped. She held him in her arms while she wept over him, her eyes and nose running, her words flowing out with their rivers, awash with love and pain. It seemed she had been sitting there for eternity; her leg, underneath Wu Lei, was asleep, but she did not want to move it out from under him. She did not mind the pain; her leg absorbed the last warmth Wu Lei's body would ever give her. Dimly, she heard people moving around her; some of them called to her and then fell silent, seeing what she held in her lap. One or two curious faces came near; she snarled at them, and the rest stayed back out of respect.

Flashes of their past together went off in her mind like fireworks: The first day they met and how she had admired his fine brown eyes, how she was promised to him by her male relatives, the training they underwent to fight side by side, the unexpected joy and passion of their wedding night, how they had sparred in training and how he had spared her hurt until she told him not to, as no enemy would spare her. The countless missions they had carried out, their lives in one's another's trust, the great victories they had brought to the Son of Heaven and his Empress, and how many times they had thought death was theirs and had faced it hand in hand, side by side. Their dreams of retiring from the battlefield while they were still young to start a family of their own, a farm out in the countryside where at last they could know peace…

All broken. Shattered dreams.

"Had I not allowed myself to be separated from you during battle, I would have shielded you with my own body, my beloved," she cooed to her pale, dead husband. "I will shortly join you in eternity, Wu Lei."

Clinging tightly to him, while trying to see through blinding tears, Jade Flower shifted her weight and his and reached for her husband's sword. She was determined to cut her own throat with its razor-sharp edge.

It was then she noticed something out of the corner of her eye: a crimson ribbon unfurled from underneath her husband's left shoulder blade. She gently tugged at the ribbon and dislodged a metal-ringed, bloodstained, silver dart that was bound to it. Wu Lei's wound wept blood and water, and now she knew the source of his death.

Holding up the dart and examining its markings closely, Jade Flower quickly concluded that her husband wasn't felled by an enemy's glancing blow but by this assassin's dart. Although the silver dart had penetrated Wu Lei's skin and had resisted being plucked out, it was clear it had not punctured any vital organ. It must have been poisoned.

The dart slipped from her suddenly numb hands. While some enemies might use poisoned darts or flaming arrows, it was not usual at all. What was more, she could tell by its markings that this silver sliver of death was a Serpent Shadow dart, forged long ago by blacksmiths in their own empire. No rebellious local army, such as they had been fighting, could have possessed it. All known ones were museum pieces, accessible only to the loftiest of the nobility or the most ancient and trusted of scholars and curators. A traitor had felled her husband, a traitor with remarkable access to the archives of the empire—someone who was trusted with the keys to the deepest, most secret chambers of the ancestral palaces, where these ancient darts were housed.

One of our own nobles betrayed us. The thought was devastating. It had to be someone very high up. But who—who could have done such a thing? And why? *Why to my Wu Lei?*

She collapsed over his body, sobbing uncontrollably.

CHAPTER 1

When they tried to raise her to her feet, she was filled with white-hot rage. "No! No!" she protested, as her comrades pulled her up by the arms from Wu Lei's body. She was ready to take vengeance on any and all of them. She would kill all of them, then herself, in a bloodbath of sorrow and despair.

Her husband's murderer was not fleeing for the wooded foothills among the enemy tribe—he or she was here, somewhere, posing as a comrade. Since it had to be a member of the nobility, the murderer might even be a commander of some sort. Whoever it was, the person was diabolically clever, it seemed, and a master of dissembling and disguise. She had to calm herself so as not to show her knowledge of the true state of affairs.

All desire to end her own life was swallowed in a dark, heated, all-consuming desire for revenge.

I can't take my own life without first bringing my husband's killer to justice, she reasoned with herself. *Wu Lei would never forgive me if I did that! And with a traitor amongst us so highly placed, I owe it to the empire to live and to discover him. Wu Lei died fighting for the empire. He would never forgive me if I didn't save the empire from this person — if I didn't discover and expose him. He wouldn't forgive me, nor would the gods — in this life or the next.*

Jade Flower surreptitiously slipped the bloodied dart into her belt as her fellow warriors debated how to transport Wu Lei's body.

"I will take care of it," she told them coolly.

She surveyed the corpse-littered battlefield. She sighted Young Eight Eyes, not far off and called to him to come with the closest horse he could find so they could hoist her husband's corpse onto it and quickly get off the battlefield and back to their unit's base camp.

Jade Flower looked around uneasily as she waited for Young Eight Eyes and the horse, trusting no one. Although the battle was over, it wasn't safe to be here. There was a murderer about. This killer was clever enough to do his or her dark deed in the midst of a battlefield so riddled with wounded and dead bodies that no one but a loving wife would cradle a corpse so intimately as to discover he had been assassinated, not felled in battle.

Young Eight Eyes, so nicknamed because his eyes darted in every direction with constant wariness, was the right person to be with her right now. She felt safe with him on the lookout, and she knew he was trustworthy. When he came with a war horse in tow, she helped her comrades-in-arms drape her husband's body over the horse's back. Her heart wrenched within her at the sight of her young husband's long black hair hanging down toward the ground. Grief clogged her throat when the movements of the horse, set in motion by a gentle slap on the flanks by Young Eight Eyes, caused Wu Lei's head to bob up and down in an almost life-like way. She walked by his side solemnly, matching the rhythm of her steps to the sad nodding of Wu Lei's head and the helpless dangling of his arms.

It took a long time to get to their woodland camp; she and Young Eight Eyes walked as if in a funeral procession. When she entered camp, solemnly leading the horse with her husband's body slung atop, the warriors who were not having wounds tended encircled her and mourned aloud the loss of her husband. She thanked them, tried not to seem suspicious of anyone, and brought her husband's body to an attendant's tent, where she dismissed everyone and washed and dressed his body herself. He would be transported to his hometown for burial. He looked untouched and beautiful to her; his face at peace, and no wound but the small pinprick of the silver dart. After washing him as much with her tears as with water, Jade Flower emerged from the tent for the dead, clutching his battle sash to her breast. Refusing all offers of food, she went into the tent that, until that day, she had shared with Wu Lei.

Other warrior wives offered to remain with her, but pain and anger were her handmaidens as she undressed to rest. Although their bed was a heap of furs, warm and soft, and she wore a comfortable sleep shift that moved with her when she was restless, Jade Flower could not fall sleep. Her mind was alive with the desire for vengeance. She rose and picked up her husband's sash. In it, she had wrapped the evil dart. Now, she unwrapped it slowly and carefully and poured water from her drinking gourd over it to get rid of any residual poison. She coated the sharp tip with wax from a burning candle, then ripped a long, thin swath of cloth from her husband's battle sash and looped it through the metal ring at end of the dart. She tied this around her neck and let the dart dangle coldly between her breasts.

She would never forget this. She would find out who did this and plunge this same dart into his or her life's vein. It would be coated with a special, slow-acting poison she knew how to make. She smiled a little at the thought of watching her husband's killer die in agony. The desire for vengeance filled her heart like a dark flood, blotting out her grief.

Jade Flower lay in her tent, gazing at its ceiling, twisting and turning as adrenaline coursed through her. The desire for revenge was like an opiate over the chasm of pain at her loss—a chasm so deep she could see no path up its steep walls. Her eyes were dry. Her heart raced. Sleep was impossible.

She understood, now, the wisdom of the ancient saying: "Vengeance does not sleep." The raw darkness of her mind would not allow her to slumber. There was no point in even trying.

There was a village just down the foothills from their camp. They had stopped there to buy food on the way up to their woodland lair. Wu Lei had bought her a silly toy—a child's drum rattle. It was cunningly made, and he had joked that she should keep it for their future child.

There had been a tea house in the village. As she recalled, it was the kind of establishment that served tea and food by day and wine and women by night. There were hand-painted portraits of pretty women on silk banners hanging along the back walls. These were not just for decoration, Wu Lei had told her. Patrons pointed to a silk portrait and were led to a room where the real woman (probably older, more heavily painted, and much less attractive than the silk portrait, Wu Lei had speculated) waited in a bed. It was a place of complete debauchery, and Jade Flower had been shocked by the very thought of it, only this afternoon. Now, since Wu Lei's death, a new hardness and cynicism took her over. Such a place would have plenty of wine, she reasoned, and that was what she was after. Rice wine would dull her mind and bandage the raw wound of her pain. She would buy a bottle and bring it back to her tent in camp, drink it all, and maybe then she would be able to sleep.

Jade Flower knew how to pad as softly as a cat hunting prey. She was an expert at the sudden strike, seeming to come out of nowhere. Now, she used her feline ability to move in total silence to steal out of the camp without the sentries noticing.

Once she was out of earshot, she straightened up, squared her shoulders, and took deep breaths as she walked under the night stars. The cool night served to numb some of her pain, and she was grateful for that. She wished it was freezing out so she could throw herself into a snowdrift and go out on a white cloud to oblivion. She had heard that freezing to death became pleasant after a time — that all a person wanted to do was to drift off to sleep. Yet it was not that cold; there was no snow. She would have to numb herself the way she had chosen; the way of rice wine.

It was a challenge to make her way down the dark hillside, but she dared not strike a light. She was sure-footed; her feet were like one of the dancers of the imperial court, so skilled was she in the grace of the martial arts. It took her twenty minutes, but she made it to the village.

From its main street, she turned to look back at the wooded foothills. Her unit's camp, like the camps of their comrades, was completely invisible. The land under the moonlight appeared to be deep in undisturbed slumber. She smiled, and for a moment she felt very proud of the elite corps of husband and wife warriors she belonged to, specially commissioned by the Empress. There were several divisions of them, and even the most discerning eye would not be able to tell they were encamped all over the foothills outside Beijing this night.

She saw the tea house ahead, with a few lights still on. The noise from the building was muted. The patrons had that much regard for the village the tea house was situated in—or that much regard for their own reputations.

Jade Flower was dressed in simple, black, fitted trousers topped by a tunic. Spare and boyish, it made fighting much easier. With a hood pulled over her hair and held close to her face, she knew she could be mistaken for a slender young man. Still, she carried weapons—a small dagger tucked into her sash, and a sword no longer than her forearm concealed in a thin scabbard along her thigh beneath her trousers. She did not expect to have to use them. Still, she checked that it was reachable through the bottomless pocket before she pushed open the door from the cold, dark street and walked into the light and warmth of the tea house.

CHAPTER 2

Jade Flower found a small, uneven table in a dim corner and eased herself onto the rickety wooden stool. Her whole body was sore from the day's exertions; her heart and soul were battered by loss. As soon as she sat down, she realized how exhausted she was, and she had a fleeting fear she would not be able to make it back to camp. Why hadn't she felt this tired as she lay on her furred robes in her warm tent? Maybe sleep would have claimed her after all, had she simply waited.

An indifferent server came to her table and asked her what she wanted.

"Rice wine. The best you have. A bottle, not a glass," she said gruffly.

He shrugged and moved off. She listened to the click of bone dice and the thunk of glasses being put down on the wooden tables. A smiling, sly-looking woman passed among the tables, pointing to the fluttering silk portraits of women. She was arranging trysts. Jade Flower felt a wave of revulsion curl in her stomach. Most of these were married men, she surmised from their ages. Why were they so disloyal to their wives? Wu Lei had never been disloyal to her.

Jade Flower watched the smiling procuress make her way through the tables urging men to buy women. *It's all right,* her gestures seemed to say, *this is simply a business transaction to fulfill your desires. No different from paying for rice wine or food.* The tea house was, after all, a respectable business establishment, was it not?

The server placed a bottle of rice wine and a cup on the table. Jade Flower hardly noticed him. As she focused upon the female merchant of flesh, she began to grow resentful. What did such a woman know of the passionate attachment that could grow between man and wife, in which one's every cell vibrated with the life of the other, in which it was painful to part even for a moment?

Jade Flower felt a tear cascade down her face. *Wu Lei!*

No, this she could not allow. Tears were weakness. She uncorked the bottle of rice wine on the table and drank from it a great draught.

The room buzzed and swayed, lamp seemed flicker, and the sly, silken lady seemed to be standing at an angle. Jade Flower never drank, and the wine hit her hard. Yet the pain inside receded as the liquor clouded her mind. Good. She took another swig.

In her alcohol-soaked daze, she soon decided that these men were not such bad fellows after all. They were probably just lonely and hurting — like her. As the rice wine dwindled in the bottle, she felt a sense of benevolence toward all around her, and when she found one man staring at her openly, she smiled at him. She drank the rice wine to the dregs, then ordered another bottle to take with her.

Her benevolence toward her fellow man increased, and soon she found herself throwing dice with the men at the next table, making bets and laughing until her sides hurt. The man who had stared at her before insinuated himself into the group around her. Perhaps he was lonely, too.

Many of the men jested with her, saying such things as, "This one is so young, he hasn't even got a beard! What a lovely youth!" When Jade Flower heard such comments, she drew her face more closely into her hood and tried to stand nonchalantly, like a young man, rather than modestly, like a woman.

Someone was banging a drum and playing a wooden flute, and she clapped her hands and stamped her feet in time, trying to stomp the pain out of her mind and heart. She whirled and danced. The sly, silken lady kept working, working the tables, and men disappeared every few minutes, climbing the creaking stairs to the upper loft where the women were.

As the hour grew later, Jade Flower realized she should leave. She had to get back to the camp before there was even a whisper of dawn in the sky, or she would be spotted by the sharp-eyed sentries. The tables were emptying, and her head ached. She said goodbye to all her new friends, shushed all their protests at her leaving, and tucked a bottle of rice wine into her sash. Then she went out into the cool, fresh air.

Dizzy, she swayed on her feet, trying to orient herself by looking at the moon. She was pretty sure her camp was in that direction — or was it? This village was surrounded by wooded foothills! In which direction was her camp? She was blinking up at the sky, trying to discern the shape of the woodland she had left, when she felt a man's arms come around her from behind, squeezing her in a wine-reeking embrace.

"Hello," he said in a too-smooth, suggestive voice.

Jade Flower was drunk or her elbow would have finished him with a sharp jab to the solar plexus. As it was, her gesture only melted into his chest and its momentum managed to turn her around to face him.

"I have been watching you," he said. "You are no man. And if you are, you are going to have to prove it."

She was too hazy to do an appropriate foot stomp, knee to the scrotum, or even to twist properly to break his arms' grip on her. He lifted her off her feet, still embracing her, and carried her into an alley.

"Nooo!" she howled, kicking her feet uselessly. Her feet seemed very far away from her, and she could not get them to connect with either her brain or the man's shins. "No, I don't want this!"

She could feel his shrug. "That is what all the maidens say. They are pleased afterward."

"I am a married woman, and my husband is a warrior. He will wreak vengeance on you—"

"I see no husband here. Where is he?"

He is dead, Jade Flower thought, her breath catching in her throat.

The thug walked her into a wall, banging her head against it. Jade Flower began to slip downward, and he was right with her, bending over her. She both heard and felt the hem of her tunic being rent. His weight was upon her, his liquor-soaked breath heavy in her face, as he worked to undress himself. All her strength seemed to be gone; she could not coordinate her moves. She was of the Tiger school of self-defense; yet instead of a tigress, alcohol had made her into an almost helpless pussycat, caught in the jaws of a common dog.

Her mind screamed. *No! No! Wu Lei! Wu Lei!* She could not let this cur penetrate her.

Through the clouds of darkness in her mind came a stream of light, cold as moonlight. Her training was drummed into every fiber of her consciousness and into every muscle of her body. It permeated her, and it was designed to withstand and overcome pain, to think clearly in spite of near unconsciousness, and to battle the despair of defeat. The cold light of discipline broke through her cloud of vagueness and weakness. Her muscles answered to her brain's suddenly sharp commands. She remembered the dagger she had in the sash at her waist. She became crafty.

"Oh!" she said, as if she were experiencing pleasant anticipation at his fumblings with her clothing.

She felt him relax his forceful grip on her, and he kissed her as she fought her revulsion.

"That is more like it," he said.

Since he had relaxed a little, she was able to shift around more under him and her fingers wrapped around the haft of her dagger.

"Take your tunic off," he ordered her. She wriggled as if to free her sash and raise her tunic, smiling at him all the while and making breathy noises as she subtly positioned the dagger. She loosed the sash and used it to hide the dagger, the began to slowly raise her tunic with one hand, titillating him.

Before her breasts would have been revealed, she paused and said, "Kiss me again before we begin." He leaned his weight on her, drawing his face close to hers; she drove the dagger into his belly. She grunted as she heard the sound of blade meeting and tearing through flesh and muscle, and she viciously twisted the blade again and again, enjoying his gasps of agony as his warm blood flooded over her.

He screamed; he called her terrible names; he hauled himself upward, and staggered about, grasping the dagger with both hands to pull it out of his belly. Quick as a cat, she was on her feet. She unsheathed the sword whose cold steel ran the length of her thigh beneath her leggings, and held it aloft with both hands. As the man struggled with the dagger in his belly, she stepped behind him and plunged her sword into his back, just below the neck, and watched as more blood spurted forth.

All her pain, fear, and anger rode the point of the sword as she plunged it again and again and again into the now helpless man. The last time she plunged it in, she pulled it out so forcefully that it spun out of her hands. She heard it clatter somewhere farther down the alley and marked the spot where she thought it had fallen. She would find it later. Now, she rolled the man over onto his back, pulled her dagger out of the cavern of his rib cage, and wiped it on his jacket. Her clothes might be soaked with this man's blood, but her dagger was clean and shining in the moonlight, and she was still a faithful wife.

By now, people were pouring out of the tea house, having heard the shrieks of the dying man. She heard the bought women upstairs screaming and crying out too, and saw them looking out their windows.

Turning her face from the moonlight and the lights of the tea house, she slipped into the shadows and retreated down the alley to retrieve her sword and make her get-away. Her hand came up empty when she touched the place she was sure her sword had fallen. Her mind was clearing now, and she knew where it should have been; her senses—as deft as a bat's echolocation—had never failed her. That it had now was mysterious, but there was only emptiness where the sword should be and there was no time to search for it.

Jade Flower secured her bloodied sash around her waist, tucked her dagger into it and melted into the dark streets of the village.

CHAPTER 3

By the time Jade Flower had made her way safely up the foothills to their woodland camp, eluded the sentries, and had stolen back into her tent, her whole body was trembling. She was horror-stricken at herself. She had never killed anyone for personal rather than patriotic reasons and certainly not with the unreasoning frenzy she had felt when she had plunged her sword into the rapist again and again.

Maybe this is practice for when I meet my husband's killer, she thought grimly. *I don't care who he is or where I encounter him, I will kill him, and for personal reasons.*

Yet she could not console herself. Now she was a widow and a murderer, all made so in the same gruesome and awful day. Covered in blood and soaked with rice wine, she threw herself down on the furs in her tent.

Somehow in her dreams the would-be rapist became the same person as her husband's murderer, and she felt comforted by having taken vengeance. When the painful consciousness rose up in her dreams that it was not the same person, and that her husband's killer remained undetected and her husband unavenged, and that she was now a murderer of a civilian, she told herself she would face those thoughts on the morrow; she would sort it all out after some much-needed sleep.

Somehow she awakened in the morning, and no one commented or wondered at her grim face and utter lack of appetite. No one even wondered why she kept vomiting. Jade Flower and Wu Lei's devotion to one another was well known among their comrades, and no one was surprised to see her sick with mourning.

She made the journey to her husband's hometown in a blue haze of pain. Her husband's body was drawn in a wagon, and she forced herself to stop looking behind her to see its solemn aspect. She was exhausted in every way, and the day was fittingly dim and clouded.

The funeral itself was like a bad dream. Jade Flower walked behind the ornate coffin as it was borne by pallbearers. She felt as if her heart was inside the coffin with her beloved. A procession of mourners, wailing and beating drums, walked behind her.

It was a lacquered coffin, covered in bright-red, embroidered silk. Jade Flower was considering doing what she had heard other loving and virtuous wives had done upon their husbands' deaths: swallow opium and kill herself then and there.

In front of her husband's tomb—the tomb filled with his ancestors—she saw some of Wu Lei's relatives. Wu Lei's nephew played the traditional part, since they had no son to do it. He waved a flag and called forth the spirit of the dead man. Then, as the coffin was brought forward by other relatives, Wu Lei's nephew knelt next to it, all according to custom, and cried out to Wu Lei's body in the coffin, "Avoid the nails!" as the coffin was set down and attendants hammered the lid down.

Jade Flower winced with every blow, as if each one was a nail in her mind and heart. Then the coffin was put inside the tomb, and the funeral was over.

The mourners, many of them nobles of the empire whom Jade Flower recognized, turned away to disperse. She felt her teeth grind with suspicion. Which one of them had murdered her husband—which one wore a false mask of grief over the man in the coffin, whom he or she had murdered?

Wu Lei had been buried within view of a mountain (it was believed this would give the dead person something to lean on for strength.) His coffin faced the rising sun to signify rising fortune. A pearl was placed in his mouth, also for good fortune, and all the customs for a man of his stature had been observed.

Hollow as Jade Flower felt, and filled with mourning as she was, she understood that the awful customs were meant to comfort and provide closure. There was some of that, she had to admit. It had all happened so quickly. She was deeply wounded, but these rituals were some faint salve upon her inner cuts. It was comforting to know where her husband was, among his ancestors, with a solid place on earth she could always recall. Yet her loneliness consumed her, even among the crowd of people who came up one by one to console her and to murmur words of praise for her husband.

In the distance she saw the royal palanquin moving away. Even the Emperor and Empress had attended. That was some comfort too, she supposed, and ragged sobs shook her as this balm settled in her heart, over her wounds. Then, seeing her father-in-law approaching her, his body bent over with age and sorrow, she tried to control her tears.

She bowed to him from her waist, and he reached out with wizened hands to clasp both sides of her face.

"Yawen," he said over his shoulder to his wife, Wu Lei's mother, whose face was wet with tears. "Bring the gift forward."

Yawen carried an ornate box of gold filigree—a jewelry box. The gold filigree was studded here and there with precious gems.

"Our son wanted you to have this upon his death," Yawen said.

"Upon his death?"

Jade Flower's mind worked rapidly. Wu Lei's parents were quite aged; why had he entrusted them with this box to give to his young wife? It was almost as if he had known he was going to die early.

Of course, thought Jade Flower, they were warriors; their lives were dangerous. They might be killed at any time.

Yet …

She bowed again to her in-laws and stayed low as they touched her hair and shoulders sympathetically. They pressed a money purse into her hands. It was weighted with gold coins. Then they drew away, a portrait of two old people united and bent in their sorrow. At the same time, a certain patriotic pride seemed to surround them. Their son had died a warrior of the empire.

Jade Flower opened the box to see if there was a message inside. There was nothing. The box was lined with red, new-looking silk, but the box itself was antique—the kind that was archived, like the silver dart that had caused Wu Lei's death. It was a museum piece. How had her husband procured it? What did this gift mean?

There was a slight opening in the red silk lining, and she poked a finger into it. Something dry touched the tip of her digit, and she drew it out, hearing it crackle and tear as she pulled it through the opening in the lining.

It was a dried, golden ginkgo leaf. She could almost feel Wu Lei's touch upon it. He must have placed it there. But why? What did it mean? What message was he sending? Had he known he was going to die? Did this leaf have something to do with who had killed him?

Jade Flower's head began to ache with puzzlement and sorrow. She was distracted when a royal courier came into her field of vision and gestured to get her attention.

"You are ordered to appear before the Emperor and Empress," he told her. "They will send attendants to prepare you and a palanquin to transport you."

"Prepare me for what?" she asked with an uncharacteristic edge of suspicion in her voice. She trusted no one these days.

The courier dismissed her question. "I am not privy to that information. I am a mere messenger. The Empress also told me to tell you to be in good looks and, as much as possible, good spirits."

The last thing she wanted to do was to appear at court in good looks and good spirits, when her heart had just been buried. She clung to the gold filigreed box as if it were a lifeline to her husband. Yet she had been expecting to be summoned to Beijing. There would be condolences, tributes paid to her husband, and probably reassignment in the field.

"When am I to report?" she asked mournfully. She was utterly exhausted and wanted nothing more than to rest for a few days before doing anything.

"Tomorrow."

Jade Flower frowned, shocked. What could their majesties possibly want that was so important they would summon her the day after her husband's funeral? She had never heard of such a thing. Yet an imperial summons could not be ignored. She would have to go to Beijing on the morrow.

It occurred to her that the imperial palace might be a good place to begin nosing around for clues to the identity of her husband's murderer. With its endless parade of nobles and its snarls of gossip, intrigues, and power plays, Beijing was the perfect place for a highly placed assassin to hide. Hungrily, she thought of the palace's archives and museums and wondered if any of them contained the ancient silver Serpent Shadow darts, the store from which her husband's murder weapon had come.

CHAPTER 4

T he curtains of Jade Flower's palanquin were drawn, for the winds sweeping Beijing carried a fine grit. Jade Flower was used to wind and dirt in her hair and face from her outdoor life, but her hair had been specially dressed for the occasion and she was wearing finery she was not accustomed to for her meeting with the Emperor, the Son of Heaven, and his wife, the Empress.

The thoughtful Empress Xinyi had sent a legion of handmaids to help bathe, dress, and fit her into the green silk brocade gown she had also sent to her. Xinyi had sent several hairdressers — eunuchs, whom the men of Jade Flower's warrior band had sniffed at critically — to tame her hair, which was usually smashed into unsightly submission by her leather helmet. After a great deal of brushing, combing, oiling, and muttering under their breaths about wild Mongolian horses having nicer manes, the eunuchs had fashioned her locks into something resembling a court style. The dark tresses were spread out over a board and festooned with flowers of jade.

One of the eunuchs addressed her. "You actually have fine and lovely hair, once it is brushed and oiled. And beneath all that dirt, you have quite a pretty face."

"And a good form," said another eunuch who carried in the dress, though he appeared completely unmoved by her "good form." "The handmaidens will alter this to fit you perfectly. It looks like the Empress guessed correctly what color would go best with your complexion."

"I have met the Empress before," Jade Flower said curtly. "And the Emperor. Many times."

Jade Flower was uncomfortable going to the palace in the Forbidden City of Beijing. Of course, she was uncomfortable in the elaborate court clothes and hairstyle, but she did understand the reason for them. The identities of the warrior elite husbands and wives were not known, except as various nobles of the Empire who sometimes were summoned to the Dragon Throne. She could not appear in Beijing in warrior garb.

Yet far more uncomfortable than the clothing and the manners she would have to adopt was the fact that court was known to be rife with conspiracy and suspicion as its thousands of eunuchs, handmaidens, concubines, wives, and attendants all vied for power and influence with the Emperor. There were rumors of poisonings and murders, compelled suicides, and sexual liaisons that led to political intrigues. Jade Flower hated all that, but she reasoned it might be a hotbed of potential information about her husband's assassination.

In her heart she preferred the arena of battle, where status was determined by bravery, skill, and merit. In her world, the one with the best strategy, the best command over the hearts of others through valor, justice, self-sacrifice, and honesty rose to power. The respected ones were those with the most strength or accuracy with an arrow or sword, the ones most schooled in the techniques of ancient kung fu and its precepts for internal discipline. Things were fair and good on the battlefield. In the palace she knew she would be entering a world where the appropriate manner of behavior seemed foreign to her.

She had met her husband in an army camp on its windswept plains. She had joined the army in disguise as a man to keep her delicate younger brother from being conscripted. Every family was required to give up a male to the army. Her father was dead; he could not go. She knew her young brother, sixteen years of age, would not be passed over by the impressment agents, but she also knew he would not survive the army. He was a frail boy who loved poetry and birds; farm work exhausted him. More than that, he had a bleeding disease. The slightest rending of his skin would cause him to bleed for hours before it stopped. He had nearly bled to death on several occasions, when a simple cut that another boy might cover in dirt and forget about, bled profusely. If he were nicked by a spur or a sword while in the army, let alone severely wounded, it would be a death sentence. Only their mother's herbal compresses and prayers had saved him time after time, and Jade Flower did not think the soldiers would be so careful of him.

So Jade Flower, physically strong and resilient, strapped down her bosom, hacked off her hair, smeared her face with dirt, and dressed in her brother's clothes the day the impressment soldiers came. Thus she had joined the army—and found freedom.

Jade Flower managed to go almost a year without being discovered, and when she was, she was immediately sent to the Emperor and Empress for punishment, which she feared was death. However, Jade Flower's life was spared because the Emperor, at the Empress's urging, had decided that an elite corps of husband and wife warriors would be trained in swordplay, horsemanship, and kung fu.

Empress Xinyi had reasoned that these marital teams would display the kind of oneness of purpose that was needed to defeat the dynasty's enemies, both internal and external. They would defend one another on the battlefield, and support one another in planned assassinations and the dissolution of plotted coups against the Dragon Throne. Jade Flower, with her military prowess, appeared to be an excellent candidate for this corps. She was matched in marriage to Wu Lei, an excellent swordsman, and they became one of the Empress's warrior couples.

Gratitude had thumped in her bosom to be given a new life instead of death. She was ready to give her life for the Emperor and Empress because of it. What was more, they had matched her with a man who suited her perfectly.

Wu Lei had been an unusual man. He reminded her of her brother—her brother as he might have been, had he been a strong warrior as well as a sensitive boy. Wu Lei quoted poetry to her; he loved art and music; and unlike so many men, he also loved conversation. She was able to tell him all her thoughts and dreams, and he told her his. He was boyish and innocent-looking yet surprisingly strong and ruthless when he had to be. Wu Lei was her soul mate, brother-warrior, her window to the world of artistic beauty, her lover, and her friend.

Now tears dripped down her cheeks and dropped on her silken lap as she remembered him. She gently rubbed the little drops into the silk with the tip of her finger. She hoped the tears did not form visible rivulets in her white makeup, but she didn't really care if they did. A woman should be allowed to grieve her lost love without being expected to look like a perfect courtier.

The noise around her palanquin increased, and she surmised that they were deep into the city of Beijing. She peeked out of the curtains to see.

Beijing was ever-changing and never-changing, at once. She was quite sure that there had always been the same streets crowded with vendors selling the same rice, millet, bean curd, cabbage, green beans, bean sprouts, celery, radishes, and sweet potatoes. She was sure there had always been the open sacks full of spices; and the large, swimming vats of shining fish and darting eels, and the barrels-full of entangled, fighting crabs. There had always been roasted ducks, and live fowl, as well as their precious eggs for sale. Vendors of medicinal herbs and steaming cups of tea, of porcelain vases and dishes, and of furniture plied their trades as they had done for centuries.

There were plays being enacted in the streets, children playing and darting about, squealing and screaming, and there were circus performances with animals, jugglers, and fools. There was the old man, beating his drum endlessly, reciting the ancient tales.

Jade Flower took it in, bemused. They approached one of the gates of the Forbidden City, which was so tall, it seemed to block the sky. The gate was made of copper-colored cups hammered down over bolted wood. The cups looked like a thousand shields. Beyond the gate were the vermilion walls of the Forbidden City, the Emperor's extensive compound of gardens, courts, and pavilions.

When she felt the palanquin lowered to the ground with a soft thud, she went forth, hiding the great trepidation, sorrow, and dread she felt in her heart. She walked like a noblewoman, with her head held high, even though she was dying inside. Exhausted, still feeling the after-effects of too much drink, and still tormented by the memory of murdering a civilian, her emotions almost overcame her. Yet she was an elite warrior, able to publicly dissemble. Behind the mask of makeup, she schooled her face and eyes to betray no emotion.

Once inside the scarlet walls of the Forbidden City, she was led into the Hall of Harmony where she was left to wait—and wait. This provided her ample opportunity to get her emotions under ironclad control. To pass the time, she began counting the dragons that adorned the ceiling of the Hall of Harmony.

Five hundred and sixty-one, five hundred and sixty-two —

There were two thousand of the dragons, so she still had plenty to occupy herself with when the doors opened and Liu Huimin came in.

Liu Huimin was the Empress's main female attendant. She had no title that Jade Flower knew of; her name said all that was known of her. She was wise, quick, and clever, with a knife-like aspect to her sharp personality. "The deer with velvet antlers.," some said of her. Jade Flower had never known Liu Huimin not to be smooth and velvety; if her antlers had sharp ends, they were well swathed. Liu Huimin's influence ran deep and wide, mostly because she had the Empress's ear.

How Jade Flower wished she had a smooth face and countenance like Liu Huimin's! She'd had to school her features rigidly to keep her careering, impulsive emotions from showing at every juncture, but a face as smooth as cream-colored silk seemed to come naturally to Liu Huimin. Liu Huimin's movements and expressions were all economical and neat; bespeaking a character of both discipline and grace. She plucked the very strings of the Empire with her silken hands, and everyone attached to the court knew it.

It was an honor to be greeted in person by Liu Huimin.

"Ah! Jade Flower!" said Liu Huimin, bowing with a flourish. "My condolences over the loss of your precious young husband."

Jade Flower bowed stiffly in return. She was reining in her fear and trepidation as to why their majesties wanted to see her so soon, as well as her doubts about whether she should tell the Emperor about the silver dart, and the jewelry box with its strange message of a ginkgo leaf. Her palms were sweating and her heart was palpitating—she hoped its pulse was not visible in her throat.

"You are always a welcome sight at the palace," Liu Huimin continued in her liquid voice. "The Emperor said so himself, just a moment ago. Now, please follow me. Their majesties have been eagerly awaiting your arrival."

Jade Flower bowed again, less stiffly, as Liu Huimin, her figure encased in a column of ocean blue silk, turned and led the way out of the Hall of Harmony toward the imperial receiving chamber in the Inner Court. Liu Huimin turned once to make sure Jade Flower was following, gave her a shimmering smile, and passed out of the room between two vermilion pillars. Ahead of her, Jade Flower saw Liu Huimin's silk clad figure bow to make obeisance as she herself entered the presence of the Celestial Son of Heaven, ruler on the Dragon Throne.

CHAPTER 5

The Son of Heaven and his wife, the Empress, were seated on a large, round, bed-like chair atop a dais. Covered in silk of imperial yellow, the chair looked immensely comfortable. It was flanked by perfectly symmetrical, identical porcelain Ming vases, which were the height and breadth of a man and backed by a sumptuous silken tapestry.

Jade Flower's discerning eye noticed the same patterns and colors in the silken tapestry and the finely wrought Ming porcelain. There were flecks of imperial yellow in both to accent the yellow bed-chair. In contrast and in harmony with the setting, the Emperor and Empress wore vermilion and yellow robes of silken brocade, heavy with elaborate embroidery and encrusted with gold and gems. They were an impressive sight, and Jade Flower felt her sense of trepidation increase. Whatever the pair wanted, she was bound to do, no matter what state of mind and heart she was in.

The Emperor dressed his hair in the traditional Manchu style. The Manchus had ruled China for hundreds of years, and their styles differed from that of the Han Chinese. The Emperor's forehead was shaved to appear very high, and his never-cut braid of long hair, sprouting like an island on his otherwise shaven, bald pate, trailed down in his back in a queue. The Empress's hair was combed and splayed over a thin but wide board attached to the back of her head. This had the effect of showing her hair's quality and beauty, and indeed her hair shone, picking up the faint glow of adorning ornaments of jade, gold, and fine gems pinioned on the board and artfully surrounded by strands of smooth black hair.

Jade Flower paid obeisance, kowtowing to the Emperor and Empress and striking her forehead on the floor. She was told to rise and only then, slightly dizzy, did her surroundings come into full focus.

There were many attendants in the room, probably one hundred in all. The women were concubines, she thought, with the red dot on their lips, their hair wound around their heads in various shapes and coils, anchored with decorative pins and hung with Burmese jade, coral, precious jewels, silk flowers, and real blooms, too. Each woman wore an elaborately embroidered red silk robe. Platform shoes, peeking out from under their robes, adorned the concubines' feet. The shoes were sewn with pearls and jade and embroidered with symbols of good luck, happiness, fertility, and longevity.

Jade Flower teetered on her own similar platform shoes. They gave Manchu women like her, who did not bind their feet, the appearance of the titillating, small feet that Chinese men seemed to love so.

She was grateful it was not Manchu tradition to bind the feet or she would never have survived so long in battle. Chinese men referred to bound feet as "three-inch golden lilies" and enjoyed watching and playing with them (as long as they were carefully bound with lengths of cloth and covered in delicate embroidered shoes—unbound, such feet showed deformity and decay).

In fact, Jade Flower did not like the uncomfortable and unnatural platform shoes, either. She surreptitiously slipped them off. She liked to be steady on the feet that Heaven had given her. The idea of falling down in front of the Son of Heaven and his wife from teetering on ridiculous shoes did not appeal to her. More comfortable, Jade Flower breathed a sigh of relief, the sound of which she stifled. As long as she could stand still, her abandoned shoes remained under the hem of her lengthy and heavy dress, hidden from sight. She was a tall woman anyway; people would not know she was not wearing shoes if she kept still.

Her eyes met Liu Huimin's. The Empress's handmaiden, in her deep blue silk, was dressed more austerely than the other attendants. Her hair was tastefully ornamented, but, as always, Liu Huimin was the soul of discretion. She was appropriately dressed for court, but gave the impression of a minister or an adviser rather than of a court celebrant. Her seemingly far-seeing gaze was, as always, calm and inscrutable. Liu Huimin was impeccable and impenetrable, yet her glance contained a look of gentle welcome, full of sympathy, and Jade Flower remembered her kind words about being welcomed by the Emperor. It was always good to see Liu Huimin again; she was such a familiar face, almost an institution at the palace.

Aloud, Jade Flower wished their majesties long lives and long reigns in the usual exaggerated terms.

Empress Xinyi had a colorful history. She had been chosen to be a concubine of the twenty-one-year-old Emperor when she was a mere fourteen years old, and had trained in the palace for four years before assuming her place in his harem. An Emperor was supposed to have one Empress, three first wives, nine second wives, twenty-seven third, fourth, and fifth-rate wives, and then eighty-one concubines arranged in ranks of sixth, seventh, and eighth ranks. Overall, the Emperor was to have at his disposal one hundred twenty-one women. The Empress, who had been unusually beautiful and poised even at age fourteen, had been the daughter of a minor official and had begun life in the Forbidden City as a seventh-rank concubine.

This was not a bad social position. Chinese women, in general, had harsh lives, and it had always been this way. In the third century, poet Fu Xuan had written: "How sad it is to be woman! Nothing on earth is held so cheap." The very word for "woman" was synonymous with slave.

Royal concubines, however, were honored, even ones of the seventh rank. They lived in the pavilions of the palace and were waited upon by handmaidens and eunuchs. They were served the daintiest foods and dressed in the finest clothing. At the same time, they could not make an improper move at court without risking life and limb. There was certainly no freedom in it, and freedom was something so important, Jade Flower had discovered, that men—and women—were willing to die for it. She certainly was.

The Empress had been elevated quite quickly through the ranks of concubines and wives after having had the extremely good fortune of conceiving and bearing healthy twin sons to the Emperor. She became the most admired and powerful woman in China, beloved by all, including her husband.

Xinyi's luck had held out, too. She had borne a third and fourth son to the Emperor and, what was more, the Emperor and the Empress genuinely liked one another. In fact, rumor traveled all over Beijing and the country that the concubines and other wives in the Emperor's harem simply had nothing to do now that the Emperor and Empress were so in love and because Xinyi had produced four healthy heirs to the Dragon Throne.

The couple's ease with one another was palpable even as they sat in their heavy yellow and vermilion robes in the presence of hundreds of people. A warm parental love emanated from the pair, and Jade Flower found herself breathing easier. Suddenly, she felt that the kingdom — and her fate — was secure in the couple's hands. Remembering the rumors of the couple's devotion, and seeing it displayed before her eyes as the Empress's fingers idly intertwined with the Emperor's, she sighed a deep sigh of relief and longing.

Liu Huimin suddenly crossed in front of the royal throne to take a tray from a concubine who had come to offer it. Almost as an afterthought, Liu Huimin turned to bow to the Emperor and Empress before taking the tray. Jade Flower was startled. No one walked in from their majesties or turned their back to them, even for a second. Yet their majesties said nothing.

Liu Huimin has risen high in their estimation indeed, thought Jade Flower.

The Empress addressed Jade Flower formally, "My deepest sympathies and condolences to you, Jade Flower. I know how you loved your husband. I cannot imagine the depth of your loss."

The Emperor chimed in. "He was a good man. A good man and a good warrior."

"A good husband?" the Empress asked, raising her eyebrows.

"Yes," said Jade Flower. "He was an excellent husband. I loved him dearly, and I will miss him for all my days."

"As is proper," said the Emperor. "If I died, I know the Empress would be buried in sorrow. As you know, none of my wives or concubines would be eligible to remarry, and it would be assumed they would not want to."

"That is not your case, however, Jade Flower," said the Empress with emphasis as Liu Huimin took a step forward. The Empress's hand idly gestured for Liu Huimin to stand back, and Liu Huimin did. Jade Flower suddenly sensed that the meeting was coming down to its purpose, and that this purpose was well known to the people on the platform of the Dragon Throne, including Liu Huimin. She, alone, was not in on the secret.

The Emperor said, "Due to pressing national matters, you must continue to serve the kingdom as part of a warrior couple partnership."

The Empress said, "It is time for Jade Flower to begin to look toward the dawn of a new day of life, for the sake of the nation."

Jade Flower felt confused. Those did not seem to be the Empress's own words; it was as if she was repeating something someone else had said. Automatically, she looked to Liu Huimin, who, as usual, showed no emotion, but whose eyes were heavy with satisfaction.

"You have suffered a great loss indeed," murmured the Emperor. "Now we want you to experience a great gain. You will prepare for remarriage this day," he said sternly, looking at Jade Flower. "I will choose a suitable warrior to be your spouse. You are to meet him and marry him before the sun sets tonight."

CHAPTER 6

Jade Flower felt her face drain of blood. Her face would have been pale had it not been powdered. She was absolutely dumbfounded. Dimly, she realized there was no arguing. This was an order from the Son of Heaven and his Empress. To dispute it could mean losing one's head. A gong sounded, and the shifting of feet among the dozens of attendants in the room meant the interview was over. Liu Huimin looked meaningfully at Jade Flower, as if to impress upon her that it was time to exit.

Dazed, Jade Flower knew she was supposed to make obeisance to the Emperor and Empress, sinking to her knees many times over, expressing effusive gratitude and knocking her forehead on the ground while speaking of the royal couple's wisdom, insight, brilliance, and good rulership and to wish them prosperity for ten thousand years. She could not do it. She could not even close her mouth.

Liu Huimin approached her with the air of a clucking hen rescuing a wayward chick and gently took her arm. As if she were showing a child what to do, Liu Huimin bent her own body and made obeisance, pulling Jade Flower down with her and speaking the appropriate words, which Jade Flower dazedly echoed.

Then, with a firm grip, Liu Huimin conducted her out of the chamber, murmuring loudly enough for their majesties to hear: "Of course, you are not yourself, being so freshly bereft. Some concessions must be made for your state of sorrow."

Jade Flower was grateful and she leaned on Liu Huimin, who exuded a faint floral scent, as Liu Huimin escorted her from the chamber. Jade Flower realized that, with her movements, her platform shoes were no longer under her dress but had been left somewhere in front of the Emperor and Empress. Such a breach of court etiquette would cause a furor to break out, she knew. She hoped some concubine or other would not be blamed for her mistake. It could mean death.

I hope they realize it was me! She raged inside. *Let them kill me,* she thought defiantly. *They might be doing me a favor! In fact, if I still had my sword, I would run myself through with it rather than marry so soon after the death of my beloved!*

Her warrior's mind was not dead within her; in the same instant she thought of killing herself to protest their majesties' decision, she also thought she needed to ask the Emperor for a new sword. She began to imagine the type she would like; what kind of blade it would have; she imagined herself touching the blade to test its sharpness, drawing her own blood willingly, and then making the sword sing in the air as she weighed its heft.

Unconsciously, thinking as a soldier, she matched paces with Liu Huimin, who had a soft, controlled tread. With a mere glance, Liu Huimin indicated to her attendants that she wanted to be alone with Jade Flower, and they discreetly withdrew.

"I would speak to you," Liu Huimin said to Jade Flower. "On behalf of their majesties. Perhaps I should not, but I know their hearts. Sometimes one must do something for one's sovereign's own good, even without the sovereign's knowledge. That is the highest kind of loyalty, don't you agree?"

"It depends upon what one does, of course," said Jade Flower.

She was recovering somewhat from the shock of what she had been told, her soldierly self-dominating her more emotional side. Thoughts of procuring a new sword filled her mind. She had loved her sword — it had saved her life many times. She wished she could have her old one back, but a part of her wanted to try a new one as well.

Liu Huimin smiled. "I just wanted to reassure you of the Emperor and Empress's extremely high regard for you. They may seem to be pushing all this through quickly, but they have their reasons. The Empire is in great danger. You will hear of it soon, I fear. Their majesties know they will need every man and woman warrior in place, closing the gaps in the ranks. Yet I wanted to express my personal regrets and condolences that you must go through so much so soon. You look tired too, poor child."

Liu Huimin's smooth hand gently touched the side of Jade Flower's face, moving a stray strand of hair away from Jade Flower's eyes. Her gentleness and sympathy almost brought tears to Jade Flower's eyes.

"Indeed, if I let myself, I would break down," Jade Flower admitted. "I have not had much sleep and no respite from fast-moving events."

"Rest now," said Liu Huimin warmly. Here is your chamber." Liu Huimin pushed a red enameled door inward to allow Jade Flower to enter a room. "Here I will attend you personally, and make sure you look perfectly lovely for the wedding without taking the usual hours of time getting you dressed according to court requirements. I can cut corners, and no one will ever know."

"You are kind," said Jade Flower.

Liu Huimin's sympathy seemed to seep into her heart and Jade Flower found herself starting to cry. She tossed her head, reminded herself she was a warrior, but Liu Huimin's sympathetic gaze and the comforting, sumptuous surroundings of the bedchamber Liu Huimin had ushered her into worked to break down Jade Flower's defenses.

It was a large and beautiful chamber. Fat red candles burned in all corners, throwing light and heat onto the yellow silk curtains that covered every wall, making them glow golden. Embroidered silk sheets and comforters were arranged invitingly on the large bed, which was in the middle of the room and swathed in acres of yellow silk, coyly parted to reveal the glory and comfort of the bed. Gilded furniture, carved and ornate, lined three of the silk-covered walls. The gold shone in the light of large lamps suspended from the ceiling.

Jade Flower threw herself down on the bed and, in a spasm of sorrow, began to sob into the silk pillow. She heard Liu Huimin clucking again, sympathetically, moving about the room, drawing curtains and folding linens. Jade Flower was glad she was there. Liu Huimin was utterly trusted by their majesties as a courtier, an adviser, and even as a friend. It was said that Liu Huimin and the Empress spent hours playing mahjongg together, exchanging gossip almost girlishly. Jade Flower knew she was vulnerable emotionally right now, and sometimes even a soldier needed a friend.

She cried for a long time and was grateful that Liu Huimin did not offer to hold her in her arms or do anything more sympathetic than pass her fresh silk handkerchiefs every few minutes.

"Oh, dear," Liu Huimin said when Jade Flower had stopped crying temporarily. "Your face looks like someone threw a pomegranate at it! We've so little time to prepare you for your betrothal and wedding! Go out on the balcony and get some cool air on your face, won't you? That will tame the red. I must go and get some preparations for your bath and dress. Please go take some deep draughts of fresh air while I am gone."

Jade Flower nodded, still miserable, and then got up out of the bed and began to search through the maze of silk curtains all along one wall. She found the opening just as Liu Huimin closed the door behind herself, going out into the corridor. Jade Flower slid open the rice paper door to the balcony and stepped out.

The balcony overlooked a courtyard—a rather vast, walled courtyard of vermilion brick. There were some guards about but they clustered around the entrance to the courtyard, which was a wrought iron gate, almost half a mile away. They seemed much more interested in what was going on outside the courtyard walls than within them as they peered relentlessly through the gate. Jade Flower stepped closer to the filigreed railing.

The hard surface of the courtyard looked lethal.

If I get dizzy and fall, I shall not regret it, she thought, shaking off a touch of vertigo and wondering if the bricks would dash her brains out if she fell from this height. She was almost certain they would, especially if she stepped back and took a running leap over the railing so as to give herself momentum.

Forced to marry a man I barely know and do not love, with no choice in the matter, so soon after my husband's funeral? So I am to be no more than a concubine!

Death seemed preferable. Then it would be all over. The thought grew upon her. She would be with Wu Lei. She would not have to go through the bathing, the dressing, the primping, the engagement, wedding, and banquet, facing a new man, and all of it to be crammed within the next few nightmarish hours. She would not be given to someone she could not possibly love, no matter who he was, whom she felt would be nothing but an encumbrance on her self-appointed new mission in life—to find and kill her husband's assassin. Her suicide would be a death with honor—everyone would know she did it out of love and devotion to her late husband.

Jade Flower stepped back and pulled aside the yellow silk curtains, which were fluttering and wafting around her. Then she went deeply back into the room, so far that the backs of her calves touched the sides of the silken bed. She stood, her muscles taut, facing the balcony, and then she began the slight sway of the hips, like a cat positioning itself to pounce on its prey, to give impetus to her running leap. She closed her eyes. Within seconds she would be on the brick stones, brains dashed out, all of it over—

She opened her eyes to gauge the length of her running leap one last time, and coiled to spring. She heard someone plunge across the silken bed and catch her by the arms from behind, arresting her flight and flinging her with well-calibrated violence sideways onto the silken bed.

It was Liu Huimin. For once, Liu Huimin's hair was mussed and her face was contorted with fear.

"I will prepare you to be wed now," Liu Huimin said through gritted teeth.

Liu Huimin was amazingly strong. Jade Flower could have outmaneuvered her, but she was caught by surprise and the muscular woman pinned her arms down by straddling her and planting her knees, painfully, on Jade Flower's triceps.

"You will meet the man you are to wed and proceed immediately into the wedding ceremony as ordered by the Son of Heaven and his wife. I will brook no disobedience."

Recovering herself, Liu Huimin got off Jade Flower, crossed the room, and stood between Jade Flower and the open balcony door.

"I think you have had quite enough fresh air now," she said, and she pulled the rice paper door shut firmly and adjusted the silk curtains over it.

"I could run right through that door," Jade Flower said defiantly.

"I would not advise you to try it," said Liu Huimin. "The curtains would entangle and hinder you. It would be a clumsy, not a noble, death. In fact, I do not believe you would die; you would probably just break your limbs and hobble like an old woman for the rest of your life."

Jade Flower sighed. She knew Liu Huimin's assessment of the situation was probably right.

"I act and speak for your own good, Jade Flower. I hope you know that." Liu Huimin spoke like a firm mother. "Now I will bathe and dress you. You will meet your new husband one hour from now."

Liu Huimin held out a silver goblet to Jade Flower. "Drink this and take a brief nap. You will arise feeling like you had a full night's sleep under a pleasant sky full of pearl stars and black velvet skies."

Jade Flower doubtfully accepted the draught.

CHAPTER 7

It seemed she had not even finished drinking the liquid in the silver goblet before her head hit the silken pillow and she was indeed drifting in the depths of a pleasant night sky. The black velvet of evening enveloped her softly, tenderly, and she drank deeply of a restful, peace-filled sleep. She could not remember handing the goblet to Liu Huimin. She could not remember anything, except—

Her eyes flew open. "I must prepare for the wedding!" she cried out.

"Oh, so you want to be married after all," came the soothing, comforting voice of Liu Huimin, sitting at her side.

"Their majesties have ordered it—I have never slept through an order from the Son of Heaven!"

"You have not slept through this one," Liu Huimin smiled. "You slept but five minutes. Are you refreshed?"

"I am," said Jade Flower in surprise. "I feel—wonderful." She waited for the onslaught of her grief to hit her—it was held at bay. She was in no pain or discomfort anywhere, mentally, physically, or in her heart.

"Good," said Liu Huimin, smiling again. "Now let us get you ready to be wed."

Liu Huimin prepared Jade Flower for the rite of marriage by her own hand, as she had promised. She poured a cistern of hot water into a hammered copper tub, which she helped Jade Flower into.

"Ah, you are very beautiful," Liu Huimin commented, pouring jasmine perfume into the water. Jade Flower breathed it in. It seemed to clear her mind.

"Put the past behind you," soothed Liu Huimin, rubbing Jade Flower's shoulders with a soft, warm, wet cloth.

Jade Flower then washed herself, as Liu Huimin discreetly and carefully added hot water just when the water cooled slightly. Jade Flower leaned back in the tub and heaved a great sigh. Liu Huimin poured more jasmine perfume into the water, and again Jade Flower had the sensation of it chasing the clouds out of her mind.

After she had thoroughly bathed in the lulling, perfumed water, Jade Flower rose. She was feeling refreshed in body and soul. Liu Huimin enveloped her in absorbent cloths and helped her dry herself. Then she slid a fine, white silk slip over Jade Flower's head. Jade Flower noticed the slip was embroidered with small white flowers at perfectly even intervals. She was still admiring the handicraft responsible for such flowers, wondering how anyone had enough time and patience to do such things, when Liu Huimin swathed her in a red silk wedding dress. It felt marvelously smooth and luxurious against her clean skin. Then, using strings in a masterful way, Liu Huimin plucked the hairs of Jade Flower's forehead to make a perfect hairline and shaped her brows over her eyes into startlingly lovely arches that brought out Jade Flower's eyes provocatively. It hurt—a little—but Liu Huimin rubbed her forehead with a gentle powder that seemed to sooth Jade Flower's skin. Looking in the mirror, she saw no red marks, and she admired Liu Huimin's handiwork.

"You make me quite beautiful," said Jade Flower.

"You are quite beautiful," said Liu Huimin warmly. "It is a good thing too, because we haven't much time to transform you. I am glad we have the good foundation of your natural loveliness to work from."

She powdered and rouged Jade Flower until Jade Flower no longer recognized herself. Certainly there was no trace of the warrior in her appearance. Yet she did not look like a courtesan either. She looked like a nobleman's wife.

"Oh, these hands!" exclaimed Liu Huimin. "They have seen too many horses' reins and sword hilts! Never fear. I will get your hands to match your face and figure in nobility."

With enough filing, buffing, exfoliating, and oiling, Jade Flower's hands emerged, soft and graceful. Liu Huimin got down on one knee to fit embroidered slippers upon Jade Flower's feet. Jade Flower wondered idly what had become of the platform shoes she had kicked off in the receiving chamber next to the Hall of Harmony.

Escorted into the same chamber she had been in earlier that day, dressed in her wedding finery, Jade Flower gave the wedding vanguard of courtiers a disdainful look. They were carrying banners and shouting joyfully about the wedding to come. More gracefully than before, Jade Flower did her obeisance to the Emperor and Empress. The draught Liu Huimin had given her and the jasmine perfume continued to keep her mind clear and to fend off emotional pain. She felt quite wonderful, in fact.

The Emperor gazed at Jade Flower for a moment in a fatherly way. Then he clapped his hands. Eight warriors emerged from behind the imperial yellow silk curtains of the hall. They were all dressed resplendently in wedding garb of red silk with their hair shining in well-knotted braids. Jade Flower was taken aback. It was like looking into a hall of mirrors where one person was reflected over and over again.

Two of the warriors looked boldly at Jade Flower, as if appraising her. They seemed to think very well of themselves, Jade Flower thought, and were measuring her to see if she was worthy of them. She hoped neither of those two were chosen! Two others looked at her appreciatively, fire in their eyes, as if they could not wait to sweep her off to the bridal bed chamber. Jade Flower felt herself trembling before their gazes and wondering if they would ever seek to know her heart and mind as well as her body. Wu Lei had.

She could not keep a frown off her face at these thoughts, and, when she looked up, she saw the Empress watching her. She tried to rearrange her features into a look of receptive obedience to whatever the Emperor and Empress would order. Two more warriors looked solemnly at their Emperor and Empress only, as if disdaining to look at the prospective bride because it would be disloyal. Jade Flower did not like their air of mindless obedience. Her heart was sinking within her. The only two she thought she could stomach would be one of the last two, and in spite of their warrior garb, they were so obsequious to the Emperor and Empress she wondered if they had any spirit at all.

She looked helplessly at the Emperor and Empress. Which one of these undesirable men was going to share her bed this night and her life all the nights after? She tried not to show her anguish on her face, but she was near tears.

"Jade Flower, step forward to receive your husband," ordered the Emperor.

With leaden feet, Jade Flower stepped closer to the Dragon Throne.

CHAPTER 8

Jade Flower bowed her head, unable to look up to see the man chosen for her. After a whispered conference between the Emperor and Empress, the Empress airily waved her hand at the row of eight men.

"You will not be wed tonight," she told them. "None of you. Be gone. General Luan Yu Luan, come forward."

Jade Flower had not noticed General Luan Yu Luan near the dais, blending in with all the attendants there. He stepped forward. Jade Flower followed his movements with interest. Why was he here? General Luan was already married. Feeling safe on that score, Jade Flower looked at him openly, with frank curiosity. He was quite famous, this man, and she had never seen him in person before. No one could deny that he was handsome and strong-looking with an impressive stamp of good character on his features: a mixture of sternness and kindness that gave the impression that he was stricter with no man more than himself.

Wu Lei had spoken of him once and had said he was a good man. He had said that General Luan Yu Luan was known for his honesty and use of diplomacy to win the peace after the battle. He was also known to hate wasting lives, even if he had to put his own in danger to protect others. The men and women under him were known to adore him for this.

General Luan, Jade Flower noticed, seemed to have a silent but special relationship with the Emperor, the nature of which she could not guess, but the two men's eyes met every few seconds or so in what seemed to be silent understanding. Yu Luan was rumored to have great influence, even though he was also known among the warriors as being no toady before the throne. It was said he preferred camp to the court and found most court frippery intolerable, although he was expert at court manners.

After what seemed like a lengthy silent exchange between the two men, the Emperor said, "Yu Luan, are you acquainted with Jade Flower?"

"We have never met," said Yu Luan simply. "I knew your esteemed husband." He bowed slightly to the memory of Jade Flower's husband, and she bowed, too.

The Empress commented, "A man of few words. That can be a virtue." She seemed to be talking directly to Jade Flower.

"Truly, it can be," nodded the Emperor in agreement, "although in matters of love, it is generally better to be a man of many words, is it not?"

The Empress giggled. "Well, you certainly are, my dear," she said fondly. "Your outpourings—" Checking herself, she rearranged her royal robes and cleared her throat. "Our condolences to you, too, General Luan Yu Luan. Jingwei was an excellent warrior and diplomat."

With a stiff bow and a face that revealed nothing, Yu Luan acknowledged the sentiment.

Jade Flower stared at Yu Luan. Had his wife died, then? She had not heard so. A military partner like Jade Flower, Jingwei was known to be a good fighter, but as it was with her husband, it was said that she preferred to preserve life rather than shed blood. She was rumored to be behind much of her husband's deft diplomacy. When it was necessary, however, Jingwei had a reputation as a brave warrior and an expert in the martial arts. Jade Flower had never heard anything but praise for the couple, and she had not heard of Jingwei's death.

The Empress noticed the look of puzzlement on Jade Flower's face and said, "Had you not heard that Yu Luan's wife, Jingwei, died in childbirth?"

Jade Flower turned to Yu Luan fully and said, "My condolences. A great loss."

Yu Luan glanced at her, seeming almost to study her.

After a moment, he murmured, "The boy child died, too."

Jade Flower was surprised he could even bring himself to mention it, and in so stoic and factual a way.

He must be a cold man, she decided. What she had taken for self-discipline in his rugged facial features was indifference to human feeling, she thought. She tried to keep the disdain she felt for such a man — so different from her expressive Wu Lei — from her face.

"Proceed to the wedding chamber," ordered the Emperor suddenly, making a waving gesture with his right hand that indicated Jade Flower and Yu Luan.

Jade Flower's jaw dropped. The next moment she was caught under the elbows on either side and escorted from the chamber, completely dumbfounded. Was she to marry Luan Yu Luan? Or was it possible there was yet another man waiting in the wedding hall, chosen to be her new husband, and another woman for Yu Luan? Would it be a double wedding?

Jade Flower almost went limp between her escorts. Why were the Emperor and Empress putting her through all this? Was it just a royal game to them? Some sort of test? Her despair and sense of rebellion almost overwhelmed her as the attendants almost carried her out of the room and into another.

*   *   *

General Luan Yu Luan watched his bride-to-be being swept away by the courtiers. He was a practical man, and he had gathered a great deal more from the meeting than Jade Flower had. He knew that he was to be wed to Jade Flower within minutes. He was not opposed. He had long admired the couple Wu Lei and Jade Flower, who were well known as individuals and as a fighting unit. He was not entirely displeased that he was now to take Wu Lei's place in that unit, and he knew the times called for the husband and wife teams more than ever before.

Yet he was not entirely pleased either. Jade Flower was known to be a fire-cat; very different from his gentle Jingwei, whose spine of steel was hidden in layers of softness, and whose passion was so well-disguised under rigid propriety. From the many facial expressions he had seen flitting across Jade Flower's face, propriety was something she needed more schooling in.

Thinking of Jingwei and contrasting her to the fiery Jade Flower, he felt tears slide down his cheeks. He wiped them away quickly. He would do his duty. Thinking thus, he strode toward the wedding chamber to be wed to Jade Flower in obedience to the Emperor and Empress of China.

CHAPTER 9

edding custom dictated that Jade Flower be paraded through the streets of Beijing in a sedan chair, red lanterns bobbing from its sides, with cartloads of her expensive wedding presents from the Emperor and Empress following her on display. Yet all custom seemed to have been thrown away in the haste about the marriage. Why were their majesties in so much of a rush?

Liu Huimin was waiting for her in the wedding chamber. Her smooth silken hands took Jade Flower's, and she kissed her gently upon each cheek.

"I know your mother and father passed away years ago. I will act as your parent this night. Yet I hope you will also continue to think of me as a friend."

Jade Flower pursed her lips. She remembered the pain of Liu Huimin's knees on her triceps, pinning her to the bed. At the same time, she realized that Liu Huimin had done it to save her life. She nodded, and Liu Huimin smiled.

"Your husband awaits you," Liu Huimin said warmly.

There was General Luan; he was dressed in a red silk robe. So it was to be him after all. His hair was freshly combed and arranged, and his face was shaved clean. Against her will, she felt her eyes lingering on his good looks and manly bearing. Well, he might be acceptable as a husband—someday, she thought. In any case, he was highly positioned and respected, and he might be a useful instrument to help her avenge her true husband's death.

He met her gaze calmly—coldly, she thought—and between this and the Chinese orchestra in the room, playing flutes and banging on drum, her head began to ache. Yet she could sense, once again, Yu Luan's almost palpable unity with the Emperor, and the tranquility and simplicity of doing one's duty as an elite soldier swept over her and she became more serene.

Soon others led them side by side to a table where elders sat. Liu Huimin sat in the place where Jade Flower's parents would have sat had they been alive. Two elderly but kindly-looking people sat in the place where the bridegroom's parents should be, and Jade Flower surmised that these were Yu Luan's parents. The couple bowed to the elders and to the tablets of their ancestors, which were carved with family names and which had been set up on separate tables.

Hot wine was served to them in separate bowls. They drank from their bowls, the hot wine singing down Jade Flower's throat and tasting so good and royal, it made her feel like singing. Remembering Wu Lei, she choked on it a little, then cooperated with a solemn Yu Luan to mingle the contents of the two bowls together. Then they drank the mixed wine to symbolize their new union. They performed the same ritual with rice, eating first from separate bowls, then mixing the rice together in one bowl and eating again, once more in symbolism of joining together. Jade Flower tried not to think of the consummation of their union to come later that night, the oneness that all this symbolized.

They bowed to the Emperor and Empress and again to their elders. As a pair, they bowed to the assemblage of guests and then went to the feasting hall with everyone, where there was much eating, drinking, and laughter.

A massive platter of the special celebration rice sat in the middle of each table, steaming hot and full of cold, bursting, sugared fruits. It was a delicious dish that made Jade Flower's taste buds dance, and the sight of it brought a small, almost involuntary smile to her face. Of course, everything in the palace was of the finest possible quality. All the delicacies were perfectly prepared.

Luan Yu Luan glanced at her, seeming to note her enjoyment of the food. Yet he said nothing. He certainly had a reserved manner, Jade Flower thought. Wu Lei would have filled such moments with poetry and song, in celebration, like this was supposed to be. He would have decorated the occasion with beautiful words, moving her heart to its depths. Was this all Yu Luan had to offer? Inscrutable silence? Would life with him not be dull, then? Or did he disapprove of her relishing her food? He could not know, she thought, how much her heart grieved for her boyish, sweet, poetic young husband. Yet she was not dead herself. She was still very much alive. She felt resentment toward Yu Luan, thinking he was judging her. She would never be able to love him; never. Theirs would be a marriage of convenience and obedience; that was all.

"You are a person alive to the senses," Yu Luan said to her.

"Yes," she agreed. "Is there something wrong with that?"

"Of course not."

"I shouldn't think so. I am not a slave to my senses, that is certain."

"You could not be part of the warrior troupe if you were."

Was that a warning? What was this mysterious man thinking about her? Did he dislike and disapprove of her already?

They were called to go before the Emperor and Empress, so they rose and made their obeisance, kowtowing and touching their foreheads on the floor. They both wished their majesties ten thousand years of glorious rule.

"Yes, yes," said the Empress impatiently. "And how do you like one another?"

"Dear, it is so early," the Emperor murmured. "They are both but recently cut from their beloved spouses. A bone does not mend in a day." He turned his full attention upon them, commanding them to meet his eyes. "Time will be your friend in this marriage. Let time do its healing work."

"Be good to one another," advised the Empress. "Love is built," she admonished them. "Build your love with kindness to one another."

The couple bowed in obeisance.

"You will stay here together tonight," said the Empress lightly, waving her hand as if the matter of their accommodations was of little importance. "In the chamber Jade Flower has been occupying. It is near ours, and you will begin your marriage there, with us nearby, as your celestial parents."

"Dance for a time," the Emperor said. "Then retire to your bridal chamber and consummate your new union."

Jade Flower blushed at this frank command.

The newlywed husband and wife were commanded to lead a dance. Jade Flower kept her eyes cast down.

Once their movements had set the other dancers in motion, Yu Luan asked her, "Why do you blush?" It seemed a question of aloof curiosity, nothing more.

"I do not blush," she said, raising her face to him defiantly.

"But you do," he said. "There is certainly nothing to blush about."

Resentment rose in her. Who was he to tell her what she could and couldn't feel?

"You would wish to control the very blood that runs in my veins?" she asked distastefully. "And command it to freeze?"

"No," he said, startled. "I merely meant we will do our duty, as commanded."

Jade Flower thought for a moment, then she said, "Even a man cannot perform the act merely out of duty."

"Tell me, Jade Flower. Which did you love more — China or your husband?"

Jade Flower thought for only a split second. "China," she said.

"Ah. Then you will be able to love me. For I too, above all else, love China. In many ways, I am China."

He stepped back from her as the dance ended, and others surrounded them, pulling them separately into more feasting, drinking, and dancing. Jade Flower was flummoxed by their conversation. What did he mean — he was China?

He is utterly inscrutable to me! She fumed. Wu Lei would have told her everything he was thinking and feeling. There was no guesswork with him. Yu Luan she had to discern — and he seemed to keep himself very well hidden. This was going to be difficult.

When the feasting and drinking and dancing were ebbing, Yu Luan turned to Jade Flower and told her they should rise and go to their bedchamber.

"Why should we?" she wanted to know.

"Because the Emperor and Empress expect it."

She kept her facial features under strict control, not for Yu Luan's sake and his dislike of her blushing, she thought, but because she did not care to show her feelings in public. She rose, bowed to the Emperor and Empress, and followed her new husband, who was led by eunuchs lighting the way to their honeymoon chamber, the room in which Liu Huimin had prepared her for the wedding.

Jade Flower approached its red enameled door with dread.

CHAPTER 10

Inside the lovely and now familiar room, its comforting red candles throwing warm haloes against the yellow silk walls, Jade Flower turned to Yu Luan. She had no intention of allowing any advances he might make, for the sake of China or not. She steeled herself to fight him to the death if she had to. Her hands formed into claws.

He met her gaze directly. "I have some duties to perform this night. I shall return later." His voice was quiet, neutral.

Jade Flower felt her jaw drop. He was leaving her alone? She was not sure if she should be grateful or insulted. She opened her mouth to speak, to say she knew not what, but Yu Luan had already departed, leaving her alone in the bridal chamber.

Jade Flower fretted. Soon she was bored—and lonely. Liu Huimin came to her room for a while and helped her undress, placing her in a gossamer sleeping gown that was so sheer it was almost transparent. There was no decoration on it at all—she realized that her body, in almost plain sight, was supposed to be the decoration. There was her blush again.

She begged Liu Huimin to stay for a while, but Liu Huimin said she could not, and tucked her into the bed, bidding her to wait for her husband. Soundlessly, Liu Huimin closed the door behind her.

Sleep was impossible, of course. Jade Flower was on tenterhooks about Yu Luan's arrival. What would he do when he re-entered the room? What would he say? She steeled herself to be ready to accept anything, but she wanted to be loyal to Wu Lei for the rest of her life.

She had placed the silver dart in the drawer of a red lacquered chest when she had entered her bath earlier. She had not wanted anyone to see it on her person. She rose and got it out of the drawer, holding it in her palm for a long time, the hot tears trickling down her face, wetting the ribbon of Wu Lei's sash that held the silver dart.

This is what killed my husband, she thought, over and over again. *This tip pierced his flesh and conducted the poison to his heart.*

She slipped it over her head and climbed back into the bed, holding the strand of ribbon in her fingers, the dart cold against her skin.

A fitful, uneasy sleep claimed her. When she awakened, still waiting for Yu Luan, her tears had dried. She moved restively in the bed. It would be good to have someone near her, to snuggle up to the warmth of a fellow human being. She would not object to being held in Yu Luan's strong-looking arms. Yet Yu Luan was male and young, and she was female and lithe, and she was sure the comfort she longed for would soon turn into something else. Perhaps if she closed her eyes and gritted her teeth, her body would be able to experience the solace of being held and made love to, even as she kept her mind away from it all, in a compartment that would ever belong to Wu Lei.

Do it for the sake of China, Yu Luan had seemed to be saying to her, and the Emperor and Empress as well.

The door opened and Yu Luan strode in. "Oh!" he said, as if he had not expected to see her.

Guiltily, Jade Flower realized she had left the covers off and was quite exposed to his gaze. Instinctively, her hands protected the silver serpent dart, one hand covering the dart itself and the other clamping around its ribbon.

Yu Luan gazed at the length of her for a moment, then he unlocked his gaze and reached toward the bed, flipping a silk-covered comforter over her body. She could not help but wonder, as a woman, whether the sight of her had displeased him somehow. His eyes had certainly been riveted for a moment—in attraction or disgust? His facial expression had been (she sighed with the growing familiarity of this) unreadable to her.

Beneath the covers, she slipped the serpent dart from around her neck and slid it under the pillow. She did not want it to scratch him should he embrace her. She was surprised at herself for having this consideration for her new spouse. Wu Lei had always said she was a considerate spouse, but she had never believed him.

Taking a deep breath, holding her muscles taut, closing her eyes, and speaking through her teeth, she said, "I accept that you must do what you will."

"Do what?" he asked.

"You know what," she hissed, opening her eyes to glare at him.

"I think it might be easier to make love to one of those rigid standing pillars in the Great Hall. Really, Jade Flower," he said in a light, teasing tone, sitting on the bed and smiling at her. "You are right that I cannot do this out of mere duty. And certainly not with a woman who is like a stone lion guarding the entrance."

She couldn't help it; she started to laugh. The absurdity of the situation struck them both, and they kept laughing. As soon as they would stop, one would start snickering again, and they would both start laughing again. Jade Flower felt the laughter release some of her grief and tension.

"It is a bit absurd, isn't it?" he smiled sympathetically. "It is far too soon for either of us. A few hours ago, I did not think I would ever laugh again." He looked surprised at himself.

"Nor I," she said, equally puzzled.

Yu Luan went to one of the gilded wardrobes and opened it. He took comforters, cushions, and sheets from the deep shelves and proceeded to make himself a pallet upon the floor, next to the bed.

"I will sleep here tonight," he told her.

"All right," she agreed.

Something like a friendly feeling toward him filled her. She was grateful to him. He was right; it was too soon, and she was surprised to find humor and kindness in him.

She was also slightly affronted, she had to admit. Didn't he want her? Had she looked ridiculous, lying there so rigidly? Had he not found her attractive enough to tempt him? Weren't men supposed to be able to overcome all circumstances when it came to making love? What if he did not find her attractive? Life together might be difficult then.

Slowly, Yu Luan began to make the rounds of the room, extinguishing the rest of the candles with his fingertips and then she heard him sigh as he eased his body onto the makeshift bed he had made on the floor.

"Thank you," she said, but she was suspicious of him. What if all this was a ploy, and he meant to come at her in the night, when she was sleeping and off her guard?

An even more horrific though struck her, chilling her to the core. What if he was the murderer of her husband? It had to be a nobleman with great access to the archives of the palaces. She knew that General Luan had such access.

She slipped her hand under the silken pillow and gripped the silver dart. Its sharp point would meet his life's vein if he tried to sneak up on her.

He made no such move. In fact, he said, "I wish you a good sleep," so kindly that Jade Flower was soothed to the point that she could no longer fend off her weariness. She was exhausted from the events of the past few days. She felt like she could sleep for a week, Yu Luan or no Yu Luan.

CHAPTER 11

Early in the morning hours, before dawn, Yu Luan decided to rejoin his troop of elite coupled warriors. He supposed the Empress would want to spend more time with Jade Flower—she seemed to like her very much—and then would have his new wife delivered to his camp when she thought it proper.

It took him a full day to reach the desert camp by horseback. When he arrived, Jingwei's spirit seemed to permeate the atmosphere of the camp, more so because he had been away, Yu Luan supposed, and that gave him solace. He felt quite himself today, with a wife in waiting who was an excellent warrior, and he held Jingwei in spirit. He stood now at the verge of the encampment where the scrub ended in a ragged line along the edge of a low bluff. It was a place he and Jingwei had liked to come in the morning hours whenever they were camped near Beijing. Now, he must come here alone.

The hills beyond were feathered with color as the leaves turned, and the sky was clear but for a few diffuse, soft white clouds. Cranes were in flight, and the air had a sharp edge of crispness to it. It was the perfect weather of early autumn.

Yu Luan believed very much in finding the good and beautiful in each day, mostly in the small things. It was not a conscious practice of a religion; it was just the way he kept himself full of appreciation, when there could be so much to complain about in life: the taking of his wife and child from him; the hardships of camp and warrior life; the fact that his new wife seemed to embody a banked fire of hostility of against the world.

It was better to concentrate on the trees and the sky and the way the leaves waved in the wind as if in greeting. A crane flew right in front of him, and he was startled. Was it carrying the spirit of his wife into the realms of immortality on its back? So went the legends about cranes, that they carried the souls of the dead into the eternal realms. He was bemused. He watched the flight of the crane for some minutes.

"Ah!" he said, hearing and seeing the approach of his chief lieutenant, Lieutenant Ching.

Besides being his best warrior, Lieutenant Ching was also his best friend. Yu Luan was standing apart from the camp, contemplating the skies and hills, and Lieutenant Ching knew him well enough to know where he could find him.

"I see Jingwei is leaving us," said Lieutenant Ching softly, nodding toward the crane's flight. "Perhaps to make room for your new wife."

"Perhaps," said Yu Luan.

"What is she like?"

Yu Luan shrugged. "Beautiful. Emotional. Tempestuous."

"But a good warrior, if her reputation is deserved."

"I assume her reputation is deserved."

Ching looked thoughtfully at the crane, which was still visible in flight. "How very different from Jingwei. That is good for you," he added, clapping Yu Luan on the back. "The Son of Heaven is wise beyond wise."

"Yes," said Yu Luan, raising his eyebrows. "We have our differences, but every once in a while, I see that he truly is the Son of Heaven. It is like a mantle on his shoulders—he may not deserve it, but he does all he can to live up to it, and more often than not, he does."

"I hope your new wife comforts you in your loss," said Ching sincerely.

"I would not characterize Jade Flower as comforting," said Yu Luan, pursing his lips. "You will understand when you meet her. I wonder what exactly the Emperor saw in her for me. Yet—she has beauty and spirit—" He broke off and became lost in thought.

"It sounds like she will indeed comfort you," Ching said. "A spirited beauty is not one to be passed over lightly."

"No," said Yu Luan, still thoughtful. "No, no one could pass Jade Flower over lightly."

He remembered her upturned, blushing face while they were dancing, her pique in the bedroom, which had deeply amused him. The sound of her laughter and the way her mirth had reached her dark eyes intrigued him. He realized that a tiny part of his heart was looking forward to seeing her again.

His eyes traveled over the hills where the crane had flown and disappeared.

"Goodbye, Jingwei … my love," he whispered. Then his heart cracked, and Ching solicitously left him to his tears.

CHAPTER 12

Jade awakened from her slumber. She had slept like one dead. For a moment she was disoriented, but a warrior's sense of time and place was keen, and she soon recalled exactly where she was and what her circumstances were. Out of curiosity, she looked at the floor toward the side of the bed where Luan had camped for the night. With a start, she realized the floor was empty. There was no trace of him. All the bedding had apparently been neatly disposed of, too.

Was it all a dream? No. The agony of her husband's death descended on her like an anvil. The last day came rushing back in a cascade: the funeral, the hasty wedding, the cacophony of celebratory drums, bowing to their elders, and the feast, delicious beyond resisting; then later, laughing with Luan — how had she been able to eat, to enjoy food, to laugh? She had thought she would never enjoy anything ever again.

There was a knock at the door, and a group of six attendants swarmed in. They were eunuchs. Jade hastily covered herself with the silken quilt.

"Don't worry," said one. He seemed to be in charge. He directed the others with gestures to draw a bath and bring fresh clothing out of the wardrobe. "We are unmoved by your beauty — and if we were not, we would be unable to do anything about it anyway!"

"I would have women servants nonetheless," said Jade.

"Why, we attend to all the women on the palace grounds!"

"Not to me. Bring Liu Huimin to me," said Jade.

The head eunuch shook his head. "Liu Huimin is with the Empress." He hesitated, then gestured to one of the other eunuchs. "Tell Mother Liu Huimin that General Luan's wife wants her."

The eunuch bowed and left.

Jade smirked. This was a mark of her high standing with the Emperor and Empress — or, at any rate, the high standing of her new husband with them. Still, she reconsidered her stubbornness.

"If you will all turn your backs, I will enter my bath," she offered.

Sighing, the eunuchs obliged. Gingerly, Jade approached the bathtub and dangled one foot over the water. None of them turned. Gratefully, Jade slipped into the water and began to bathe. Whenever one of the eunuchs would shift position, as if to turn his face in her direction, she would say, "Uh-uh-uh!" and waggle a finger at him.

Muttering slightly, the eunuchs stood with their backs rigidly turned toward her.

"I need a towel," she said, when she was finished bathing.

The head eunuch was positively comic, she thought, as he sidled toward an enamel cabinet, opened it, and retrieved a fluffy towel from it. He thrust it toward her with his back still turned, and the towel dipped into the water.

"Clumsy!' said Jade, quite enjoying her power over these men.

Just then, the messenger eunuch returned with a frowning Liu Huimin behind him.

"What is this?" Liu Huimin cried out, noting the eunuchs lined up with their backs turned on Jade.

"A noble woman's modesty," said the head eunuch, and Jade was grateful that he put it that way.

"Well, there is no use in all of you just standing around. You're dismissed. I will attend to Jade."

The eunuchs filed out and closed the door behind them.

"Can you get me another towel?" Jade asked Liu Huimin. "The clumsy eunuch dropped this one in the water."

"Not surprising, given the fact that he couldn't see where to put it! Were you this modest last night, Jade?"

It was a joking question, and Jade could tell Liu Huimin did not really expect an answer. Yet Jade was suddenly overwhelmed with guilt over not performing her duty to obey the Emperor and Empress. Along with the guilt came the desire to confess.

Jade took a breath. "Oh, Liu Huimin, we did nothing!"

"Hm. The Emperor and Empress will not be pleased."

"Must they know?"

Liu Huimin appeared to be thinking deeply. "You are asking me to lie to their majesties?"

"What business is it of theirs anyway?"

"Everything to do with the Empire is their business. But, given the circumstances, perhaps I will be able to keep your secret."

Jade sighed in relief. "You are a true friend to me, Liu Huimin."

"I mean to be," said Liu Huimin smoothly. "Now let us get you dressed. A breakfast tray is coming as well. You will appear before their majesties shortly, to be discharged to join your husband's warrior troop."

"Where is his troop located?" Jade asked. "Oh, you probably don't know."

"Jade, I know everything that goes on in this Empire. But I am not authorized to tell even you. You will be given escorts who know the way to conduct you safely. Now, hurry. Here comes the breakfast tray. Make short work of it, and we will go see the Son of Heaven."

Jade ate quickly and then followed the stately silk column of Liu Huimin's figure to the reception chamber of the Emperor and Empress. She wondered how, so early in the day, Liu Huimin was so perfectly groomed and coiffed. She sighed in admiration.

After the proper greetings and obeisances were made, the Emperor abruptly gave Jade the order to join her husband at his unit's camp. The Empress, however, studied Jade's face thoughtfully. Her probing sympathy seemed to get behind Jade's defenses and crumble them from within. Jade felt a tear trickle down her cheek. She dared not wipe it off and draw attention to it; it spilled onto the white embroidered silk of the dress she was wearing.

The Empress leaned over to the Emperor and gave him whispered counsel. Jade bowed her head. She was breaking down before her Celestial Parents. It had all been too much for her.

The Emperor looked at her curiously. "Do you have some concerns, Jade?" he asked with such solicitude that Jade's reserves completely crumbled. She fell to her knees before him.

"Oh, yes, I have, wise Son of Heaven!" she cried. "In addition to its suddenness, my husband's death was terribly suspicious! I do not believe it was the result of battle. He gave me — he arranged for me to receive a jeweled box after his death that contained a single golden ginkgo leaf. I believe it was some sort of sign or signal. I believe he was assassinated, and it had something to do with a golden ginkgo leaf — something that leaf symbolizes. I think he knew he was a target and wanted to let me know that his death was not accidental."

To her shock, she had their majesties' total attention. Did they think she was insane — just a babbling wench barely able to get her words out over tears and sobs? But no, the Emperor half rose from the dais, staring at her open-mouthed, as if she had given up state secrets that even he did not know.

Encouraged, she spoke rapidly: "There are hints of special dangers to the Empire, are there not? Could his murder be connected to that? Perhaps he knew something."

Liu Huimin, standing in back of their majesties, frowned and shook her head at Jade, as if warning her to stop speaking and angry that her own confidences in Jade were being betrayed. Jade could not stop herself.

"Is that not why I was remarried so quickly, without any time for mourning? Are there not special dangers threatening the Dragon Throne? Could this golden ginkgo leaf be related to those dangers? My husband did not die a warrior's death in battle," Jade emphasized. "He was assassinated — deliberately — with this!"

She tugged at the red ribbon she wore around her neck and brought forth the silver dart.

The Emperor gasped and rose fully to his feet, staring at her. Then he raised his yellow-silk-clad arm like a long wing and swung it in a gesture to encompass the entire room.

"Leave us!" he thundered at his attendants.

With a flurry of clothing and a tromp of shoes, the score of imperial attendants fled the room.

"I said leave us!" he roared, red-faced, at Liu Huimin.

The Empress said, "Surely Huimin can stay."

Liu Huimin, looking pale and shaken, said, "I am happy to obey the Son of Heaven," and she too sped out of the room on soft-padded shoes. She did not even glance at Jade, but Jade could see that her face was full of fear.

CHAPTER 13

S how me that dart," growled the Emperor. "Bring it forth." Shaking, Jade approached the dais. She had never been so close to their majesties before. Bowing, she lay the dart in her Emperor's hands and watched as his face went through many changes. A flicker of the Empress's eyelid reminded her that she should bow, over and over again, as she backed from the dais.

Jade assumed a meek kneeling position, ten feet from the dais on the platform. She had clearly displeased the Emperor mightily. She was terrified. Leaving her platform shoes on the floor could have incurred a death sentence in the rigid demarcation of manners that characterized a Manchu imperial court. What would her latest breach of etiquette bring? Had she gotten Liu Huimin in trouble too?

Luan, you may soon be twice a widower, she thought, her heart sinking as the Emperor's glinting, slanted eyes slowly rose from the silver dart to her own face, latching eyes with her.

"This is an ancient Serpent Shadow dart," the Emperor said to her carefully, then asked in the slowest and most deliberate voice possible, "You know what this means, do you not, Jade? Speak! Speak frankly now!"

Jade's courage came back to her. "It means that someone very high up in the empire — someone with access to the ancient archives — killed my husband."

The Empress said soothingly, "My dear husband, we are always subjected to intrigues by the people surrounding us. Treachery on the part of the nobility is, unfortunately, nothing new. Curators of the ancient archives are not immune to bribes either. These unfortunate truths are abated by the fierce loyalty of most of our subjects, who would gladly lay their lives down for us."

"No," said the Emperor thoughtfully. "Wu Lei's death, combined with the sign of the golden ginkgo leaf, means that they — *they* —

have extended their reach into the secret places of the Empire and are able to target our best warriors in seemingly minor skirmishes."

Jade swallowed and dared to speak. "Who are *they*?"

The Emperor could not seem to bring himself to speak. He merely sat on his throne-like dais, slowly shaking his head.

The Empress leaned forward and whispered, "The Golden Ginkgo Society. They are a rebel society bent upon overthrowing the Dragon Throne. Us. They are bent on overthrowing us."

"Their reach has grown long," mourned the Emperor, coming out of his state of shock.

"A ginkgo leaf could have fallen inside an old jewelry box—" The Empress was still trying to be soothing.

Jade reported with the crispness of a warrior: "It was inside the lining of the box. It had to have been placed there. Deliberately."

The Empress sighed while the Emperor nodded glumly.

Seizing the moment, Jade begged, "May I stay in Beijing for a few days? Under your imperial protection? Perhaps I can use my eyes and ears to pick up conversations. Everyone in the palace knows I am in mourning and freshly wed. No one will suspect that I am spying on conversations. I will stay three or four days, pick up what I can within the palace and in Beijing itself, and make a full report to you. Then I will rejoin my—my new husband." Jade was glad she could get those last words out. They were not easy to say.

The Emperor nodded slowly. "Yes. Yes, that is a good plan, Jade. You are keenly motivated to discover this, and the Empire is in dire need of any intelligence it can find about the positions and plots of these evil people. Yes, you may stay in Beijing for a few days."

"If I can find my husband's murderer, I will have found a key person in the Golden Ginkgo Society, which is pledged to overthrow your majesties."

"Yes, but don't let your personal desires becloud your military judgment," counseled the Empress. "And," she all but wagged her finger at Jade, "Personal vengeance has no place here. If you find him—or her—the person must be brought to us for justice."

Jade felt her own eyes flash and her mouth turn down in a grimace. She bowed her head in obedience, though.

"They do not just want to overthrow us," the Emperor told her. "They want to overthrow the Manchu dynasty. That means our sons could not succeed us. We would become exiles, a family without honor, wandering and homeless, unable ever to assume the rule we were born to, the rule we were destined to by Heaven."

"They have serious motivation, indeed," said Jade.

She suddenly had misgivings. Hopefully, she thought, they did not show on her face. Although the Emperor and Empress were the wisest of rulers, made excellent decisions, and had brought prosperity and relative peace to the empire, their sons were nothing to be proud of. Spoiled, vain, dissolute, and immoral, she did not think any of them worthy to inherit the Dragon Throne. It was a matter of murmured concern among all the nobles.

As if reading her thoughts, the Emperor said, carefully and slowly, "I have a reserve arrow in my quiver, Jade."

The Empress's hand on his arm signaled him and Jade that the Empress thought the Emperor was treading on dangerous ground in revealing any more.

"Do you understand me, Jade?" the Emperor pressed on. "I am not stupid. I am not blind. I know what is best for the empire, and I have a spare arrow in my quiver. Now take your questions and know well that there is a line to the Dragon Throne well worth fighting for. Your personal motive—revenge for your husband's death—might mingle with other personal motives at some point in the future. Your interests lie, in every way, with preserving the Dragon Throne. I will give you four days to try to penetrate the mystery of your husband's assassination and link it to the Golden Ginkgo Society. After that, I can spare you no longer from the field."

The Emperor rose and walked behind the dais. He lifted a silver stick and struck a suspended golden gong; the sound reverberated throughout the palace, and within seconds the doors to the chamber flew open. Attendants filed in and assumed postures of obedience.

Liu Huimin came in last, shuffling slightly on her silk-clad feet, making obeisances before the throne.

The Emperor has taken her down a peg or two, Jade thought. Perhaps she needed it.

Jade bowed her way out of the room. She was not at all sure what the Emperor had been hinting at with his carefully repeated mention of the 'spare arrow' in his quiver. He must have been reassuring her in general that he knew what he was doing, that he had forces in reserve, and that he was encouraging her to redouble her loyalties and let her personal motives for revenge mix — for four days — with the interests of the empire. That must have been what he meant.

Four days! Four days was nothing to uncover an intrigue and an assassination plot. It was a very small boon. Yet she felt a glow of satisfaction that her words and thoughts had swayed the Son of Heaven.

CHAPTER 14

That night Luan stood a little beyond the halo of the campfire, in the coolness of the night. His troop had supped, cleaned up, and were now enjoying an hour before everyone retired to sleep. Some were practicing fighting techniques. Someone was stroking a qin, a silk-stringed, fretless, board-like instrument. The notes seemed to fly away gently into the night. Several couples had gone off to end their day in prayer. It was a peaceful time, with varieties of soft sounds: the murmur of voices recounting stories, the swish of clothing rustling as people practiced their kung fu arts, and the melodic notes of flutes and the qin punctuated by the pops of the embers of the fire. It was Luan's second favorite part of the day. Dawn was his first, when the soul was fresh and ready to embark upon the battles within and without by arming the inner self with meditation.

Luan heard the footfalls of horses displacing the dirt of the ground with soft thuds. Glancing around, he saw that no one else in the camp seemed to notice. His senses went into high alert, and he rose to the balls of his feet, all his muscles tensing. Yes, there were at least four horses, and all had riders. Four people, then. He relaxed, as his unit was composed of nine couples, all well-trained in both martial and military arts. They would be more than a match for the visitors if the visitors meant harm to them. Also, he could tell from the depth of one of the horse's footfalls that one rider, at least, was a youth. He felt of the subtle energies — no, not a youth, a woman.

He turned to his comrades, several of whom had heard or sensed the incoming presence by now. This was one reason why he was the commander of the group. A few seconds could be crucial.

"Three men and a woman," he told them. "We are more than a match for them, and they do not seem to be hiding their approach."

He heard the sentries hail the visitors, who by their murmurs announced themselves peacefully. As they entered the encampment,

Luan saw the woman's face catch the firelight. It was Jade. She had arrived with an escort of three eunuchs. They were well-trained, Luan could tell by their military postures in their saddles. To be sent to guard a noblewoman like Jade, he assumed they were trained in expert swordsmanship. Their majesties would not have left her vulnerable in any way.

Jade dismounted, thanked the eunuchs, and paid them with what looked like a generous amount of gold and silver, while Luan stepped forward to invite them all to share dinner.

"We have just stored the food; much of it is still warm," he urged them. "We have tea and fresh water as well."

Hospitality was important in the desert. There was no other place on earth where people needed one another so much to survive.

The eunuchs thanked him, and others of his encampment introduced themselves to them, found seating for the men around the fire, and brought out food and skins of water and warm tea.

Jade faced Luan with her features smooth and seemingly under control. He admired her for that and bade her welcome, which she acknowledged graciously, but she was glancing around, and seemed to be deciding how to make do with the terrain at hand, like a true military woman. When he offered her food, she refused, accepting, however, a cup of tea.

"Let me warm it for you," he suggested, and he found her a comfortable place by the fire.

The eunuchs brought news from the court at Beijing, and the fighters, who had been in the desert for several weeks, listened with grave attention.

A eunuch asked, "Are you all masters of kung fu then?"

The others looked to Luan to answer.

"Kung Fu is a broad term," he answered carefully, "encompassing many arts. But, yes. There are two general schools of kung fu. Our encampment here are experts of the Wu Dung school."

"And what does that mean?" another eunuch asked.

"It means that we deal with energy and, in general, use an attacker's own force against him or her."

"I have seen exhibitions at court," said the third eunuch, "in which the warrior maneuvers until the enemy tires from his own efforts to land blows. Is that what you mean?"

"That would be one strategy, yes. We live out the maxim that the martial arts are for self-defense, or for defense of the weak or of the nation's integrity. It was originally developed by the monks for such purposes. That is why we choose the desert to train in. The solitude and silence are most conducive to learning about the art."

Jade snorted with a sound of contempt. When all eyes turned to her for an explanation, she said proudly, "My troop was of the Shaolin school. We use the muscles Heaven gave us. But we are in agreement that martial arts are primarily for defense, not aggression. Sometimes defense calls for strategic aggression, however."

Since she was staring at him, Luan commented mildly, "I don't disagree."

"May we have a demonstration?" the head eunuch begged. "It will be better than a Beijing opera!"

Jade snorted again. "I will demonstrate Shaolin technique! My favorite is the Tiger. I don't know if any of the Wu Dung school can stand up to me, though."

"A woman tiger?" teased a eunuch.

Luan said, "Actually, it is very fitting. The aggressiveness of Shaolin Tiger fighters is meant to conclude a fight quickly. It is highly suitable for a woman, who might not have the same stamina as a man in a fight."

The Tiger style was the exact opposite to Luan's own style. His was almost entirely a defensive method that sought to wear out an opponent through making them waste their force. Since the Tiger relied on attack and aggression and force to subdue its foe, a match between a Wu Dung warrior and a Shaolin Tiger warrior would be interesting indeed.

Jade announced proudly, "A tiger is never prey but always a predator. I am ready to demonstrate, should a worthy opponent step forth!"

Laughingly, the entire group began to chant, "Luan! Luan! Luan!"

It was the group's first acknowledgment of their connection in marriage. Now the group broke forth riotously with teasing.

"You seem to have caught a tiger by the tail, Luan! Watch out!"

"Ah, yes, you must look out for the tiger wife!"

There were many other teasing remarks, and Jade stared steadily, almost fiercely, into the firelight. Luan had an almost irresistible urge to take her down a peg or two.

"All right," he agreed. "I will fight the tiger — or tigress, in this case."

Jade rose, amidst cheers, and removed her outer garments to help her movements flow. Luan did the same. Then they circled one another around the firelight as the eunuchs and other spousal teams cheered.

Jade formed her hands into claws. Her thumbs and first fingers curved into crescent shapes, while the other fingers were arched and held apart, almost as if she were stiffly holding two balls. There were raucous cheers at the sight — appreciative ones from the fellow fighters and somewhat mocking ones from the eunuchs — but Luan took those hands quite seriously. He could see she had good form. What was more, Jade had assumed the basic stance of the Tiger, with her back erect, her waist locked into her hips, her head upright, and her weight settled low. He detected the faintest movement of her tailbone, as if there were a tiger's tail attached to it, the slight movement giving her the leverage to fling herself into motion at any moment. Her teeth were showing in what looked like a tiger's snarl while her eyes assumed the dangerous depths of the big jungle cat.

Jade was probably about his age, in her mid-twenties, Luan guessed, and she was in her physical prime. It showed. Quite the lovely — and dangerous — feline, he thought, as he assumed his own Wu Dung battle stance to take on the tigress.

CHAPTER 15

As Jade leaped from her haunches, one could almost see the body of a tigress and its muscles rippling beneath her skin, as if the animal's spirit was superimposed on the form of the woman. She was as powerful and fluid as the lordly beast for which her art had been named.

With suddenness and a roar, she delivered a jaw-cracking blow to Luan's face. Her aggression had worked just the way it was supposed to, surprising him and catching him off balance. Its swift and fearless application was intended to end the fight early, before her energy gave out. He realized that he had been lulled into a unguarded moment of admiring her martial beauty; warrior-like, she had taken advantage of that moment.

His teeth gritted with grudging respect for her as his jaw hardened against her classic, tiger-claw strike. It had a twist on the end that increased its impact, and true to its form, the blow from the heel of her hand was the first contact, and it was hard as Gobi Desert stone. The downward swipe of her fingernails would score his cheek with four long, bloody stripes, as if he had encountered a real tiger.

To his surprise, however, he felt only her fingertips graze his face, almost gently tracing the arc of her attack. He must have looked startled, because she backed off into her stance and seemed to communicate, through a noble restraint of expression, that this was demonstration only, and she would never hurt a sparring partner who was on her side in the larger scheme of things. His respect for her grew.

Luan's Wu Dung movements were different. His body did not settle into its muscles as hers did; he was light on his feet and seemed to dance, flow, and almost fly. There was a measured grace to his movements, underpinned by the force and flow of qi — energy — seemingly harnessed by the economy of his movements. He tempered his strikes and did more blocking and sidestepping than delivering his own blows.

Her mouth lifted at one corner in a kind of contempt. He realized she had fought men before; men who were genuine opponents, not inclined to let her win easily. He let the energy wind of his movements increase and saw sweat break out on her forehead as she countered his blows.

Another tiger-claw strike landed, this time on his neck, and again he was surprised that she did not use her nails, although she did growl fiercely while applying it. This gave him the opportunity to grasp her wrist and twist enough to flip her off her feet, all the while guiding her fall with his qi so that she was not hurt upon landing. She sprang up from her prone, crab-like position, and Luan let her do so, although he could have easily put his foot on her back and pinned her down.

The other couples and the eunuchs cheered for both of them. As the eunuchs began to complement their demonstration, Luan thought it was a good opportunity to end the fight, and he bowed to Jade.

"Worthy opponent," he said, and she bowed stiffly in return. Then he suggested the two of them go over to the other side of the camp to have a restorative cup of green tea. Other husband and wife couples were now on their feet, joking with and demonstrating their skills to the admiring eunuchs.

"You let me save face back there," Jade said to Luan when they were out of earshot of the others. "You let me rise that last time. You had me."

"Well, you saved my face too," said Luan, running his hand along the place where her fingernails should have left marks but hadn't. "Literally."

"It was only a demonstration," she said, and sauntered off with her tea.

Luan had hoped for some sort of harmony between them based on this positive interchange, but as she sat staring into the fire, nursing her cup of tea without companions, it appeared that Jade's loneliness was increasing. Unhappiness marred her features. She looked very much as if she wished she were somewhere else.

He supposed it was foolish to do so, but he approached her again. She sullenly made room for him to sit next to her on a log, and kept staring into the fire.

"You were in Beijing for four days," he opened the conversation. "May I ask what you were doing there?"

"I had an assignment from the Emperor," she said briefly. "To find something out."

Luan accepted this with a brief nod. "Did you find out what you needed to?"

She sighed. "No. I tried, but I uncovered little intelligence for the Son of Heaven."

"I am sure you did your best," Luan said offering comfort.

"I don't need your pity," she said stiffly.

"Ah!" said Luan. "It is not pity. It is empathy. I have failed in some errands for the Emperor, too. We warriors do not consider failure acceptable, do we, in spite of its occasional inevitability?"

Jade said nothing. Then she looked at him. Her expression was so easy to read. He was beginning to appreciate how her emotions played on her face.

"You are—" he said, and he tilted his head a bit to gauge more accurately— "Afraid? Something has frightened you?"

Jade said, "I have not come as far as I have in life because I am a coward."

"Of course not. Yet feeling fear is not the same as cowardice."

"I know that," she said. "I have not been in battle as many times as I have, conquering my body's fear, not to know that."

"Your fear has paralyzed you this time, though," he said, certain he was right. "Your energy is boxed in. I can feel it."

She looked at him, annoyance on her face. He was not sure if it was because he had guessed the truth, or because she thought he was still insinuating that she was a coward.

So much prickly pride she has, he thought. Yet, both of them struggled with raw emotions, he knew. He had the advantage of having been out here in the wild and mountains for a few days, letting nature soothe his sorrow. She had been at court, surrounded by people with little time for reflection.

Jade rose abruptly, tossed the remaining contents of her tea mug onto the ground, and walked away from him.

The edges of night had encroached upon the campsite, like cold fingers stealing their way into tunics and feet. The fire could not keep the warriors warm now; the temperature was dropping too quickly. Even as their faces flushed in the firelight, their backs were so cold they shivered. It was time to retire to their bedding of quilts and thick furs to ward off the coldnight.

Jade pitched her tent on the other side of the camp from Luan, so that they slept closer to the rest of their comrades than to one another. It was a public insult—one Luan did not expect after she had expressed her gratitude to him for letting her save face.

Why didn't she return the favor and let him save face by coming to his tent, as a wife should? He'd had no intention of making her feel cowardly. He had been trying to help her overcome what was blocking her inside. Wasn't that what a husband should do? He and Jingwei had often liberated one another's pent-up energy with understanding conversation.

She is different. I must accept that, he told himself, but he felt anger burning deep within him. The other warriors were right. He had caught a tigress by the tail all right.

The question was whether he should let go or pull.

CHAPTER 16

A woman was sobbing in the predawn darkness. Luan could hear it all the way across the camp. For a moment he feared one of the husband warriors had been killed; perhaps the camp had been invaded and taken over. His senses came alive, and he untangled his muscular limbs from the fur covering, ready to spring into action. He took a moment to sense the energy around him before bolting out of his tent.

No. He sensed there was no takeover. The sobbing was definitely a sole woman in mourning. It must be Jade, her brave front crumbling in the long, lonely night. Some of his anger at her melted. The tough little tigress was not so strong after all. Left on her own, she could not cope with her sorrow.

He snorted. She should have come to his tent last night. Then this public shame would not have happened. Still, it helped him forgive her for flouncing off far away from him to her solitary tent.

The sobs ceased suddenly as if cut off by a knife. Frowning, he strode to Jade Blossom's tent, passing by a handful of early risers, who huddled around the fire. They watched, but held their peace.

Luan entered the tent to find Jade in a heap under her furs. He could barely see her, but the slight curve of her glistening cheek reflected the first glimmers of dawn that crept through the tent flap. In the surrounding darkness, it shone like a crescent moon. As he approached, the furs heaved, and his own breath came easier at the sight. She was alive, at least, and breathing.

He pulled the furs away to reveal Jade, shivering in her night clothes, trembling and gasping between sobs.

"Jade?" he inquired softly.

"I am so ashamed to let other warriors hear me crying, but I could not stop myself. I tried to stifle my sobs with the fur robes, but then I couldn't breathe and I began to gasp and panic." Her voice lowered in shame. "I am not acting like a warrior."

"You are acting like one who has suffered a great loss," Luan said, sitting down beside her and patting her shoulder kindly. "We do not expect the wounded to act as warriors until they have recovered. Your heart—your energy—is wounded. It is more painful than a wound of the flesh."

She raised her eyes to his, the lashes dark and wet. "You are wounded, too."

"Yes."

"And yet you do not show your weakness."

"If I did, I would cry a river. My heart seeps constantly within me."

"Why can I not keep my own river of tears inside like you do?"

Luan smiled. "Men and women deal with sorrow differently," he said. "You know the ancient tale. A husband and wife have lost an infant child to death. The wife sobs openly and wants to talk about it; the husband says nothing day after day. The wife begins to think he is insensitive and does not care, and one night at dinner she accuses him of being unfeeling. When he opens his mouth to speak, blood pours forth, for he has bitten his tongue to keep from crying aloud."

"Yes," said Jade. "I have heard the tale. Certainly I cannot hold my sorrow in like that."

"You carry more weight than your sorrow. I can tell. You are carrying a heavy burden of knowledge and fear."

"You are right," she sighed.

He felt she was on the brink of confiding in him, but Luan became distracted by something he sensed outside the tent. He raised his head as if listening. There were few sounds from the warriors gathered outside the tent, but he sensed their curiosity, still unsettled. However, the camp was safe.

"That sensing of yours," said Jade, considering his face with a shrewd eye. "I wonder if our troop had been trained in Wu Dung rather than Shaolin, whether we would have sensed—whether my husband would have sensed—whether *I* would have sensed..." Her voice trailed off.

"Sensed what? Your husband died in battle. It is unfortunate, but every battle holds that possibility for all of us."

"No," said Jade. She shook her head sadly and slowly. "My husband was betrayed. I pulled this out of my husband's dying body." She fumbled at her neckline to pull out on a length of sash and a silver dart.

Luan's brow furrowed. He reached to take the dart in his hands.

"It has a poisoned tip," she warned him. "Be careful. I have washed and sealed it, but still..."

"Thank you for caring about my welfare, Jade." He was sincere. He raised the dart to the height of his eyes and examined it closely by moonlight.

"This is a Silver Serpent Shadow dart," he whispered in wonder. "No enemy would have access to one of these. This dart belonged to someone—"

Luan paused, and Jade filled in: "Someone in the empire. Someone with access to museum stores of the empire's glory. Someone inside and high up. Someone of the nobility."

Luan sighed heavily. "It is not unusual that the greatest enemies of a realm are sometimes within it. I would hope that everyone near the Emperor is loyal, but clearly they are not. However, this Serpent Shadow dart is not from Beijing. Whoever this traitor is, he or she has access to the royal museum stores in Nanjing. That is where the Serpent Shadow relics are stored, in the ancient palace."

Sudden light poured into the tent as the flap was opened. They could not see who it was, silhouetted as thy were against the growing dawn.

"People are wondering if she is all right," said a gruff voice.

It was a woman named Willow, and she indicated Jade with a nod of her head at the word 'she.'

"That is no excuse to rudely invade someone's tent!" said Jade indignantly, snatching the dart from Luan's hand and shoving it under the covers.

"Please, ask permission to enter next time," Luan said mildly.

Willow nodded and the tent flap fell back into place as she left them.

"That is all the rebuke you have for her? She saw the Serpent Shadow dart!" protested Jade.

"I trust Willow implicitly. I am not sure she saw it, and even if she saw it, she will make nothing of it. Her loyalty is unquestioned."

Jade seemed to take him at his word. "I should have known—I should have seen—I should have sensed someone was his enemy," she mourned, pulling the fur back from the dart and weeping over it.

"You must absolve yourself of guilt in your husband's death," Luan scolded her gently. "There was an intrigue or a plot afoot, and you could not possibly have known about that."

"I should have."

"No one can know everything." He sighed heavily as he said this. He knew he should take his own advice. It haunted him that he had been away on a solitary mission when Jingwei had come to term with their baby. Of course, there were women to help her, but he could not help thinking that if he had been there, and she had known of his presence, she might not have succumbed to death. He knew the needs of the nation came first, but regret still gnawed him. He had known she was sick all throughout her pregnancy, but womenfolk assured him this was often the case, so he had not thought any more about it.

Jade narrowed her eyes at him even more, and for a horrible moment he thought she was reading his mind. He did not want anyone to know the depths of his guilt.

"Excuse me for a moment," he said to her, rising, and he saw disappointment and frustration on Jade's face, as if she had just begun to read an interesting book and it was snatched from her.

He went outside the tent where he took several restorative gulps of fresh air.

CHAPTER 17

All the other members of the unit were up by now, gathered near the fire. Willow stood at the center of the group, and turned to look at Luan as he left Jade's tent. He sensed among them a mixture of emotions — concern and empathy a certain amount of disapproval toward Jade.

"Brothers and sisters!" he addressed the other warriors. "Jade mourns her first husband, a great, fierce, and loyal patriot whom we all miss. Taking up arms with a new partner at her side is difficult for her, and I myself still mourn Jingwei. Please be patient with us as we find our way together."

The warriors quietly dispersed, throwing looks heavy with sympathy at Luan himself. He sensed their deep respect for him and the heart-wound he carried. He knew they had loved Jingwei. His speech seemed to fill them with respect for his new wife too, for in moments their disapproval changed into acceptance and he smiled at them all, showing his thanks. He also felt that the shame of Jade sleeping so far away from him was blotted out by this latest incident — she clearly needed someone with her, and he was the logical someone. He felt an indulgent sense of compassion for Jade, so unable to control her emotions, and he was ready to go back to talk to her.

He overheard Ching say to his wife, Anbai, in passing, "It appears the tigress has quite a soft heart after all."

"I like her better now that I know a tender heart beats beneath the tough tigress hide," agreed his wife.

The encouraging words exchanged between two of his warriors, one of them his lieutenant, emboldened Luan to re-enter Jade's tent. Jade looked at him gratefully and as if she had been expecting him. Encouraged, he sat next to her.

"Tell me what happened last night," he said, for he knew women must talk about these things. "How did your sorrow overwhelm you?"

"I had a dream," she said and shuddered. "I dreamed I was at my husband's funeral again. There was the lacquered coffin, covered in bright-red, embroidered silk. I could not believe he was in there and that I could never reach him or touch him or talk to him again. It was all just exactly as it was. I felt all the same things, saw all the same sights, and heard all the same sounds. I was proceeding along, wondering if I would not be wise to swallow opium and kill myself."

At Luan's head shake, she waved her hand, as if the thought were safely dismissed.

"There was the tomb in front of us," she continued. "There was the boy waving the flag and calling forth the spirit of the dead. It was Wu Lei's nephew, as we have no children to do it. The boy did his duty in the dream just as he had done in real life, and just as it happened in real life, he knelt by the side of the coffin and called out, 'Avoid the nails!' when they began to hammer the coffin lid down." Jade shuddered and winced as if hearing the hammer blows once again.

"It was a traditional funeral," commented Luan.

"Yes, traditional. Everything was done according to tradition. But in my dream, as they hammered, my husband—oh, excuse me! Of course, you are my husband now."

She made a bowing motion with her head, which both surprised and pleased Luan.

"As they hammered," she continued, in a whisper of horrified awe, "he began calling out: 'I am alive! I am alive!' and I began to fear they would pierce him with the nails, as they kept hammering diligently, as if they did not hear him. I was the only one who heard. I pushed the men aside, I fought them off, and I tried to raise the coffin lid, all the time hearing him call out, 'I am alive! I am alive!' but I couldn't get the coffin open, and no one helped. They all thought I had gone mad with grief. Then the next thing I knew, his cries faded away, and I think … I think he suffocated and died inside the coffin."

"Ah," said Luan. "There is meaning here. I can feel it in your energy as you recount the dream. There is meaning, but I must discern it. How was he buried?"

"He was buried where there was a view of the mountain behind him, for something to lean on, and with the sun rising in front of him to signify rising fortune. Everything was done according to tradition for a man of his standing."

"Then he should be content, not restless, as your dream indicates. Did they place mercury and charcoal within the coffin to prevent rotting?"

"Yes. As I said, everything was done according to form."

"And a pearl was placed in his mouth?"

Jade nodded vigorously to show that this traditional custom, too, had been properly observed. "What is the meaning?" she begged to know. "You are a discerner of energy—tell me! Do you know?"

"I think I do know," said Luan. "But I am not sure you will want to hear it."

"Tell me," she said, rising to her knees and clutching his arm. "I must know."

He said, softly, "It means your husband does live."

"Lives … how?"

Luan sighed. "Your husband lives in me."

Jade's mouth opened, then snapped shut. She removed her hand from his arm and straightened up.

"That is a very convenient interpretation," she said.

"Accept it or not, as you wish," he told her. "It is what I discern. What more evidence do you need, Jade? Our marriage was ordered by the Son of Heaven, the Emperor, and the Empress. You dreamed that your husband is alive and trying to get out of his coffin. Of course, we know he is dead and buried, as is my wife, Jingwei. The energy of a live husband is trying to resume its place at your side but you are resisting."

Jade's arched brows drew fiercely together over her large, brown eyes. Luan himself knew there was some hypocrisy in his lofty words. He, too, was struggling to accept the sad events that had brought them together, and he knew it all too well.

Jade lifted her chin. "You would be resisting, too, had you suffered a loss as great as mine," she said, her words clipped.

Anger rose in him. His face reddened, his body trembled, and his hands clenched. His usually calm veneer broke, surprising him at the angry tide that flooded out of him toward her.

"Do not dare to misinterpret my resilience and silence!" he said through his teeth, mindful of those outside the tent. "I grieve my wife as deeply as you grieve your husband. You are selfish to think you are the only one suffering. I also lost a child! My wife and I were looking forward to the birth. We knew love — more love than I ever hope to have with you! I didn't ask to be married to you; I didn't choose you. I took you as wife in obedience to my Emperor."

Jade had been stunned into silence, but it didn't last long.

"So the calm, stoic, Wu Dung warrior has feelings after all," she hissed, sounding exactly like the cat she pretended to be.

Without a word, Luan got up and strode from the tent, growing even more angry as he marched away. Jade was a selfish woman! The vain tigress seemed to think her grief and feelings surpassed all others. Did she really think he was ready to joyously receive her as his wife, with no misgivings or regrets about his own loss? Could she not understand how wounded he was still, and how difficult it was for him to be a strong leader to the warriors? Did he have to be the target of her resentment and conceit, on top of his own sorrows, cares, and responsibilities?

Luan gazed at the calm, silver, crescent moon that still hung in the gray dawn sky as he returned to his own tent, trying to calm his anger at his new wife. He should send her back to the Emperor with a note stating his displeasure. They would not receive her with much kindness then! Maybe that would tame the tigress once and for all.

He willed himself to patience. He could not remember the last time he had lost his temper like that, with anyone. It was the river of sorrow within him, no doubt, that could not release itself in weeping. He must march on and lead. He felt badly to have lost his temper with Jade, and he wondered if anyone suspected their argument. The warriors' eyes had been on him when he left Jade's tent, though no one had spoken.

Silently, he tried to emanate a peaceful energy throughout the camp, striving to achieve it over the growing pool of resentment he felt toward his new wife.

CHAPTER 18

Jade was conscious of the warriors' consideration that morning at breakfast, although she still felt ashamed of her early morning display of emotions. They seemed to be offering her nothing but patience and empathy. She felt a grim satisfaction that she had provoked Luan to reveal some emotion. He wasn't as stoic as he pretended to be after all! Yet she wasn't happy he was mad at her, and she did realize she had belittled his loss.

As she approached the group sitting around the fire, she murmured an apology for her behavior the night before. The warriors protested.

"A loyal wife might swallow opium upon her husband's demise to end her own suffering," said Ching. "It is perhaps even more painful to go on living, and we respect you for it."

"A wife could grieve for the rest of her life for her dead husband," his wife, Anbai, said. "Your grief is understandable."

Jade sensed that some of the other women were slightly less sympathetic, especially Willow. She overheard Willow murmuring to the other woman charged with cleaning the dishes after their meal. She caught a snatch of their conversation as she brought her own bowl and spoon to them.

"Luan is a good man," Willow opined. "Any woman should put aside her sorrow for him."

The other agreed. "A great warrior, a kind man — and handsome, too!"

"He is all those things," agreed Willow.

Jade wordlessly handed them her dishes, then came back to sit down before the fire. She looked at Luan, who gave her a polite but distant greeting. He seemed to be waiting for everyone to finish eating and to put the food away. The warriors, attuned to his special energy, made short work of it all. Once the ritual of eating and clearing away the mess was complete, they again gathered around the fire and looked at Luan expectantly.

"A courier came in the night," he announced. "A group called the Golden Ginkgo Society is gaining in power and influence. They gather more followers every day. They are in rebellion against the dynasty and wish to see its downfall."

Jade's mouth opened and closed. She frantically gestured at her new husband to tell him she knew something about this already. He ignored her.

"There was a self-immolation by one of the Golden Ginkgo Society's female members just outside the Forbidden City last night," Luan told the troop. "She set herself on fire and burned to death. The act has, as may be expected, generated some sympathy, and the Emperor fears the Society's recruiting efforts will begin to bear many more fruits."

Jade again tried to get her husband's attention; again he ignored her. Instead he called on Ching.

Ching said, "Setting one's self on fire is a noble act, as it shows one's unflagging commitment to a cause."

The other warriors nodded.

Luan said, "As I mentioned, it has generated some sympathy. We have an eyewitness report of the incident."

The warriors were silent as they listened and squinted as if trying to envision the scene according to the eyewitness report Luan read aloud to them.

It related how a woman in the midst of a crowd, held aloft a jar of inflammatory oil, and cried out, announcing to all what she intended to do. The crowd drew back, scarcely believing what they had heard. She seemed hysterical, the report said, and many doubted she would go through with the act once she faced its stark reality, but still they jostled for a better view.

The woman was no warrior, nor did she seem lunatic or drunken. She was a perfectly ordinary, middle-aged woman, and that added to the horror and unreality of the proceedings. No one imagined that she could be a member of a secret society.

But she told all within hearing that she was member of the Golden Ginkgo Society and she did not waver. She doused her clothing with the oil while decrying the regime and screaming for justice. Some supporters in the crowd cried aloud with her, agreeing with her, and some began to sway and sing a holy song for her martyr's death. They were beginning to believe she was serious.

When she drew out flint and steel and struck a spark, the crowd drew back, gasping, fearing the flames that began to lick at the woman's dress. People were confused about what they should do. Some cried for water, or argued that they should throw the woman on the ground and roll her over in the sand by the road to smother the flames.

The report said the woman smiled as the folds of her dress caught fire, but that her smile contorted into a rictus of agony as the flames engulfed her. Still, she did not move. She did not scream. She did not beg for rescue. The crowds around her murmured with respect for her martyrdom.

Jade could imagine the woman's silhouette twisting and shrinking as the flames devoured her, her humanity and vulnerability offered up to her cause with a silent scream. For the careful reporting said there was no sound but the hungry crackling and the hollow, thirsty whoosh of the flames as they consumed her.

When at last, she crumpled, she was a shrunken thing. The report described how she lay face down on the sand, limbs flailing, looking like a baby just learning to crawl. At last, she ceased moving and the flames slowly died down, leaving her charred corpse frozen in its unnatural posture. The crowd had melted away. When the heat had cooled, soldiers had come and carried what was left away — a blackened, distorted, husk.

Luan stopped reading and, for a moment, there was complete silence but for the whisper of wind through the scrub.

That husk, thought Jade, said more than any words that could have come from her mouth. How would the people of Beijing read this silent protest? How would they respond?

"Naturally," said Luan, at last, "any such scene awakens our human sympathy for the person who victimized herself so. We are moved and touched in our hearts, as were many of the onlookers, according to the report. That does not mean the cause the woman died for is one we should be sympathetic to. This woman was sadly deluded. However, her act has had some effect. Her immolation left a scorch mark on the stones outside the gates." He looked down at the page in his hands and read: "'Some are gathering around this mark to pray. This is, of course, quite uncomfortable for the Emperor and Empress. Supporters of the Golden Ginkgo Society are passing out leaflets among those praying, explaining their grievances and goals.'"

Luan fell silent. His listeners remained quiet, too, enthralled and disturbed.

Impatiently, Jade waved her hand once more to get her husband's attention. A moment later, she dropped it to her side again, knowing that Luan was going to ignore her, which he did.

"What are their specific grievances and goals?" inquired Ching.

"They wish to overthrow the dynasty. Their grievance is that the dynasty is Manchu, not Han Chinese. Many members of the Golden Ginkgo Society are young people, although they have older leaders too. They say that the Manchus invaded China and have dominated it for hundreds of years without legitimacy. They say that the Emperor is not the Son of Heaven, but that their own Han leader is. Their Han leader, Wei-Ling, claims his own divine right to the Dragon Throne."

"That is treason!" exclaimed one of the warriors.

"He should die the death of a thousand cuts!" snarled another.

The group came to life. Several of them sprang to their feet, ready to fight at that moment, and the ringing of speedily unsheathed swords and daggers rent the morning calm.

"Luan! Luan!" Jade called from amongst them, waving her hand to get her husband's attention. He ignored her.

CHAPTER 19

eace now!" Luan calmed his warriors with pacific hand gestures. "Such a grave situation requires cool heads and calm hearts. The Emperor and Empress have been very patient with the Society, and no one has yet been arrested or killed. There are many such secret societies, but the Golden Ginkgo Society is the largest and most dangerous. Its members say they are immune to the sword and cannot be harmed, and that they have spiritual powers beyond our imaginations. Of course, they have not been tested in battle yet, so the masses are beginning to believe their claims of divine immunity to all weapons."

"When they encounter the blade of my sword," Willow growled, "they will not be immune. I guarantee you that."

Jade suddenly thought of something. She needed a new sword! The Emperor had not bestowed one on her. She again tried to get Luan's attention, but again he ignored her. Instead, he nodded at Ching, who spoke up again.

"Do they, themselves, believe this—that they are immune to the sword's blade? Or do they use it as a mind weapon to confuse their enemies?"

Luan answered, "They believe it, and this belief will inspire them to deeds of foolhardiness, which some may mistake for courage."

"The woman who self-immolated was not immune to fire," Ching pointed out. "Can the followers of this Society not understand that such people would not be immune to the sword either?"

Jade's hand itched, thinking of a new sword for herself. She raised her hand again, but Luan turned his features toward Ching to address his point.

"They claim that her body will soon reconstitute and she will once more walk among the living. They can explain away a great deal. At the same time, because they have not been tested against the Son of Heaven's troops, the Golden Ginkgo Society does, indeed, have the mental advantage of which you spoke. Believing them immune to weapons strikes doubt into enemies' hearts and trembling admiration into the hearts of the gullible. They are fortunate to have found, in their own sincere beliefs, such a powerful weapon of the mind. They are also fortunate to have attracted such devoted followers."

Jade was secretly fuming. Ever since he had begun to speak, she had been trying to get Luan's attention. She was not used to being ignored like this; Wu Lei always had been scrupulously attentive to her, even in group settings.

Luan went on. (Was he never going to stop speaking? Jade wondered. For someone so stoic, he was certainly waxing eloquent this morning!)

"The stroke of Fortune is at times unpredictable. At this time, it appears that fortune favors the Golden Ginkgo Society, for they are growing rapidly in numbers and influence. An incident like this swells their ranks remarkably. There must be an imperial response." He studied the group of warriors and then said abruptly, "We are breaking camp immediately. Although the courier who came in the night was trustworthy, he might have been traced or followed here. You must prepare."

He looked directly at Jade.

"You will saddle your horse and ride next to me," he ordered her.

Finally, he was paying her some attention! Jade was displeased, though; it was certainly Luan's prerogative both as her husband and as the camp commander to order her thus, but he had so far not exerted his authority over her and given orders like this. Her face flamed a little. Wu Lei had been a unit commander too, but he had never pulled rank on her like this.

Her thoughts went to Wu Lei, with his musical, soft voice, how he always explained everything in eloquent words and in detail so that she understood exactly what he was thinking and feeling and could easily go along with him—so unlike the cryptic Luan.

She bowed in outward acquiescence anyway, trying to keep her lips from tightening visibly and giving him a hint of her resentment. She did not like being spoken to in such a peremptory tone. Still, she was glad that he had acknowledged her subtle signals and that she would now have an opportunity to talk to him about a new sword and about what she knew of the Golden Ginkgo Society. Her lips turned in with resentment, thinking he had not called upon her when she had valuable information to impart.

As the others packed up the camp and loaded their horses, Luan approached Jade. "We will ride ahead, a bit apart from the others," he informed her.

"As you wish," she said stiffly.

Luan was apparently an efficient packer and traveled lightly. He was ready to go in minutes. Jade felt a grudging respect for him. She also traveled lightly and could pack up at a moment's notice. When she appeared, with her tent struck and her belongings compacted into a portable bundle, Luan nodded, mounted his horse, and gestured for her to mount hers. She did, and the two set off.

In passing, Luan addressed Ching. "We will scout ahead," he said, and Ching nodded.

Ching was standing with his wife, Anbai, and as she and Luan passed the couple, Jade thought she detected a bit of disappointment in Anbai's face. She looked at Anbai inquiringly and reined her horse to a stop before her.

Thus encouraged, Anbai came forward and stood next to Jade's horse, blinking up into the sunshine. "I hope we get an opportunity to talk sometime soon," she said, her expression friendly.

"Why," said Jade, surprised at the woman's good will. "Why, I do too," she said politely.

Anbai then stood back from Jade's mount, and Jade turned her horse to face and follow her new husband, hoping their short conversation was the budding blossom of a potential friendship.

"You've a new friend, it appears," commented Luan, when she guided her horse to walk next to his.

Jade could not decipher the expression on her husband's face. "I hope so," she replied.

"Friendship is one of the great treasures of life," Luan said.

"I know that," said Jade, a little impatiently.

Did this man think she was a fool to be lectured to from on high? He was about her age, she gathered. Why did he take the position of one so wise and all-knowing—and bossy? His ignoring of her during the meeting set her teeth on edge.

"I need a new sword," she blurted out to him. "And I know something about the Golden Ginkgo Society."

"Indeed," was all the reply she got, and he rode so placidly and imperturbably that fury rose in her breast.

She would not let him see it.

CHAPTER 20

uan made small talk for a time, pointing out this and that natural feature of the breathtaking but harsh desert landscape, and Jade's impatience and anger grew within her. Why was he not letting her get a word in edgewise? Could he not tell how upset she was? Finally, she reined in her horse and stopped.

"What?" Luan asked, surprised. "What are you doing?"

"You are so insensitive—you who always think you know everything about the qi around you! You certainly don't pick up much on mine! You must know I have something to say to you—I've all but waved a flag for the last hour!"

Luan looked astounded, then hurt, then angry. Then he explained himself, very carefully, as if controlling himself with every word to keep his composure.

"Your behavior during the meeting means that everyone in camp knows you have some information to impart. I am certainly aware of that. But my warriors are highly attuned. We were not quite out of earshot from them. That is why I have not yet solicited the information from you."

"Oh," said Jade, deflated. "I did not realize."

"There is much you do not realize," he said in a steely tone. "Now please, let us ride on and tell me what is so important that you have been jumping out of your skin to tell me. You utterly lack subtlety, Jade. You have no idea how much my personal prestige has been stretched to cover your many blunders so far."

"My blunders?" Jade's breathing accelerated. "Who among us does not make blunders, especially in his or her first moments in a new situation?"

"Being in a camp such as this is not so new to you that you should forget your manners. You are not a child. Stop acting like one."

Jade felt like wheeling her horse and galloping away from Luan, away from the other warriors, away from this new life she did not want. Yet she knew a person could not survive alone in the desert. That was the only thing that held her back.

"I am in mourning," she said coldly.

"As am I! Are you so entirely self-absorbed that you cannot at least try to bear your sorrows with as much dignity and patience as I bear mine?"

"It is for others — not you — to comment on your dignity and patience," she retorted.

That seemed to strike Luan deeply. To her surprise, he bowed his head penitently. "You are right in that," he said humbly. "I do apologize. You are absolutely correct. Let us keep riding, or in a moment the others will catch up and hear every word we say."

Jade was surprised by his sudden humility and the chagrined look on his face. Apparently he had taken her offhand rebuke very much to heart. That showed her he was sincere about being a man of good character. Remembering her own words and actions, she felt rebuked too.

She bowed her head too. "I apologize for reacting so to you leading us out of earshot before hearing me out. I was mistaken in your motives."

"Jade," Luan sounded like he was relieved, "let us drop our weapons against each other — as we now both have — and try to live in peace."

"Agreed," said Jade. "There are too many enemies arrayed against us to be fighting one another. The empire is more important than our differences."

They looked at each other out of almond-shaped brown eyes. Jade suddenly felt hope in her heart, and she almost unconsciously moved her horse closer to his.

"Please impart your information," he invited her.

"Wu Lei," she said carefully, instead of 'my husband' — "Wu Lei was assassinated, as I told you. I am sure it was the Golden Ginkgo Society."

Luan looked doubtful.

Jade, carried away by excitement, cried, "I want to be chosen as the infiltrator! I am driven to find things out. I —"

"You have emotion too," he said quietly. "Perhaps too much for the subtleties of the mission."

Jade felt utterly punctured by his words. "You do not think much of me," she said huffily.

"On the contrary. It is interesting to meet someone who cannot hide their emotions. I can see that, with your passion, you would be excellent in battle. Yet missions calling for more subtlety might not be your strong point."

Jade sighed deeply. He was probably right.

"I have been these last four days in Beijing, trying to discover things about my husband's murder," she told him. "I turned up very little — people were very close-mouthed."

"People will say more if they believe the information means little to you," he said.

"Maybe you are right." She felt her shoulders slump and her face fall. "I was very disappointed in my own espionage. I found an ancient blacksmith's shop on a side street where similar darts were forged long ago. He told me that the mold was in the archives in Nanjing. That is about all I found out."

"I told you the darts were forged in Nanjing. You spent four days to learn something I already knew."

Jade's mouth tightened. "I cannot read your mind to fathom all your knowledge."

"Time wasted never comes back," he said. "And we live in perilous times."

"Stop chiding me! I am worried and frightened enough!" Her throat filled with emotion and tears stung in her eyes.

"What are you so worried and frightened about?" he asked, a little more gently.

"I found a note," she confessed, choking a little. "It said, 'If I wanted to kill you, you'd already be dead … just like Wu Lei. If you want to live, stop asking questions.'"

He glanced at her sharply. "Where was the note?"

"It was in my rice bowl."

"In the palace?" Luan pulled on the reins of his horse, stopped, and stared at her, full-eyed, his attention completely riveted on her.

"Yes."

"Did you tell anyone?"

Jade shook her head sadly. "It was a personal threat. It seemed better to keep it to myself than bother the Emperor with it. He had already allowed me four days to investigate Wu Lei's death."

"I think the Emperor should know about this. Someone in his court has threatened the life of a noble woman. Someone evil is close to the Dragon Throne. He must be warned at once."

Luan swung his horse about and spurred it into a gallop. Jade spurred hers to follow. A part of her was piqued that he seemed to care less for the threat to her welfare the note had presented, than for the threat he saw to the empire.

Then she thought of what else she had wanted to discuss with him.

"Luan! Luan!" she called after him, and she spurred her horse to go faster, but he had disappeared in a cloud of dust from his horse's hooves. "I need a new sword!" she called out to emptiness.

Then she burst into tears of frustration.

CHAPTER 21

Jade wiped her eyes, spurred her steed harder, and charged after her new husband. Blinded by the dust of is passing, she almost rode into the column of their fellow warriors, who had drawn their horses to a stop near a grove of cypress trees. Some had pulled off to the side of the road and were dismounting, but the rest were still in the center of the road.

Jade pulled her horse's reins so suddenly he skidded and reared. Sawing the reins, she got the horse back down on four hooves, reined him to one side and looked about for Luan. Not seeing him, she assumed he had made haste for Beijing.

As if reading her mind, Anbai approached her and pointed to a small rise where Luan could be seen tending a camp fire.

"Does he mean to cook a meal?" Jade asked in confusion.

"No," said Anbai, smiling. "He is sending smoke signals to Beijing. He is a master of it. It seems he has an important message to impart."

"Oh," said Jade. She shrugged, as if it was of little concern to her, yet inwardly she felt gratitude that Luan had taken the information she had given him seriously.

"Is that not a security risk?" she asked, gesturing toward Luan and his fire. "Anyone may read it."

"Luan uses a variety of herbs to cause subtle changes in the color of the smoke to fit a color-coded alphabet. He is a master of it, as I said."

"What should the rest of us do?"

"Wait. Come," said Anbai. "Eat. I have some dried fruit and some bao. They are cold, but still good."

Jade dismounted, tied her horse to a cypress sapling, and seated herself next to Anbai on a small boulder. The other woman offered her food. She nodded, accepted it, and began to eat. The bao were filled with aromatic rice mixed with chopped meat.

"How are you getting on?" Anbai asked in a friendly way.

"All right, I suppose," said Jade.

She looked restlessly over at Luan and his signal fire. "My new husband doesn't listen to me, though. I mean, he does and he doesn't. Everything I say that has bearing on the empire, he listens to almost too keenly. Anything personal, he doesn't seem to want to know about."

Anbai smiled. "He is a typical man. I will say that General Luan Luan is the most dedicated man I know, with the possible exception of my Ching. It is a virtue in a man."

"Yes, but it is uncomfortable sometimes. My husband — Wu Lei — managed to care about me and the empire, both at once. Neither was left unattended to in his care."

"We have all heard he was a fine man," said Anbai consolingly.

Willow, who was sitting nearby on the other side of Anbai, snorted.

"Do you have something to say, Willow?" asked Anbai sweetly.

"Maybe he was paying too much attention to her on the battlefield," said Willow, "and that's how he got himself killed."

Jade sat very still. She thought but for a moment, finished chewing, and rose.

"You will back up those words with your sword," she said, with growing fury, to Willow. Then she stopped short. She had no sword with which to challenge Willow.

Willow placidly kept eating.

"Let us fight empty-handed!" Jade cried in challenge, and she assumed the stance of the tiger, forming her hands into claws. She stamped the ground in front of Willow as if throwing down a gauntlet.

"All in good time," said Willow, refusing to rise and continuing to fill her mouth with food.

Willow looked like a man in the bulky, shapeless clothes she wore. She was neither fragrant nor orchid-like, Jade thought, in spite of that being the meaning of her name. Of indeterminate age, her face was lined with an expression of ill nature. She reeked of smoke, horse dung, and seldom-changed clothing.

"By all means," said Jade. She was almost crowing since Willow had not taken up her challenge. That meant she was the victor by default. "Don't let me interrupt your eating. From your size, it looks like you rarely let anything interrupt that."

Willow snorted and Jade sat down again, feeling confident. Anbai murmured to Willow that she should apologize to Jade.

Willow merely repeated, "All in good time."

"What have you got against Jade?" Anbai scolded her. "You said something very hurtful to her, and the whole camp knows she is mourning her first husband mightily."

"She has a second husband to comfort her," said Willow.

"Ah, are you jealous?" asked Anbai. Her brow furrowed with what looked like genuine concern for the mannish, bullish Willow.

Willow scowled. "Why was she matched to someone new within hours of the departure of her husband?" she growled. "I am still single these several years since my husband died in battle."

"I didn't ask to be married again," said Jade. "I didn't want to be."

"But why? Why do you enjoy such favor with the Emperor and Empress?"

Jade shrugged. "Some might call it favor. There is some political purpose behind it, I am sure. Sometimes I feel like a pawn in a chess game. I am not happy with my situation. Do not think I am glorying in it."

"Well," sighed Willow. "I am more valuable as I am. There are parts of my mission that require an attractive, unattached woman."

She rose abruptly and walked to the other side of the fire, stooping to get herself more food from her saddle pack.

"If her mission requires an attractive woman, I don't see how she will fulfill it," sniffed Jade, and Anbai barely stifled a guffaw. "The Emperor probably had too hard a time finding a man who would accept her."

"Now, let's not be unkind," admonished Anbai. "Willow has her secrets and sorrows, as do we all."

"You are a nice person," said Jade appreciatively. "You are very easy to like. Oh!" she broke off. "Here is Luan, back from his smoke signaling. Luan! Luan!" She called to him. "I need a—"

He moved to the other side of the clearing to where he'd tethered his horse. He ignored her, digging into his saddle pack for something to eat. He sat with Ching and some of the other men until he had finished his sparse meal. Finally, he rose and came to address Jade.

"Jade, you have lost your sword. In this unit, a warrior who has lost his or her sword must earn it back."

"My service to my country has earned me many swords," said Jade stiffly. She realized that all the warriors were beginning to listen to their conversation with interest.

"Your service to your country has been great," admitted Luan. "Yet it is a mark against you that you have lost your weapon. You must wipe out that blot on your record by winning a sword in a fight."

"Then what will happen to the person whose sword I win? What sword will that person use?"

"That person will have to win a new sword in a fight as well."

Jade rose. "So your company always has one weaponless warrior?"

"Until we go into battle and the person wins a sword from an enemy."

"Your rules are harsh," Jade said. "But I can see that they make for good discipline."

She rose and accorded her husband a slight bow. He returned it in equal measure.

Jade looked around. "Whom shall I fight to gain my sword?" she asked.

Luan's gaze lingered on each of his warriors, going from one to another, his face showing that he was weighing the merits of each as opposed to Jade's. It took him several minutes to decide, and Jade swished impatiently, standing on her feet.

"Willow," Luan's jaw snapped in a curt order. "You will fight the tigress to keep your sword."

CHAPTER 22

Willow strode forward, planted her feet wide apart, and faced Jade mockingly. "As I told you, all in good time," she said.

She drew her sword from its leather scabbard, making it sing. She sliced at the air, sweeping it from side to side. Then, placing both hands on the hilt, as if she were going to use the sword as a club or an axe, a demonically grinning Willow moved toward Jade.

"Bow first," said Luan laconically. "And move further away from the other warriors."

Jade stared at him open-mouthed. He was allowing a woman of much heavier weight, and an armed one at that, to threaten her viciously, and that was all he had to say?

Jade glared at him. Willow shuffled her feet in the dirt and moved apart from the other warriors. Angrily, Jade followed. They were where they could be seen but out of range of anyone else getting hurt by accident.

Jade bowed with her teeth clenched. Her hands formed into crescent moons and she assumed the Tiger's fighting stance. She had to breathe deeply to overcome her fear of the blade in Willow's hands.

Jade thought to herself: *She is wearing thick clothing and carries too much weight.*

Her warrior's mind calculated the length and breadth of Willow's sword and her potential reach, including the woman's weight and the cumbersomeness of her rough clothing. She would stay out of that reach until she could get behind Willow, force her hand down, and bend her wrist to the breaking point to make her drop the sword.

Willow licked her lips as if relishing the prospect of the fight. She settled into a stance unseemly for a woman. She spread her legs wide apart, her feet splayed outward. She lowered her body almost into a squat and then swayed from side to side, brandishing the sword.

She will fight like a man, thought Jade. *I will sweep those feet out from under her.*

Jade held her stance and began the tail-moving motion of the feline. She thought she caught a look of appreciation on Luan's face before she launched herself, dove through the air, and landed between Willow's splayed feet, using her hips to pummel one of the heavy woman's knees so as to make it buckle, thus throwing her off balance.

But Willow was planted on the ground as solidly as an oak tree, and with a growl that was more like a cry, Jade had to scramble through the door of Willow's legs as fast as possible to avoid the quick downward thrust of the sword. She then barreled her full weight backward into one of Willow's legs. This time she succeeded; Willow's leg buckled at the knee, and she went down, crashing onto Jade's body in the process. Jade twisted and rolled out from under the flailing woman. She sprang to her feet and then pounced on Willow, who was trying to rise from the dust. Dimly, she heard the other warriors cheer.

Encouraged, Jade pinned Willow's limbs down and bore down as forcefully as she could on the wrist of her sword hand, hoping to loosen its grip. Willow bucked mightily and threw Jade off, making her land in the dust on her side. Jade swung her legs and catapulted herself into a standing position. Then she crouched like a tigress. Willow had rolled into a similar crouching position, looking very much like a bear.

Jade's eyes were on the sword. She threw herself at Willow, using what strength she had left to unbalance the stalwart woman. As she tried to get a grip on Willow's arms, wrestling with her, she was surprised to find that much of Willow's bulk was clothing, and it was hard to grasp her. The woman seemed to be all clothing! Jade grabbed Willow's sword hand and pulled the thumb back so far

Willow yelped in pain. The sword went down in the dust, but just as Jade dove for it, Willow kicked it away, laughing.

"You have no sword!" Willow crowed. "You've nothing but dirt in your mouth! May you choke on it!"

Jade took advantage of the moment of celebration, pretending to be more overcome by the dust than she was. Through her eyelashes, she saw Willow relax for a moment—and a moment was all she needed to plunge toward the sword again. She was certain she was faster than Willow, and she had a one second advantage too.

She laid hands on the sword and whirled around, brandishing it.

Willow did a wide, sweeping kick. The woman's legs had to be much longer than they looked in the men's trousers she wore rolled up—her foot connected unexpectedly with Jade's wrist, and the sword went flying.

Then it was a free-for-all. The sword lay apart, forgotten by both women as Willow threw herself on Jade and they wrestled to the thrilled cheers of the other warriors. They rolled over and over in the dust. During one revolution, Jade managed to shove a skull-rattling knee into Willow's chin. She saw Willow's eyes roll up in her head for a moment and heard the crack of her teeth as her jaws slammed together from the blow. But then, an enraged Willow descended on Jade like a hive full of angry bees. She grabbed Jade's hair in handfuls at the sides of her head, wound it around her fists and pulled until Jade screamed. On her knees, Jade head-butted Willow's groin again and again—it would have devastated a man, of course—but it seemed to have little effect on Willow except to make her grunt and pull Jade's hair harder.

Jade felt distinctly outclassed. Fragrant Flower had plenty of strength left in her, and Jade was losing force every minute. Willow managed to straddle her and then punched her in the face, knocking her head against the ground. Desperate, Jade twisted her body to unseat Willow long enough to to roll face down in the dirt. Dust was becoming her most intimate companion!

She pushed up with both arms and butted Willow's face with the back of her head, aiming for where she thought Willow's nose was. She heard a satisfying thunk and from Willow's stung cry, she was sure she had connected mightily. The larger woman yelled and fell away, holding her hands to her blood-spurting nose. Jade scrambled to her feet and looked around desperately for the sword, but she couldn't find it. Was that it, by Luan's feet?

She was heading toward it when Willow, her nose and mouth bleeding, grabbed Jade's leg, stopping her, unbalancing her, and throwing her onto the ground her full length. Wind knocked out of her lungs, Jade lay prone in the dust, gasping for air, and to her horror, Willow then rose, bellowing, grabbed her hair again, and began pulling her by it toward the edge of the little bluff where Luan had built his signal fire.

Jade scrambled to her haunches to create some slack in her long, black hair and sprang at Willow's thigh, seeking to break her hip with the thrust of her own shoulder. She had little force left, but she thrust again and again, wondering when her strength would give out.

"Peace! Peace!" called Luan. "The fight is over."

Willow instantly released Jade's hair, and Jade slowly rose. Sore and dizzy, Jade went to stand in front of her husband. He looked her over speculatively, as if gauging her injuries. Evidently he decided they were not too serious, for she saw him barely able to suppress a grin. Willow looked worse than Jade did, with her bloodied mouth and nose. Willow couldn't even seem to stand up straight.

"Who won?" demanded Jade angrily.

The warriors, who had been clapping and cheering, fell silent and inclined their heads toward Luan to hear his verdict.

CHAPTER 23

hat fight was definitely not Wu Dung," Luan said, and a ripple of merriment circulated throughout the warriors. He held up his hand for silence. "Yet a warrior must be prepared for any kind of fighting. Our enemies are not sworn to abide by the principles of Wu Dung. Jade, you did not capture the sword, which was the object of the fight. Therefore, I proclaim Willow the victor."

Willow threw back her head and crowed in triumph. Then she doubled up and groaned as if she had an awful stomach ache.

Humiliated, bruised, and sore inside and out, especially at Luan, Jade started to return to her boulder next to Anbai when Luan's laconic instruction to bow to one another came again. She bowed clumsily to Willow, who bowed to her with a dignity that was somewhat impaired by the blood and snot still streaming from her nose and the groan that accompanied the movement.

Still shedding dust, Jade seated herself next to Anbai and accepted a clay mug of herbal brew from her. After a few sips, it cleared her head marvelously. It felt good to sit next to Anbai, who seemed to be radiating silent sympathy. She caught Luan watching her; he looked satisfied when she finished her tea and raised her head. She took a deep breath. She was already feeling restored. Still, she thought Luan could have complimented her on her fighting rather than just declaring Willow the winner.

"You are an excellent fighter," Anbai said. "None of us would relish going up against Willow—not even the men. Especially when she has a sword."

"I lost," said Jade disconsolately. "And I still have no sword."

"Well, you know what they say. The sword finds you. That was not to be your sword, that's all. You have won everyone's admiration today for your courage and skills. I believe you were the real winner."

That was little comfort to Jade. She glared at Willow, but all the animosity seemed to have gone out of her opponent. When their eyes met, Willow suddenly grinned at her, fresh blood pumping from her nose as she did, and Jade laughed a little. She had given as good as she'd got, even if she hadn't captured the sword, and even if Luan had not acknowledged it.

As they prepared to resume their journey in search of a more secure camp, the murmurs of the other warriors and the compliments they went out of their way to pay her, showed Jade that she had gone a long way toward winning their respect and acceptance.

In a way, she *had* won, she thought. She felt better about everything. Then, to her surprise, she saw Luan smiling at her, waiting on his horse with her horse saddled next to his. He held the reins to her horse, and with a gesture of his head, invited her to come and ride next to him. She walked over to him, trying to hide her pain as she did so, and mounted her horse. She could not keep a slight grimace from her face as she did so.

"Well done," he complimented her. "Rarely have I seen such unadulterated grit. Willow is a formidable opponent."

"I still need a sword," she said, lowering her head.

"All in good time," he said, and Jade felt the good mood between them fade as he used this phrase of Willow's.

Had he been in some sort of secret cahoots with Willow? Why had he chosen her for Jade to fight? Why had he declared Willow the winner in front of everyone when it was plain the fight had been a draw, even if Jade had not procured the sword?

She rode silently, mulling all this over and not feeling very happy about it.

"The foothills are beautiful, are they not?" Luan asked in a cajoling voice.

"I have learned to be indifferent to my surroundings, beautiful or ugly," said Jade. "That is what a warrior does."

"Indeed," said Luan quietly, and they rode in silence for the rest of the afternoon.

Everyone looked at them uneasily when the unit camped that night, as if sensing some tension between them. Perhaps Jade's expression gave her away too. She knew only too well that she was not good at hiding her emotions. She must have looked angry; she could feel her eyebrows draw together, and she was hard put to make her mouth into anything but a tight, hard line. Luan looked as impersonal and calm as ever.

They had sheltered in a grove of trees by a foothill stream and the warriors dispersed to build their new camp and erect their tents, couple by couple. Jade considered where to pitch hers. Nowhere near Luan's, she decided. As insultingly obvious as she could be about it, she moved to set up her own tent again as far away as possible from his.

Anbai hurried up to her with a concerned look on her face.

"I would not spoil the good impression you made today by appearing to be a sore loser," she counseled.

Jade's mouth tightened and she almost answered Anbai sharply, telling her to mind her own business. Yet she knew Anbai was right. Sullenly, she gathered her things, pitched her tent near Luan's, and huffily went inside it.

She was a sore loser. She hated to lose.

Anger kept her awake. She kept reliving the fight with Willow, thinking of moments when she might have broken through and captured the sword. When she closed her eyes, she saw red lights on her eyelids, caused by the blood throbbing angrily in her temples. It was impossible to slow the rapid beating of her heart and the fluttering pulse in her neck.

I wouldn't want her smelly old sword anyway, she said to herself.

Since sleep still eluded her, Jade decided to warm some tea on the embers of the dying campfire. She would walk a short space apart from the enclave of sleeping warriors, gaze at the moon, and try to find some peace of mind.

Jade crept out of her tent and approached the stores of food and drink, which were heaped together in leather bags, away from the fire. She had her own tin cup; she found a leathern sack containing loose, dry tea and reached into its depths, scooping out a small amount with her hand. She placed it in her cup and then found the water bags to fill her cup. She knelt by the fire and placed the cup among the embers, hoping to heat it enough to steep the tea.

The night sentry loomed up suddenly behind her. He saw what she was doing and, with a shrug, went off to resume his watchful post.

Soon her cup was heated, strands of steam rising from its depths. The invigorating steam rose up in her nostrils, clearing her head, and she bore her cup of tea far enough from the camp to feel she was alone, yet near enough to ensure safety should she encounter any trouble and require help.

The moon was a shimmering sliver of light, outlined against a black, velvety sky, and the deep, mysterious smell of nature as it settled down to rest filled her nostrils with freshness. Night's touch was tender on her upturned face. She felt an onslaught of appreciation for this. She had lied to Luan; she was far from indifferent to her surroundings. She loved nature and its beauties, as had Wu Lei.

I wish you were with me now, Wu Lei, she thought. *I am so lonely and so unhappy.*

It didn't help that she was still physically sore from the fight. That seemed to feed her mental soreness at Luan, who had plotted against her and not even given her a good word in front of the other warriors.

She breathed deeply, sipped tea, and began to feel calmer. No use fretting about it all night, she could almost hear Wu Lei's voice counseling her. Vaguely, she wondered if the spirit of her young, beautiful husband Wu Lei was with her, consoling her, understanding her heart, guiding her. Or was the feeling he was present just an illusion of the night?

A nearby noise startled her. Instantly, she dropped to all fours, casting her tea cup aside. Like a cat, she stayed in motion even in a crouch, slowly swaying her hips to provide the momentum she would need to spring on a foe.

A man's figure loomed in the darkness. It was not the sentry; Jade could tell from his silhouette. Jade crouched lower, her haunches moving ever more quickly and smoothly. Then moonlight fell on the man's face, and she saw that it was Luan.

She didn't know why she did it— it went against her better judgment— but she sprang at him as if he were an enemy and, with the element of surprise on her side, bowled him off his feet.

CHAPTER 24

gghh!"

Clearly caught by surprise, Luan landed on his buttocks in the dirt. Then the force of Jade's attack further powered him to the ground. He wound up lying on his back, with Jade on top of him.

"Ah, you little cat!" he said between clenched teeth.

Then something strange seemed to come over him. She felt his body relax under her. His hands rested lightly on her back, and she felt the breath go out of him. She could even see the glint of his teeth as he smiled in the moonlight under her weight.

"Here, kitty," he said teasingly.

She would have none of that. How dared he? Men were so awful that way — and both of them but recently bereaved! Her mind went back to the alley and the rapist, and, again without thinking, Jade pulled her hand back for the tiger-claw strike, with its deadly twist on the end, and after the heel of her hand connected with his face, she dragged her fingernails across his cheek.

Luan grunted with pain. His cheek looked like it had been plowed by a four-pronged rake. Enraged, he pushed her upward with a thrust of his hip bones, then twisted and threw her off him with his arm as though she weighed nothing, catapulting her over to the side. She tumbled and slid in the dust and autumn leaves, trying to rise, but he was upon her by then, straddling her, sitting on her hip, and raining blows down on her shoulders and neck.

With some satisfaction, she realized he was restraining his strength, but then she felt guilty for having raked him with her nails, because he was refusing to hurt her with his hands. His blows were only a little punishing. They were more a demonstration that he could beat her if he wished, and a frustrated expression of controlled anger. She turned to face downward and protected her face with her hands. She felt Luan's weight rise off of her, and then he put his knee on her back, pinning her down, seemingly just to emphasize the point.

He wound her long hair around his hands and gave it a substantial tug that, while not painful, humiliated her, especially when he said, "Ah, tigress! I am pulling your tail! You got your tail pulled quite a few times today, didn't you!" He accompanied this with an almost-painful knee thrust into her back.

The heat of anger rose to her face, but she also had the keen satisfaction of knowing that the entire camp would see the claw marks on his face in the morning and know that the tigress had struck. His next words, however, cut her even deeper than the marks she had administered to him.

"I don't know how your husband stood you, you are such a nasty little cat."

He threw her hair down from his hands as if in disgust and rose up and strode off, leaving her face down in the desert dust in the moonlight.

The members of the group must have seen the badges of combat on Luan's cheek as they broke camp the next morning. No one could have missed those four red streaks on their commander's cheeks, and yet they said nothing. Jade carried her wound from his words within her, but she was sure her injury hurt worse than his. They had each suffered wounded pride more than physical harm, but wounded pride was like a heart full of nettles.

Jade's only comfort was that, in spite of everything, Anbai still appeared to want to be friends. She had cast Jade several interested but worried looks.

Luan completely snubbed Jade all morning and made no sign that he wanted her to ride near him, so she plodded along with her head down. Her horse also held his head down, as if sharing her shame and misery.

Anbai pulled up alongside her and adjusted her horse's pace to Jade's. Mercifully, Anbai said nothing. Whenever Jade glanced over at her, she merely gave Jade an understanding smile. It was comforting to have pretty Anbai next to her. She smiled at Jade every once in a while. At least someone in this troop of warriors liked her, Jade thought sourly.

When they broke for an afternoon meal, Anbai prepared a particularly tasty-looking plate of food and brought it to Jade. She carried a plate for herself too. She spoke her first words of the day.

"There's a little grove of saxaul trees apart from the others, over there. Will you join me in the cool?"

"Yes, thank you," said Jade. She was so grateful to be befriended and treated kindly, she felt her eyes sting with tears.

They had left the wooded slopes of the foothills near Beijing behind and now traversed the sere, desert landscape of the Tianmo. A grove of saxaul trees — the desert traveler's best friend — showed tender, small leaves and lovely, miniature yellow flowers. The shrub-like trees caught whatever breeze there was and filtered it until it kissed the weary traveler's dusty face with kindness. Both Jade and Anbai pulled handfuls of spongy bark off the trees, squeezing and sucking on them for water. That would save the troop's water supplies, and saxaul water was sweet and highly distilled.

Jade had tied her mount to a grey tree trunk, and he was gnawing the bark as well, both for fodder and water. They would also use the bark for their campfires. It was the only tree hardy enough to be found everywhere in the harsh desert landscape, and those who traveled here owed their lives to it.

The two women found a comfortable spot in the little grove and sat down, cross-legged, and began to eat.

"Your husband is Lieutenant Ching?" Jade asked, although she knew the answer.

"Yes," said Anbai. Then, as if reluctant to bring up more delicate topics, she began to talk about Ching — what a kind and decent husband he was; what a strong and intelligent warrior; how they prayed together each morning and night, and how their spirituality drew them closer.

"So, even though I am not suffering as you are," she said, "I think I understand a little of your heart when I imagine what it would be like if Ching died suddenly and I were assigned to a man I did not know. Even if the man were very fine, I would be blind to it for some time." Anbai's empathy was palpable.

Jade swallowed, then confided shamefacedly, "I clawed Luan last night."

Anbai said carefully, "So I saw."

"It was wrong."

"Yes." The corner of Anbai's mouth curved up. "I can see your guilty conscience in your face. All morning you have looked like a little cat that swallowed a pet bird."

Jade couldn't help but laugh, which felt good. She had not laughed in what seemed like a very long time. Also, Anbai's words cast her in a naughty light, but not an evil one. Maybe the troop, and Luan himself, would forgive her.

"What should I do?"

"The words 'I'm sorry' would be a good beginning," said Anbai kindly. "When you are ready. Oh—and you might let it slip out at the campfire tonight that you two were practicing together and you did it accidentally. If I were you, I would encourage that rumor. After all, a man has his pride."

"That's a wonderful idea!" cried Jade. "Then Luan could save face."

"You would save face too," said her new friend sagely. "In fact, I will begin spreading the rumor myself as I am preparing dinner this evening with the other women."

"What if Luan already has told someone what really happened?"

Anbai studied Jade from the corner of her eye.

"You don't understand men very well, do you? Luan would not speak of it to anyone, even if it meant the death of the thousand cuts. No, we will be able to write this story ourselves, and Luan will appreciate our efforts. By the way, Jade Blossom." Anbai paused, as if unsure as to whether she should go on or not. "You realize you won the fight with Willow, don't you? Everyone knew it; Luan included. You didn't capture the sword, of course, so he could use that as an excuse not to honor you. Jade, had he proclaimed his own wife the winner there would be murmurings of favoritism in the unit. Everyone knows you won—Luan was trying to save you from envy and disgruntlement."

"Oh," said Jade, frowning. "I thought he was just being mean."

"Luan is a book you have to read carefully before you discover its contents. But you will like what you find, in time."

"I suppose," said Jade disconsolately. She never had to work to "read" Wu Lei. Why couldn't the Emperor have given her someone more like him?

Thinking about Wu Lei, Jade bowed her head. Not only was she still grieving him, but her mission to find and wreak vengeance on his killer had been totally disrupted by having to join Luan's unit. She did not even have a sword to kill her husband's killer with, should she discover who he was.

CHAPTER 25

By evening, the unit had made its way back up into the wooded foothills that offered them cover for their encampment. As the women cooked dinner that night and the men made camp, Jade watched Anbai sidle up to Willow. Jade frowned. Why was Anbai choosing to talk to *her*? What did everyone in this troop respect that wizened, acrid-faced, smelly, baggy-clothed, jealous, old widow?

Willow apparently had wormed her way to a position of social power in this troop, probably through instilling fear, Jade thought, remembering the woman's bear-like strength. Anbai had hinted that Willow was the chief gossip among them and dominated all the other women. In approaching Willow, Anbai was apparently carrying out her plan to spread the gossip that Luan's facial mars had been an accident while practicing kung fu techniques with his wife.

Jade appreciated Anbai's strategy. If Anbai could convince Willow that Luan's cheek wounds had been an accident, it was possible the entire camp would know about it by the time dinner was over. Coming from Jade's opponent, the rumor would have double force.

Indeed, it turned out to be so. Although Jade could not trace how the gossip spread, within a few hours, everyone in camp was chatty and friendly to her, and Luan looked relieved. He was not friendly to her, but he seemed his usual relaxed, calm self, basking in the high regard of his fellows and the wonderful campfire and food.

Jade sighed in relief. Perhaps she would survive being in this troop, after all.

*   *   *

As the fire died down into embers, the couples dispersed for their tents. Luan tried to convey to Anbai that he wished to speak to her, but he did not want to order a consultation and thus draw attention to it. Fortunately, Anbai sensed her commander's wish and hovered longer than the other women around the food and water stores, checking leather bags that already had been checked multiple times already.

Luan drifted, as if by happenstance, over to the water bags, and she greeted him as commander and offered to make him a cup of tea, speaking in polite and subservient terms as if their encounter were perfectly normal. He accepted the offer and invited her to make herself tea, too. Then they stood a little apart from the fire, drank from their cups, and spoke in low tones.

"You spent all afternoon with my new wife," he began.

"Yes. Jade is a fine woman," she said with loyalty.

"I think so, too. Do not imagine I do not. However, I am afraid she hates me. I don't expect her love; I only expect duty. But duty itself should have some element of love in it—love of country, love for the commander's position—some sort of devotion. I do not want her to follow or obey me gnashing her teeth."

Anbai was silent, and Luan's heart sank. He should not have tried to talk to a woman about such personal things. He was Anbai's commander, and although he considered Ching to be a friend as well as the most loyal and capable subordinate he had ever known, there was no reason to suppose his wife should be a confidante in matters of the heart.

"Well, time will do its work, I suppose," he said in a choked voice. "Thank you for the tea."

"Wait, Commander," said Anbai. "I believe you misunderstood my silence. I sympathize with both of you, and I wanted to choose my words carefully. I am not in a position to advise you, but all day I have thought of an old folk tale that I believe would help you."

Luan nodded. "There is much wisdom in old stories. I am happy to listen."

Anbai cleared her throat. "A poor young woman from the country was matched in marriage to a wealthy but surly merchant of some wealth. She was willing to learn to love him over time, yet night after night, day after day, he berated her for the smallest matters, even when she tried hard to do everything right. He was a very angry man. She was completely miserable and did not know what to do.

"She consulted with the local shaman who told her he could brew her a love potion to give to her husband if she could bring him the whisker of a tiger. Of course, she was terrified. How was she going to get a tiger's whisker without being eaten in the process? Indeed, there was a tiger known to be living in a nearby cave in the mountains, but this tiger was fierce. The entrance to its cave was strewn with the bones of those who had attempted to hunt the tiger and capture his gorgeous hide.

"The young woman went to the mountain, carrying a handful of the freshest, best meat she could find. She placed it just outside the cave and then, in great fear, ran all the way back down the mountain. Still, she was determined to get close enough to the tiger to pluck one of his whiskers, so she came back each night with a handful of tasty meat. Each night she ventured a little further into the cave, until one night she saw the tiger's eyes gleaming at her in the darkness. She dropped the meat inside the cave and ran all the way down the mountainside.

"Her husband was so cruel to her the next day, it gave her the strength to climb the mountain yet again, holding a handful of meat. This time she could see the tiger's eyes and its stripes in the small amount of moonlight that shined in the cave. This time she did not drop the meat, but lay it down gently, a few feet closer to the tiger than the night before. She walked sedately back down the mountain.

"Each night the tiger watched her from the darkness, and one night it got to its feet and approached her. She froze in place, the meat in her hand. The huge head came near to her, and she feared the tiger would bite off her hand while grabbing the meat, but to her surprise, the tiger gently rubbed her hand with the side of its face and then took the meat with a slack jaw.

"Within that week, she was sitting in the cave with the tiger's head on her lap, petting the tiger and feeding it bits of meat she tore off by hand. One time as she was petting the tiger's face, a loose whisker fell off in her hand. Now she could go to the shaman.

"She presented the tiger's whisker to the shaman and requested the promised love potion to tame her husband's temper. The shaman told her, 'My dear, if you can tame a tiger, you can tame a man. Do with your husband as you did with the tiger, and you will soon have your husband feeding out of your hand too.'"

"Hm," said Luan stiffly, after listening attentively to the story. "I suppose I am the one in the story who is trying to tame a tiger!"

Anbai smiled. "Get the whisker of a tiger," she said liltingly, "and I think you will indeed find a love potion. Jade will respond to care and kindness."

"Thank you, Anbai," said Luan. "I will consider your advice."

"You are welcome, Commander," murmured Anbai, bowing.

CHAPTER 26

J ade crept to her tent soon after dinner. She was grateful when she heard a woman's voice outside her tent flap. It was Anbai.

"I brought you some tea to help you sleep," Anbai said kindly. "I often drink this herbal tea before retiring, and it makes me sleep very soundly."

She sat companionably next to Jade on the heap of bedding, topped by furs, that was Jade's bed.

"Thank you," said Jade, accepting the tea bowl. "You are truly a wonderful friend to have." After she had sipped some, she pumped Anbai for information as to Luan's state of mind about her.

"I know he talked to you for some time," Jade said. "Is it conceited of me to think some of the conversation revolved around me?"

"He admires you," Anbai hedged. "It's just—and he didn't say this, I am gleaning it—Jingwei was such a quiet, easily tamed woman. You are almost the opposite of that."

"She was a warrior," Jade frowned.

"She was a warrior when she had to be. Surely, though, you know that she was known more for her diplomacy—winning the peace— than her warrior triumphs. She was not a tigress. She was more like a—a bird—a crane that flies above the fray."

Jade sighed. "Well, I suppose if I cared whether he cared for me, that would be saddening news."

"Whether you care or not—and I am sure down deep, you do care—you are very different, just as Wu Lei was very different from Luan. It will take some time for the four personalities to sort themselves out. I believe," said Anbai firmly, "that you have qualities Jingwei lacked and vice versa. I believe the same about

Luan and Wu Lei. Each had qualities the other lacked. Yet all four bring excellent qualities to the empire, and all four are admirable in their own way." Anbai giggled. "I have had the thought that if you and Jingwei were but one woman, with both of your strengths combined, you would be the perfect woman. I believe you would be able to take over the entire empire!"

Jade Blossom rubbed her lips thoughtfully. Then she hung her head, feeling ashamed and spoke in halting words. "There have been moments ... there have been moments when the thought has crossed my mind that Wu Lei could have learned something from Luan's reserve. Being overly expressive and emotional was a weakness we shared. Of course, I preferred Wu Lei and always will. I am not a disloyal person."

"That's not disloyalty," Anbai was quick to point out. "It is mere observation. And you owe some loyalty to your new husband too."

"I do think I have something to learn from Luan about keeping my thoughts and emotions inside."

"And he has something to learn from you about letting them out! Jingwei, too, was a very reserved person. Perhaps it is time for both of you to change and grow."

"Perhaps," said Jade. "Still, I think I would prefer to be in Willow's shoes, where I could be loyal to my dead husband and not have to cope with another."

"She would prefer to be in yours," smiled Anbai. "The other farmer's field always looks better than our own. Well, goodnight. We still have some journeying to do tomorrow, and I wish to get some rest."

"Anbai." Hesitantly, Jade held out her arms. Anbai smilingly hugged her.

"Why, you are not a tigress at all," laughed Anbai. "You are more like a little kitten!"

"Sometimes," admitted Jade.

The tea Anbai had brought relaxed Jade and made her sleepy. In fact, she was too tired to snuff out the red candle burning by her bed. She drifted into sleep, comforted and relaxed. Anbai was so wise, calm, and motherly. Jade Blossom felt cared for, and her heart opened up as if she were a young girl again. She felt she was breathing the innocence of a former self, a more child-like self. Being a warrior meant armoring one's heart as well as one's body. She was surprised to find so much feminine caring in the camp like this. Perhaps that had been Jingwei's influence. If so, it was a needed gift in their harsh life.

I *wonder what Jingwei looked like,* she thought as she went to sleep. *Was she very beautiful compared to me? Is Luan having a very hard time adjusting?* Her conscience smote her, for she knew she had not made his way any easier.

When she fell asleep, she dreamed of a crane flying from the mountains into the camp and alighting near her tent. In her dream, she rose, opened the tent flap, and the crane came into the tent. Red-crowned, with a long, black neck, tapering off into the whitest of feathers, the crane was quite stately. Its thin black legs were graceful, and its tail feathers were a rich black. The contrast of the red, white, and black was quite stunning.

To her surprise, the crane folded its legs and sat down as if nesting, looking around the room quite calmly, as if it was supposed to be there. In her dream, Jade climbed back into her bed, keeping her eyes on the crane. Then the crane rose up, spread its wings, and came over to her, enveloping her. She was afraid she would smother, yet the embrace was warm, womanly, and motherly, like Anbai's embrace. Then suddenly it seemed like she was not just being embraced by the crane—the crane had enfolded itself into her, embedded itself within her, and had become a part of her.

Then she dreamed that the tent flap opened and Luan stood over her, staring at her. Within her the crane seemed to flap to life, as if begging to be with Luan through Jade. She sat up in her bed and was thrilled when the dream Luan came to her and knelt by her side. In her dream she embraced him, kissed him, and soon she embraced him with her whole body, her legs spreading like wings to envelop him. Pleasure rose up in her; passion too.

Jade's eyes snapped open. She was shocked at herself. Where was Wu Lei in all of this? Desperately, she pulled the ribbon with the silver dart around it out from under her nightdress.

"Beloved!" she spoke to it as if it were a part of him, not the instrument of his murder. "Oh, beloved, I did not mean to betray you! I am sorry to be disloyal even in thought. I don't want him; it is my mind playing tricks on me."

A sound just outside her tent flap made her gasp and look up in horror. A man was outside her tent, asking to be allowed in. She was about to scream, 'No! No, Luan!" when the flap opened and Ching looked in.

"Oh!" he cried. 'I am sorry. I saw your candle burning and assumed you were still up. A thousand pardons! I only came to give you a message and a gift from General Luan Luan."

"A message and a gift?" she asked, rubbing her eyes and trying to sort out what was real and what was a dream.

"Yes." He stepped outside the tent for a moment and then brought in an elongated, well-padded package. "He requests that you meet him on the Yongding River."

"Leaving now?"

"Yes."

"It is growing late."

"It is still mid-evening. We can travel some tonight. I will be your escort."

Jade regarded the heavy and long package he had placed in her lap.

"Am I to bring the package itself, or…?"

"Open it. You are to bring its contents with you."

Looking at him quizzically, not understanding at all, Jade tore open the packaging and pulled its contents out.

Her mouth opened in amazement. It was her old sword, the one she had dropped in the alleyway while fighting off the rapist. It seemed like a lifetime ago, but, as she stroked the blade, there was no doubt about it: this was her old friend, her familiar battleground companion, which had drunk the blood of many a foe.

"General Luan said you have earned your sword. Come now," urged Ching. "Yes," she said. "Just give me a few minutes to dress."

How had Luan procured her sword? She was dying to ask him. Certainly that must be why her heart was beating so hard at the thought of meeting him away from the camp, away from all the others. Ching went outside to wait for her while she dressed with hands trembling with anticipation and her face flushing with excitement to be reunited--with her sword.

CHAPTER 27

Jade and Ching traveled the hard, rocky desert land until they entered dark, hillside forests along the banks of the Yongding River. Jade admired Ching's sure-footedness. His feet seemed to know the path well, although there was no path discernible in the soft blackness that surrounded them in the verdant forest. She appreciated the way Ching held some branches to the side for her while in other ways he let her take care of herself. He seemed to have an instinct for knowing when she might need help and when she was best left on her own.

One time, however, he left a large, springy, spongy young branch, curtained with green, in her way. She heard him chuckle.

"No doubt you have missed using your sword," he said.

She laughed and slashed the young branch out of her path. It felt wonderful to heft her sword again, its hilt fitting into the curve of her fingers like the hand of an old and trusted friend.

The ground grew wetter as they approached the river bank, and Jade felt her shoes dampening with cool moisture. An island was in sight, parting water and moonlight, in the midst of the softly rushing river. The water made a gurgling sound as it wallowed around the roots of the island's trees before passing on. It was a pretty spot, Jade thought. Very peaceful.

"Where is Luan?" Jade asked Ching.

"On the island."

"Am I to swim?"

"No," said Ching. He bent and reached into a thicket of the rushes that lined the riverbank. Bending and tugging, he dragged out a coracle made of animal skin. It looked flimsy but dry and bouncy.

"This will be your conveyance."

Jade frowned. "Has it an oar?"

"Two. I will steer you there."

"Then you will leave us to return to shore?"

"I do not know what Luan's plan is beyond my delivering you to the island."

The coracle was hard to steer; it was round and light and Jade was surprised that it held the weight of two grown people. Occasionally it wrestled itself free of their oars and spun in the waters, and then they would tame it again thrusting their oars deeper into the current. Fortunately, the current was fairly gentle.

The island smelled of vegetation, growing unchecked for centuries, and it breathed out at them with an earthy, woodsy smell as they disembarked from the coracle and dragged it up onto the shore. Now Jade's feet were really wet. She began to think of a warming fire, and she hoped Luan had one going. Yet there was no sign of Luan.

"Ching," Jade said, doubt creeping into her voice. "Is this a ruse of some sort? What are we doing here?"

She was suddenly suspicious of him. Had he lured her here to kill her? If the Golden Ginkgo Society could penetrate the imperial palace, surely it could penetrate the warrior troops. Was Ching an assassin? She clutched the Serpent dart around her neck for a moment before she subtly shifted her feet into a fighting stance.

Just then Luan emerged from the shadows. In the moonlight she could see that he was smiling, and his voice was calm.

"Ah, there is my tigress," he said. "Welcome to the island."

She bowed slightly. "Thank you for my sword. How did it come to be in your possession?"

"I will explain all that later. Ching," Luan nodded to his lieutenant. "You may return to the camp. Thank you for your service this night, as all nights."

Jade watched as Ching bowed and then pushed the coracle back into the water. She watched as he carefully climbed into it, balancing his weight.

She turned to Luan.

"Do you have a boat on the island?"

Luan laughed. "Perhaps."

She heard the sound of the water as Ching's oars penetrated the dark surface of the river and then rose, dripping, above it.

Luan said, "Come," and he turned and disappeared into the trees and vegetation of the island. Jade followed him, a little alarmed. He was her key to survival here, but she was not sure she was entirely ready to be all alone with him on an island without a boat.

It was dark, and the ground was spongy-wet, wetter than the ground on shore. The deep, verdant, fertile smell of untouched nature grew stronger as they made their way through a darkness choked with vegetation and growth. Suddenly the moonlight revealed a small clearing, with a tent set up in the middle of it. Now that they were close to it, Jade saw muted light glowing within its animal skin walls.

A fire! She wiggled her toes in delighted anticipation.

"Come in," said Luan kindly. "Your feet are wet. You must warm them."

She entered the tent, and the heat was strong. It felt wonderful after the long, wet slog through the forest and the island. To her delight, she smelled lemon, chicken, and eggs emanating from a small, friendly-looking pot near the fire.

She started when she felt Luan's hands on her shoulders. He gently removed her cloak and arranged its folds so that the wet hem was exposed to the fire. Luan arranged a plump, red, fringed pillow in front of the fire and not only invited her to seat herself, he took her hand and guided her gently down. The pillow was marvelously comfortable. Luan knelt in front of her and lifted her feet, one by one, gently removing each shoe and then softly stripping off the stocking.

"Oh," he said, "your feet are so cold." He spent several minutes rubbing and warming each foot in his hands before putting them down gently, close but not too close to the fire, and arranging her shoes and stockings to dry around the fire.

He had an air of a man with a secret, as he served her and tended to her.

"Why are you being so kind?" she asked him. She was starting to grow groggy and contented as the warmth of the fire wafted over her. She almost felt like purring.

"Why, I am trying to tame the tigress," he said.

"What?" she asked sleepily.

"Never mind. Soup?"

He would not let her eat the soup herself. He hand fed her, tipping the bowl of the spoon tenderly and solicitously into her mouth. The soup was marvelous. It was just tart and thick enough to be satisfying. It warmed her down to her belly. Luan opened a potted bowl with a lid, revealing steaming rice, and this too, he hand fed her.

Jade was almost dizzy. The warmth of the fire on her bare feet, the coziness of the animal skin walls, embracing them and keeping their light hidden from the night, the isolation and romance of the island setting, were beginning to be overwhelming. She was feeling quite affectionate toward Luan.

"Have you supped enough?" Luan asked her solicitously.

She nodded.

"I hope you enjoyed your meal," he said, and he gestured for her to sit still while he stowed away the food in earthen jugs, bowls, and under skins. From under a heap of skins, he produced a bottle of wine.

"Rice wine," he told her. "Will you have a cup?"

"I will," she said.

He did not allow her to drink the wine on her own either. Luan held the cup to her lips, and she drank. She tilted her head back to receive it. When he removed the cup, she licked the delicious, titillating taste from her lips. The wine, too, warmed her, as if setting a fire in her belly and causing her toes to tingle.

"May I have some wine?" Luan asked.

"Of course. What do you mean? It is your wine."

"I would have it from your lips," he said.

CHAPTER 28

He framed her face with his hands and tilted it up toward him. Jade sat stock still, unresisting. Then he pressed upon her lips a very deep and long-lasting kiss, and she was certain that if there had been any remnant of wine left on or in her mouth, his lips and tongue found it. As in her dream, she responded to him, almost as if she were someone else, not herself. The image of the beautiful white crane filled her mind, and she put her arms around his neck and pulled him closer, kissing him back. She even felt her feet loosen from her sitting position and her legs move to wrap around him.

Luan responded as a man might; he pressed her down, positioning himself on top of her so that his manliness pressed on the inner seam of her trousers. Yet when his hand moved to loosen her trousers, she rebelled.

What was she doing? She was Wu Lei's wife, now and forever.

"It is too soon," she told him.

"Your body does not seem to be saying it is too soon."

It was true; her hips were moving rhythmically under him in spite of herself. All of it—the warm, embracing tent walls, the heat of the fire, the food, the wine, the comforting and thrilling weight of Luan upon her, his handsome face, his kindness and service to her, her dream—it all seemed designed to seduce her.

Was that what he meant by taming the tigress? Was she some sort of conquest to him?

"I would be loyal to my husband," she said desperately.

"I am your husband now. We were married before the eyes of the Son of Heaven. Consummating our marriage is loyalty, not disloyalty."

Yet Luan pulled himself off her, sighed, and looked at the fire, with a resigned expression on his face as if he had known this would happen.

"I thought you didn't like me," she said.

"You were mistaken. There is much to admire about you. And you are an attractive woman."

"What about Jingwei?"

He nodded thoughtfully. "Somehow I have felt all day that she was drawing me toward you."

Suddenly Jade spotted something across the tent. It was a pair of platform sandals similar to — exactly like, she thought, as she stared at it — those she had left behind in the palace!

"Those shoes —" she said.

"Oh, do you recognize them?"

Jade rose and went to look at them more closely. She picked them up and examined them, and she noticed next to them a slim, dark volume of poetry. She put the shoes down and picked up the volume and opened it.

It was Wu Lei's favorite book of poems.

"Where did you get this?" she asked him. The hand she held it in trembling.

"It was given to me by an elderly woman in a village we were passing through. I've started reading it. I quite like it."

"These shoes — my sword —"

"Well, I picked up your shoes in the palace when I noticed you had left them behind. I did not want you to anger their majesties with such a breach of court etiquette. And your sword — well, Jade, the Emperor had asked me to follow you and guard you after the death of your husband. He feared you would do something to hurt yourself. I am sure that he already intended for us to marry, although he did not tell me that at the time."

"You were there — in the alley — when I lost my sword?"

"Yes."

"Why didn't you intervene?"

"I knew you could take care of yourself. But I did take the sword."

"Why?"

"I feared you would be identified as the killer if we left your sword in the alley."

Jade swallowed, puzzled. "You have been looking out for me for a while now."

"A little while," he said softly. And in the firelight, with his voice soft and thoughtful like that, and the poetry book in his hand, he suddenly resembled Wu Lei so much that she nearly cried out. Then she shook her head.

"Why is everything happening so fast?" she sighed. "It is like time has sped up—I am widowed, married, now you want to consummate the marriage, I see your wife in myself and my husband in you—"

"You do?"

She stopped, fearing she had said too much. She was alone on this island with him. He could do as he liked with her. She was determined to keep herself pure for Wu Lei's memory. She had to leave, even if she had to swim to shore.

Jade clambered to her feet. Luan was instantly on his as well; she couldn't help but admire the snapping movement he made to get to his full height within a second.

"Leave me alone!" she told him. "I cannot stay here with you."

She grabbed her sword, thrust it in a belt loop, tore out of the tent, and ran the short distance to the shore of the island. The soil was loose; she got her foot caught in some tangled roots and branches anchoring the island to the riverbed. She worked to disentangle her foot.

"Jade!" Luan cried. "Jade! The currents are dangerous at this time of night! Do not do this!"

He ran to her and threw his arms around her, trying to wrest her from the shore. Perhaps he was just trying to keep her from plunging into the river, but Jade's mind echoed with the darkness and fear in the alleyway near the tea house where she had nearly been raped — the aloneness, feeling trapped, the fear of the most intimate violation. She thought Luan might be trying to force her to make love with him. She kicked, fought, and cried out, even knowing no one would hear her here.

Apparently he had learned some of her fighting methods by now; she could not reach his face. He dodged her claws again and again, his head weaving. At one point he bent all the way to the right, circling her waist with his arm, and pulled her off her feet. She was quick to get her hands on the ground and to do a cartwheel away from him, but as she did so, he grabbed her leg and toppled her over. She landed with a resounding thump. He planted a foot in her back and grasped her wrists, holding them like a vice. She squealed in protest when she felt his hand on her hip, but then she felt the hard steel of her sword as it slipped out of her belt. He was disarming her. She heard the plop of her sword as he cast it aside and then he planted himself on her back, straddling her, keeping her hands and arms captive.

"You do not fight very well when you are in inner conflict," he told her.

Jade knew he was right. Even now as she tried to twist to gain some leverage beneath him, her movements were hampered by her confused emotions.

"What do you fear?" he asked her, as if reading her mind. "What are you angry at?"

"Stop!" she screamed at him, furiously twisting and, at last, being able to get on her side and then onto her back to face him. That had broken his grip on her hands and arms. Hips freed for the moment, she raised a swift knee to his back, hoping to find a kidney. She missed; she was too upset to aim well enough, but with her hands also free, she gripped him where a man is most vulnerable. She would not miss or forget that move, even in her agitation. That was always to place to aim for when fighting an unarmored man.

He slapped her face, hard; then he aimed several chopping blows at her elbows, forcing her arms to bend and her grip to loosen. She loosened her grip, but as he sighed in relief she stole the moment to squeeze out from under him. He swung his leg out wide and tripped her, but she scrambled to her feet again before he could stop her, and dove into the river.

CHAPTER 29

ade! Jade!" He broke off with an incoherent growl, then called her a salty name. She almost laughed out loud. The water was very cold, but the shore was only about twenty feet away. She could swim it easily, and then she would escape into the forest. Maybe she would never see Luan again.

Something was wrong, though; the harder she swam, the more the current resisted her, as if the very river were rebuking her for her treatment of her new husband. She could not get beyond the island; she could not get to shore.

The current was strong, and she went down once, its cold hands covering her hair and soaking it, as if the river was trying to push her head down and drown her.

She could hear his voice in her head as she struggled for air: *What do you fear?*

In her heart, she knew the answer: *I fear I can love you very much and that will be disloyal to Wu Lei.*

What are you angry at?

I am angry at myself that I feel so drawn to you so soon after my husband's death.

The waters seemed to turn more gentle, but she was still trapped in a current that held her in a cold, vise-like grip and would not allow her to move toward the island or to the shore. She did not know how long her strength would hold out.

"Jade!" Luan called again.

This time she let herself answer him. "Help me, Luan! Help me!"

"I will help you. Listen to me and you will survive this. Otherwise you will die. You must obey me before you float to the end of the island. I will not be able to help you in the middle of the river."

She gulped, nodded, and choked as she took in a mouthful of river water.

He strode along the bank of the island next to her, instructing her to turn her body a certain way, changing her orientation to the current so that the current itself turned her toward the island and lent its strength to her journey there. She was exhausted and drained of all emotion. Eventually, though, through following Luan's instructions, her spent body came up close enough to the shore for him to wade in and pull her out. She clung to him in gratitude, sobbing, and he picked her up and carried her back to the tent.

She lay on the furs shivering, while he built up the fire. He brought her hot tea and she gulped it down. She lay back and she did not protest as he stripped her of her wet clothes. She knew now that she feared she could love him powerfully. Her anger was at herself for being able to love another man so soon. She did not fear or feel anger toward Luan at all. She felt a powerful attraction.

He then stripped himself of his wet clothing and came to the bed with two large towels in hand. He dried her — every part of her — in a business-like way. She submitted like a child, allowing him to do so. He seemed especially concerned about drying her breasts and her private parts, she noted, but it made her purr like a kitten as he did so, and he laughed. Then she took the second towel and dried him similarly. Soon they cast aside the towels and embraced one another, kissing and caressing one another hungrily.

"You saved my life," she said, grateful.

"So it is not too soon?"

"For tonight, let four hearts beat as one. Wu Lei and Jingwei seem to be drawing us together."

He really was very handsome, and the fire was so warm, the tent so cozy, the island so isolated from anywhere or anyone else. It was wonderful to be held and comforted after all she had been through. She gave herself to him in the semi-darkness with abandon, knowing her cries and moans of pleasure were heard only by the island and by him, whom she now trusted with her life. Soon four became one as their flesh and spirits sealed, their bodies fused in an acme of desire and release.

*   *   *

As the fire died down in the night, Jade clung to the dart strung around her neck. She was wide awake, her eyes staring into the darkness. Luan was already asleep, no doubt exhausted from trying to tame the tigress and—to some extent, she admitted—succeeding. She had certainly been submissive to him—and more than submissive. She had been a very willing participant.

Had she just betrayed Wu Lei? And what about her vow to avenge him? Was she so disloyal that she could almost forget about finding his killer while lolling about pleasurably in another man's arms?

Frustration filled her. Events were marching on so fast. There were so many distractions in her life now that kept her from finding her husband's assassin and dispatching him with vengeance. She felt as if she were swimming the river again, grasping for something that waves and winds continually made dance away from her grasp.

Luan is my husband now, she reasoned with herself, *given by the Son of Heaven. There is something to that. I owe my Emperor and my new husband some loyalty too, no matter how quickly events are moving.*

Remembering Luan's rescue of her on the river, she found herself moving closer to him, snuggling up to him and fitting her body along his back as if they were two spoons. She rubbed her cheekbone on his shoulder gratefully.

I really am like a cat, she decided. *Feed me, pet me, treat me well, and I am yours.*

She frowned then, thinking herself no better than an animal. Yet, animal or not, she did need to keep warm, so she moved even closer to Luan and wrapped her arms and legs around him. The fire was almost completely out now, the embers giving up their burning souls in thrall to the night. Surely it was not disloyal to keep herself healthy enough to carry out her mission.

"In the morning," Luan murmured. "I am too spent now."

"I didn't mean—" She stopped herself.

She was not sure what she meant. All she knew was that her body was saturated with warmth and comfort at being so near to him. When she closed her eyes, her mind began to fill with the same comforting warmth.

Forgive me, Wu Lei, she thought. *Tomorrow I will continue my mission to find your killer and send him into the hell he deserves. For tonight, I need sleep.*

CHAPTER 30

She woke up at the first shards of dawn slicing through the seams and door of the tent. She looked around apprehensively. Was she really on the island of the Danjing fork? Had last night really happened or was it a dream?

Just then Luan entered the tent. The smell of woodsmoke wafted in with him. Jade surmised that he had been smoke-signaling Beijing again.

"We must pack up and depart now," he told her. "Our troop has been ordered back to the capital. We will go there by boat and meet them there."

"Good!" she said. "There is more hope of finding my husband's—I mean, Wu Lei's—assassin there."

"That is not our mission," he chided her. "The defeat of the Golden Ginkgo Society is our focus."

"Finding my husband's murderer is my mission."

"Self-assigned! You must obey the Emperor, not your own heart."

Jade growled inwardly as she watched him hasten to gather things and pack them into compact bundles. Luan was back to his old aloof self. Yet beneath his clipped words, she sensed a motivation of patriotism, and it made her thoughtful. To her surprise, he soon approached her and gave her a husbandly kiss on the cheek.

"We do have time for breakfast," he told her. "If you would build up the fire."

"Yes, I will make the food," she nodded, and then she wondered how she was going to get into her clothing without him looking at her. She felt shy in the daylight.

Luan answered the question by getting her clothes and tossing them gently to her.

"We really must make haste," he told her. "Warriors have no time for protracted honeymoons." Then he turned his back on her.

She struggled into her clothes under the furs of the bed and then climbed out and went to the food stores. There were eggs and rice—a perfect breakfast, she decided. Soon she had a small wok filled with snapping fat, eggs, and frying rice. She served Luan tea, kneeling to convey a bowl and its steaming contents to his seated form.

"Ah, you are a good wife," he said, breathing in the steam from the food.

"I am surprised to hear you say it," she said, sitting across from him with her own bowl. "You told me you wondered how Wu Lei could stand me." Her head hung down with the hurt of his words of the other day.

Luan pursed his lips. "I am sorry. I was angry at you and I spoke carelessly. You are delightful in many ways now that I have tamed you."

His grin told her that he was thinking of her submission to him last night. She lowered her eyes, and her voice came out softer and silkier than she had intended it to.

"Perhaps I am not yet as tame as you think."

"Good! A warrior tigress cannot be completely tame."

The meal was delicious, and she found herself enjoying the intimacy of being alone with the great General Luan Luan, laughing, eating, and teasing one another. She felt quite close to him now.

Soon, though, he finished and told her they had to make haste and return to the warriors' camp. She volunteered to pack up the food, and he nodded. Soon they brought their things outside and began to dismantle the tent together.

"Luan," she said, as they worked. "I hate to keep bringing it up, but I cannot forget that my husband was murdered. If he had died in battle or of natural causes, I think the wound in my mind would begin to close and heal. But knowing that he was assassinated by someone close enough to the throne to threaten me in the very palace—I cannot forget. I cannot begin to heal."

"I will help you all I can," Luan said, "without compromising our foremost mission, which is to destroy the Golden Ginkgo Society."

"What you don't understand is that the two are linked. I am absolutely certain of it."

"Jade," said Luan wearily. "There is no clear evidence of that." He broke the bamboo poles that had supported their tent over his knee with a loud snap and tossed them in the brush.

"But there is! There is! I told the Emperor, and he believed me!"

She recounted to Luan the mystery of the jeweled box Wu Lei had instructed his parents to give her.

"In the lining was a dried golden ginkgo leaf! That was a clue! He must have known something about them—he must have been hot on their trail for them to murder him like that. It was a sign and a signal—I just know it!"

Luan squinted, and Jade felt her heart thump with gratitude that he was at least thinking about what she had said.

All he said, though, was, "There is a boat hidden among those reeds. We will take that to shore."

Yet she knew Luan well enough now to know that he was not ignoring what she had said. She knew that her words registered with him, and that they would discuss it at the proper time. So, willingly, she helped him load the boat and launch it.

When they were in the middle of the river, he spoke above the soft lap of the oars on the water.

"The member of the Golden Ginkgo Society who killed your husband, according to your theory, has access to the archives in Nanjing where he procured the Serpent Shadow dart."

"Yes."

"This person also has access to the royal court in Beijing, for they were able to threaten you in the very dining hall of the palace."

"Yes," said Jade. "It must be someone quite high up."

They both grew solemn at the thought of what all this meant—that the tentacles of the Golden Ginkgo Society could reach to the very foundation of the Dragon Throne.

"Perhaps our missions are the same after all," said Luan softly.

"Find the mole in the palace, and you find my husband's murderer—or the one who ordered it!" cried Jade in excitement. "Don't you think so? Will you help me? Do you not see that our goals are the same? I'd bet my life on it!"

"The clue in the jeweled box does seem to indicate that," said Luan, his face thoughtful and his tone measured. "Of course, it could all be coincidence— "

"I'll wager it is not," said Jade. "Do you want to take that bet?"

"No," he smiled. "Because I think I would lose. We must make all the more haste to get to Beijing, not only to receive our assignment but to protect the Dragon Throne with our presence."

"And to seek out the traitor."

As their boat headed toward Beijing, Jade felt she had found a comrade-in-arms in her new husband. She was no longer sorry for the oneness of body she had shared with him last night, for they were of one mind and one heart now too.

CHAPTER 31

Seated on the dais of imperial yellow silk in the Inner Court, flanked by the man-height Ming porcelain vases, the Emperor and Empress regarded the couple kneeling before them. Peeking from under her eyelashes as she knelt next to Luan, Jade saw how tense their majesties looked.

Imitating the Son of Heaven and his wife, the eunuchs, concubines, and servants wore similar strained expressions as they waited in attendance, ranged along the walls or performed small acts of service for the imperial couple. Liu Huimin too, standing right next to Her Majesty, had lost some of her characteristic poise.

The Emperor clapped his hands, and a eunuch came forward.

"Bring seats for General Luan and his wife," instructed the Emperor. "And send to the kitchens for a serving woman. Then everyone leave us."

Two comfortable cushions were brought in and set upon low stands. Luan held Jade's hand to help her as she raised herself from a kneeling position and lowered herself into the seat. She wondered if he realized she was once again wearing the miserable platform shoes appropriate to court dress. She smiled at him appreciatively. He did not return her smile as he seated himself, but she thought she detected a kindly light in his eyes.

A beautiful servant, clearly angling to be a concubine by her silken dress, the big red dot on her lips, and her elaborately dressed hair, piled high upon her head and festooned with flowers, entered the room and paid obeisance to the Emperor with a flirtatious look in her eyes.

"Bring tea," he said, with a bored note in his voice. The Empress's hand covered her mouth for a moment, but Jade caught the edge of her pleased smile.

When the servant brought the tea in on a golden tray, a eunuch placed it on a stand next to Luan. With a slight gasp, the beautiful servant noticed Luan. Then, very fussily, she brushed the eunuch aside and served Luan tea herself, kneeling before him, her head bowed modestly. Then she raised her full face to Luan, meeting his eyes boldly, her smile curving flirtatiously.

Jealousy rose up in Jade's heart, shocking her. She tried to control how heavily she began to breathe, especially when she noticed the sharp-eyed Empress studying her face. To her relief, Luan could not have been more properly indifferent toward the woman. She left with disappointment clearly etched on her face, the red dot on her mouth at the center of an upside-down smile. She did not leave before casting Jade a withering glance, however. A general of Luan's stature could take several wives and many concubines if he wished. Jade knew this. She did not need to be reminded of it by the would-be concubine's contempt.

To her surprise, Luan sought her eyes and then gave her a look that could only be interpreted as reassuring. So he had noticed the woman's flirtatiousness. Jade's shoulders swayed, bringing her in closer proximity with him.

"Hmm," the Empress said out loud. She turned to her husband. "I believe our plan will work well," she added cryptically.

The army of concubines and attendants took some time to leave the hall, which they did with a great rustling of garments. Liu Huimin, the last out of the room, bowed again and again most obediently as she backed herself out of the room, a look of devotion lifting her eyebrows even as her sad smile showed concern for the empire's peril.

The next twenty minutes were filled with political and strategic discussions concerning the Golden Ginkgo Society. The Empress looked rather bored, but Jade listened attentively. The Emperor spread a map of China out before them, showing places where the Golden Ginkgo Society was evident. According to the map and the Emperor's words, the threat was growing.

The Emperor resumed his seat on the dais, looking worried and weary after communicating to Luan and Jade the growing gravity of the situation. The Empress addressed a solemn-looking Luan.

"Infiltration of their stronghold in Shanghai is necessary. We need someone, perhaps more than one, to penetrate the top within their organization and uncover their plans. We need someone who is most highly recommended, and we trust no one more than yourself to make that recommendation. Have you anyone in mind?"

"There are a number of fine warriors who have the skills and character necessary for such an important mission," Luan answered.

The Empress smiled. "That is a very proper response, Luan. Very polite and probably quite true. But do you have someone specific in mind?"

"I do, if a female warrior would be acceptable."

Jade's heart beat like a trapped bird behind her ribcage. Would he recommend her? Infiltrating the Golden Ginkgo Society would bring her closer to solving her husband's murder! She licked her lips in anticipation.

The Emperor nodded. "Women are often better at these kinds of tasks."

The Empress closed her eyes wearily and shook her head slightly. "Do not say it is because of our naturally devious natures," she told her husband with evident pain.

"I didn't. I won't," said the Emperor, showing almost childlike dismay at her rebuke. Somehow, it struck all four of them as funny, and Luan and Jade allowed themselves to join in the Emperor and Empress's laughter. Some of the tension left the room.

The Emperor addressed Luan: "On the other hand, a warrior couple might be best for this mission. Yin and yang together makes the best balance."

"Perhaps," said Luan. "An initial infiltration could be done by a lone female, however, and probably done best."

"Who do you recommend?" the Emperor demanded.

Jade raised a cup of tea to her lips to hide her eagerness, pretending to sip in a lady-like, indifferent way, as if Luan's answer would be no concern to her. She was straining to stop herself from nudging him with her elbow to utter her name.

"Willow," said Luan.

CHAPTER 32

Jade's tea spewed out of her mouth in a fountain. The Empress gave a cry, the Emperor expressed annoyance, and Luan deftly used a silk handkerchief to dab away the mess. He clucked reprovingly at Jade as he mopped up the front of her silk brocade dress.

Jade shoved his hand aside. "Willow?" she spat. "What are you thinking?"

"Don't question your husband like that," scolded the Emperor. "It is most unbecoming to you, and to him. Does she behave like this in camp?" he demanded of Luan.

"No, my lord," said Luan, pursing his lips. "I assure you, she is perfectly respectful."

What a cool liar, Jade thought. She was grateful to him, though. A word of denunciation from him, and she might be taken out into one of the courtyards and beheaded as a disobedient wife.

"Who is Willow?" asked the Empress. "I used to know all the warriors' names, but time has passed."

"She is a woman not yet in middle age, a widow. In many ways, she is the eyes of our unit. She has influence and always knows the latest gossip. Her ear is to the ground."

"Jade," the Empress said. "What do you think of her?"

Jade frowned with distaste. "She never bathes. She smells. Her features are unbecoming and her disposition is too. I don't trust her. She is more like an animal than a woman."

Jade sniffed judgmentally, then remembered her actions of the night before. She was no one to call another woman an animal! She bowed her head.

"If we use this Willow, then, as a practical matter, we will not be able to utilize a seduction strategy," said the Emperor.

Luan addressed him: "It was Willow's sister who immolated herself before the gate of the Forbidden City. She has good reason to want to penetrate and destroy the society that captured her sister's mind."

Jade leaped from her chair. "That is all the more reason not to trust her!" she cried. "Her sympathy for her sister's cause will turn her!"

Luan narrowed his eyes. "Sit down, Jade. You do not know what you are talking about."

The Emperor raised his eyebrows in seeming approval of Luan's stern voice toward his wife. He looked even more appreciative when Jade sat down in obedience to her husband. The Empress rolled her expressive eyes.

"Well," said the Emperor, glancing at his wife's expression. "Willow may be a possibility, but I believe the Empress has another suggestion."

The Empress smiled and gave her husband an affectionate pat on the hand before she spoke. "Why not test the mettle of our newest husband and wife team? This is a perfect circumstance to prove the worthiness of this concept." She turned her sunny smile on her husband, who nodded thoughtfully.

Jade was impressed again that there must be a special relationship between Luan and the Emperor. She had never seen their majesties behave and talk so freely before, and she sensed it was Luan's presence that relaxed them.

The Empress turned frankly to Jade. "This situation will call for great trust, and there is no warrior we trust more than Luan. And you, Jade, are well known as an excellent martial artist and cunning strategist. Your beauty will serve you well, too. A woman's beauty is a spare arrow in her quiver."

Jade regarded her Emperor thoughtfully. He had used that expression to her before, saying that he had a spare arrow in his quiver, once when they were talking about the succession to the throne and Jade's thoughts had gone to his intemperate sons.

It is certainly a favorite expression of his, she thought now.

The Emperor said, "As near as we can tell, Shanghai has a fairly well-structured Society presence, and for all their talk of equality, they are a hierarchical group. The leader will likely be found in their Shanghai stronghold. You will go there. You will penetrate it and make it implode from within—or, if you deem it already weak, you can signal us to overwhelm the city with imperial troops and demoralize this movement all across China."

Jade did not dare look at Luan. She could sense the excitement within him, though, at the prospect of this dangerous and important mission. She knew he would not have put himself forward, and here the Empress had done it for him.

With a glance at one another, husband and wife said simultaneously, "Yes!"

The Empress laughed heartily, and even the Emperor looked amused.

"So it is done," he said. "For now, Willow will simply have to continue wafting her personal fragrance around your unit. Go," he said, waving his hand at Luan and Jade. "Occupy the same chamber as you did the night of your marriage. We are serving a full banquet to all the warriors of your troop, to which you are both, of course, invited. Feast, be merry, and be happy here in the protected walls of the Forbidden City."

Jade's excitement subsided and was replaced by fear. She knew there was no safety here in the walls of the Forbidden City.

"Should we not remind the Emperor of the threat I received here?" Jade whispered to Luan as the Emperor and Empress put their heads together in a private discussion.

"I will remind him when I meet him in private."

"You meet with the Emperor in private sometimes?"

"Yes," said Luan casually, almost off-handedly.

"It will be a message he will not like to hear."

"He is used to plots and intrigues all around his very person. I have a far more difficult mission telling Willow she was not chosen for this mission. She specifically begged me to recommend her as a potential infiltrator."

Luan took a deep breath and Jade pondered why he was less comfortable telling Willow something unpleasant than the Emperor of all China.

CHAPTER 33

The banquet was held in the Hall of Supreme Harmony. It was so filled with serving eunuchs, serving women, and concubines winding around its engraved golden pillars that it was difficult to believe that all this was in honor of fewer than twenty people — Luan's troop of elite spousal warriors.

The room contained four large banquet tables arranged in a rectangle and covered in silk. They were set between golden pillars, leaving a large space of the blue, pink, and dragon-emblazoned carpet exposed in the middle of the room, where entertainers would perform.

The Empress and Emperor occupied their thrones, seated nine steps above their invited guests. The stairs to their thrones were scarlet and, like the carpet, emblazoned with dragons. Four jade vases stood on pillars, as if they were sentries guarding the imperial couple. Above, the elaborate gold- and green-enameled ceiling had but one central light beaming down on the carpet, like a ray of heaven. It would serve as a spotlight for the city's finest opera players.

There was enough food for a hundred people. Platters of shrimp, their black beady eyes gazing out of their heads above their tender flanks, appeared by the dozens. Succulent, almost sweet fillets of roasted duck were served, along with crisply fried wings and feet. Steaming platters of young bamboo shoots swimming in buttery gravy were on every table. There were mountains of ground poultry, beef, and spice-filled dumplings. An abundance of rice was served from hot silver bowls. There were plates of bean sprouts, spicy fried bean curd, and heaps of lettuce to wrap the duck flanks in, along with a savory sauce. Bowls of shark fin soup, hills of black mushrooms, and forests of broccoli spears appeared as well.

The warriors ate until sated and then some. Self-controlled and abstemious for so long, eating only what they could carry and prepare on the road, they now let down their guard in the Forbidden City and enjoyed the rich food, becoming quite joyous and raucous. There were several food fights. This did not matter, for except for the lush carpet in the center of the room, the banquet hall was tiled and easily cleaned. Stamping feet beat in time to music so lively, the yellow silk tapestries, with their calligraphic messages of good fortune and longevity, trembled.

The Emperor and Empress were enjoying themselves, seemingly happy that they had begun to solve the problem of the Golden Ginkgo Society with their plans for infiltration. Their grown sons appeared to be especially enamored of the warriors' revelry and joined in, traveling from table to table to get to know and admire the warriors. Prince Li, the third oldest, was particularly interested.

"Luan," Jade whispered, after a lengthy chat with Prince Li, who had stopped by their table. "I do not understand why their majesties are only now addressing the problem of the Golden Ginkgo Society. The map showed that the Society has been steadily spreading and growing in influence for some time."

Luan gave her a bemused smile. "You are still an innocent when it comes to palace politics, aren't you?"

"I suppose so. The workings of the palace have never interested me enough to study them."

"Nor I, but I have learned them out of necessity. In service to the nation, one must also be keenly aware of the nation's flaws and weaknesses."

"Humph!" said Jade, sipping rice wine from a silver goblet. "I had the impression you were blindly loyal to the nation."

"Blind loyalty is, in the end, no loyalty at all." He looked at her with humor in her eyes. "After all, a man learns the flaws of his wife over time. It is only in the first flush of love that he sees her as a goddess. Is a man then to stop loving his wife when he learns she is human and has weaknesses? Or is that when real love and loyalty begin?"

Jade looked away from his intensely dark eyes. "You ask deep questions," she said. "Of course, seeing the flaws, that is when real love and loyalty begin."

"It is the same with the love of nation, I believe, and loyalty to their majesties. To answer your question, there are many people seeking influence at court for their own benefit. They flatter their majesties and tell them only good news, praising their administration of the kingdom and acting as if everything is perfect, crediting their majesties even when it is the rain that produces good crops. I believe that map of the Society was made by one of the elite warrior corps, such as we belong to. I do not believe their majesties knew the scope of the problem until recent events drew it to their attention. An immolation at the very gate of the Forbidden City was startling to them. They have been forced to look at a problem that has gone unchecked for too long."

"Do they now understand that the Society is a serious threat?"

"Yes. Otherwise they would not assign us to it. They need intervention by the best, and they need it quickly."

"Does that mean they think you and I are the best?"

Luan shrugged modestly. "We are among the best. But you knew that."

During a break in the meal, actors stood in the center of the room and enacted the opera *Farewell, My Concubine*, about a king's consort who commits suicide when her lord, Xiang Yu, is defeated in battle. The singing and dancing, the highly stylized thick eye makeup, ornate costumes and sparse pieces of scenery made the imagination soar. Other entertainers came too: troops of dancers with long whirling scarves and sleeves and singers skilled on the qin and reed flute. At the finale, the servants brought in towers of succulent fruits.

Luan appeared to be enjoying himself, although Jade noted, with satisfaction, that there was restraint in his revelry. She felt that restraint herself. Their mission would begin soon; it would not do to completely lose sight of the responsibility, even for one evening. What was more, there was a highly placed enemy somewhere nearby, possibly Wu Lei's assassin. A warrior could never relax.

"I have noted you are a passionate tigress," said Luan. "Yet you are showing admirable restraint now."

"There is serious work ahead of us."

"Indeed." Seeing the Emperor watching him, Luan smiled, raised his silver goblet, and appeared to relax more. The Emperor raised his golden goblet to him and to Jade in response, also smiling.

Yet after a time, the Emperor, no doubt used to many such banquets, began to look restless, and the Empress gathered her small silk brocade purse as if in preparation to rise and leave the banquet hall.

Just then half a dozen eunuchs burst into the hall, ushering in their midst an imperial courier from afar. Their faces were full of fear.

"Terrible news, your majesties!" they cried.

CHAPTER 34

uan and Jade and all the warriors had risen, ready to bow the Emperor and Empress from the room. They stayed on their feet and watched as the courier faced the throne and bowed nine times, knocking his forehead on the blue and blush carpet. Then he stood and proffered a scroll to their majesties with both hands, bowing from the waist.

A eunuch took the scroll from the courier's hand, begging permission to mount the nine scarlet steps and hand the message to his majesty. The Emperor granted a hasty permission and received the missive. He unwrapped it and read its message to himself, his eyes scanning the document, as the Empress leaned over to read it too.

The Emperor rose, his face a mask of grief and anger.

"Nanjing has fallen to the Golden Ginkgo Society! Our ancient capital is in the hands of traitors!"

The room took a collective breath. Luan and Jade eyes flew to one another's like homing doves.

Prince Li slammed his fist on a banquet table so hard, he smashed the wood in two, sending the silver platters of food and drink clattering and clashing to the tiled floor. He then shoved the broken banquet table aside and addressed his father: "Let me lead imperial troops to put them down!"

The Emperor's other sons made similar requests, while the warriors vowed vengeance.

"We will besiege Nanjing!" roared Ching.

"Temperance," the Emperor said in a measured tone, clapping his hands together. "This is not the time to be hot-headed."

Prince Li bowed his head the rebuke, and the warriors fell silent.

The Emperor held up his hand, and a eunuch sounded a gong.

"We will use force when it is appropriate; first we must make plans in the light of this news. There will be many re-assignments over the next few days. You will disperse to various responsibilities. Do not question one another's destinations or whereabouts. I will have Nanjing back."

Every warrior in the hall gave a deep-throated cry of loyalty.

"General Luan, you have your orders," the Emperor said. "They are unchanged but for the location. Submit to me a plan for the assignments of your troops within the hour."

Luan bowed.

The Emperor descended the scarlet steps, and in the melee of the royal couple's departure, the warriors made their obeisance to them and to their sons and then began speaking excitedly among themselves.

Jade whispered to Luan. "Will we go to Nanjing rather than Shanghai?"

"Yes. You realize," he said carefully, studying her face, "that the danger has now quadrupled. Shanghai is still an open city; Nanjing now belongs to the Golden Ginkgo Society. What is more, hotheads may convince his majesty to invade Nanjing, or—" He glanced at Prince Li uneasily, "—perhaps even do it without authorization. We could be killed by loyal troops if they invade the city to wipe out the Society. We could be killed within by the Society if we are discovered. We will be in danger on all sides."

Jade shrugged. "What is new about our missions being dangerous? I am ready. When do we leave?"

"Soon. But you need more training."

"I? I need more training?" Jade assumed a fighting stance, and she could see in a mirrored wall that even in her fancy embroidered silk dress, the fitness of her form suggested a muscular tigress beneath its folds.

"Yes," said Luan. "You are a wonderful tigress, but you must understand more about qi. It is an infiltrator's best friend. Our mission will require subtlety—a quality I fear you lack."

Jade's mouth opened in indignation.

"Come, come," he said to her, almost humorously. "You are self-aware enough to know that!"

He then steered her by her elbow out of the banquet hall, pausing when she stumbled over her platform shoes, to the corridor where their assigned bedchamber was. She protested a little, but then she reconsidered. Luan had looked exceptionally handsome in his finery for the banquet; he was almost as resplendent and majestic as Prince Li. She had felt very bonded with him in the presence of the Emperor and Empress when they had shared laughter and understanding about marriage. She felt herself melting a little.

Then, out of the corner of her eye, she thought she saw someone standing in the shadows of a doorway.

Before she spoke, she heard Luan call out, "Who is there? Reveal yourself or be thought a coward."

Willow stepped out of the shadows of the doorway, her face distorted with surliness.

"I am no coward," she said angrily.

"Then why hide yourself?" demanded Jade.

"I cannot slip through the shadows as I used to. A few years ago, you would never have seen me."

"Why hide at all?" Luan asked. To Jade's surprise, he did not seem angry or worried that one of his warriors was stalking him.

"You have been chosen to go to Shanghai as spies. I know this. I know too that you will go to Nanjing now."

Again, to Jade's surprise, Luan did not seem upset that Willow knew of their top secret mission.

Luan admonished. "I advise you to keep that information to yourself, Willow. It is crucial to the empire's security."

"How does she even know that information?" demanded Jade indignantly.

"She has her ways," and Luan smiled, almost as if in reminiscence. "By the way, I recommended you for the spy mission before anyone else, Willow, but the Emperor wanted a couple."

"Thank you, commander," said Willow, slightly mollified. "But it is the Emperor's own fault I am not a couple. The Emperor has not seen fit to reward a faithful warrior, who has given home, youth, and husband to the cause, and whose sister was swallowed by the Golden Ginkgo Society. He has not rewarded my loyalty with a husband. He has rewarded Jade, though."

Willow looked angrily at Jade and took a step toward her.

Luan stepped between the two women as they glowered at one another. He seemed to have noticed that his wife's hands had assumed the claw shape of the tigress.

"You will have a husband, all in good time, as I have told you many times before," Luan scolded Willow lightly. "You already have an important mission. Right now you function best as a single woman, as you know. Will you keep faith in your future, excellent woman warrior?"

Willow's mouth curled up in hurt, but at the compliment her expression turned into something like a childish pout. Jade had the passing thought that if Willow smiled once in a while, she would look years younger.

"I will, commander," said Willow, taking a deep breath.

"Patience furthers," he reminded her gently. "So says the *I ching*."

"You are wise, commander, and well-schooled in the classics."

Jade was impressed. Luan touched her sleeve to go, and she quickly fell in line with his step as he strode down the corridor. Jade glanced over her shoulder at Willow. Surprisingly, for someone who appeared to be heavy and slow, the woman had already vanished. Jade remembered through fighting her that much of Willow's bulk was the heavy clothes she wore.

"How old do you think Willow is?" asked Jade. "She looks quite aged — and then at other times, almost like a girl."

"She is younger than you think. Widowhood has not sat well on her, but there is more to Willow than most people know."

Jade skidded to a stop, teetering on her platform shoes.

"Aren't you going to stop to report this conversation to the Emperor? Someone knows of our secret mission!"

"I trust Willow," said Luan. "I will not bother the Emperor with her jealousy."

"Are you not to report every single thing to the Emperor?"

"The Emperor leaves me to use my own discretion most of the time."

"I did not know you ranked so highly with him," Jade whispered humbly.

"I do not say it to brag."

"I know."

This was a large admission on her part—that she knew Luan was not a boastful man. Luan looked at her with a question in his eyes, as if to say, "Are you beginning to appreciate my value now?"

As if in answer, she slipped her arm through his and all but led him to their bedchamber. She intended to show him she appreciated him in the language a man understood. It would not be disloyal to Wu Lei in the least, she decided, as they were about to face the greatest danger either of them had ever known. They would need every ounce of unity between them they could muster.

To Jade's shock, when they entered the bedchamber, the Emperor was there, lolling on the large bed in the middle of one wall.

Luan looked amused. Jade closed her mouth, which had popped open, and the two readied themselves to do obeisance.

The Emperor waved his hand. "Just do three, not nine," he told them. "I have instructions to give you."

Luan and Jade bowed three times to the floor, knocking their foreheads on the ground with each bow.

The Emperor sat up on their bed.

"Being my Nanjing spies is the most important assignment and signifies my great trust in you. Remember," he instructed them, "what enables the wise sovereign and the good general to strike and conquer, and achieve things beyond the reach of ordinary men, is foreknowledge. Know your enemy's thoughts and actions even before he does."

Luan and Jade nodded.

"This foreknowledge can only be obtained from other men," the Emperor continued.

"And women," muttered Jade. Luan nudged her gently to be silent.

"An army without spies is like a man without ears or eyes," continued the Emperor. "You are my ears and eyes now. Do well at your task."

Luan and Jade bowed three times, with three knocks of the forehead to the ground in between, and the Emperor departed with a nod, treading softly on his silk-shod feet.

"Where did that come from?" Jade mused, turning the silken comforter back on the bed.

"*The Art of War*," Luan answered.

"I know that—I just wondered why."

"Do you know that? So you are a scholarly tigress!"

"I am a many-faceted tigress," she teased.

"You will need to be. That is why we will enter training before going to Nanjing. You need your many facets polished."

"Training!" cried Jade. "I need no extra training."

"Yes, you do. Remember, the GGS's power is not military. It is persuasive. That is why I must school you in arts you do not yet know."

At Jade's disgruntled expression, he said, "Don't worry. The training will pass quickly—and happily."

"How do you know that?" Jade frowned.

"Because we will be together." Luan's smile was warm and inviting.

Jade stared at the bed as if she could still see the Emperor in it. "I am out of the mood now," she admitted. "Thanks to his majesty. Which is just as well—you must deliver your assignments to him within the hour."

"True. Still, we will not have as comfortable a bed as this for a long time," said Luan enticingly.

Jade found her mouth, which had curled in resentment, relaxing into a smile. *I am much like Willow in some ways, she thought. Luan's honeyed tone tends to persuade me rather easily.*

CHAPTER 35

L uan was right; in the next days they were living out of a pitched tent, sleeping under furs on a straw mat, and eating meals cooked over fires. Their time in the palace now seemed like a wonderful rest stop; she could still feel the comfort of the satin sheets in her limbs and the soothing softness of the down-stuffed, silk-encased pillows in her neck and back even as they embarked on the training Luan had promised in camp.

"Willow will be an important part of your training," Luan informed her. "She is a master in the arts of dissembling and disguise."

"Willow?" Jade could feel the look of shock and skepticism on her own face.

But it turned out that Willow, incensed at the decision not to use her as the spy in Nanjing, was nowhere to be found. Apparently, she had left the camp.

Ching told Luan this when the general inquired where "Teacher Willow" was—a title that made Jade roll her eyes. Anbai, standing behind Ching, covered her mouth to repress a giggle when she saw Jade's expression. Anbai's eyes danced and then met Jade's with understanding. Then her friend sidled up to Jade and nudged her sympathetically.

Jade whispered, "Luan thinks so highly of Willow, I would be jealous if I were in love with him."

"There is nothing between them," soothed Anbai. "Luan was completely loyal to Jingwei in word, thought, and deed. He is not over her yet, even though he does not show it."

"Do you think he loves me?" Jade demanded suddenly.

"I think he likes you—and respects you—and finds you rather desirable. That's a very good start," said Anbai encouragingly. "And your feelings toward him?"

"I like him well enough—sometimes. When he is not praising Willow to the skies."

Ching asked Luan, "Should I send some troops to round Willow up? She can't have gotten much of a start. This kind of disobedience should not be passed over."

Luan looked uncomfortable.

"Ching, I trust you more than any man I know," he said finally. "Someday you will know more about Willow, and you will trust her as I do. You may be sure she is about the business of the empire in her own way. Some birds you simply cannot cage."

"I trust your judgment implicitly, Commander. I just worry about discipline among the troops."

Luan nodded, considering this.

"That is wise, Ching. Give out the word that she was under orders to gather her things and go. Remind people of the Emperor's directive not to inquire about one another's missions."

"If you are sure you trust her…"

"I do."

Jade nudged Anbai. "See? He favors her beyond all reason."

"He respects her as a warrior, that is all," said Anbai. "I have known him longer than you."

Luan planted himself in front of Jade.

"I shall have to train you myself," he said.

"All right." She shrugged.

"Anbai and Ching will aid us. They are both excellent at understanding the spiritual energy of qi."

Jade and Anbai exchanged a look of happiness under their eyelashes at this information.

"We will begin at once."

"And the others?" Ching asked.

"Tell them to train in pairs now, and after lunch we will all continue our journey toward Nanjing. When we are nearer, they will be dispersed to surrounding areas."

Ching nodded and asked to be excused for a short time to impart this information to the other warriors.

"This will work out well after all," said Luan. "Anbai is very good with qi energy, and you will be more receptive to her teaching than to Willow's."

"I should think that would have been obvious from the first," said Jade.

Jade's first training exercise was for her to sit across from Anbai, both sitting Lotus style, and to try to sense the energy nature of Anbai's thoughts.

"What is the point of this?" Jade Blossom cried out. "I want to learn to fight with qi energy, not read people's minds!"

"Can you not see how important this could be in espionage?" asked Luan. "Jade, you need to govern your mouth. I will not accept this kind of back talk from any of my warriors."

"I am not sure I believe in this," said Jade helplessly. "I'm not sure I believe it can work in myself, or in you, or in anyone."

"Anbai, read Jade," ordered Luan. "Jade, sit still and be silent."

Anbai closed her eyes and Jade sat very still. There was her friend, taking this utterly seriously. It apparently took Anbai just seconds to attain a deep meditative state through heavy, measured breathing.

Startled, Jade felt Anbai's regard, though her eyes were closed. She felt oddly vulnerable, as if questing fingers probed beneath her skin — beneath her thoughts. She felt as if Anbai was reaching into the depths of her consciousness, gently exploring her mind and heart. A part of Jade wanted to cry, "Get out!" but she kept silent.

"Your heart is locked up," said Anbai. "But little cracks of light get through. You are experiencing a great deal of confusion. You try to soldier on, but in truth you have little peace."

Just Anbai saying this seemed to lift a burden off Jade's heart. Tears sprang into her eyes as she looked at her friend.

Anbai continued: "You have too much vengeance in your heart. You must be as true as a well-aimed arrow in this mission, and your desire for vengeance may skew your aim. Your personal sorrow and anger are first in your mind. You are too glad that the mission dovetails with a possible chance for vengeance on your husband's murderer. You may kill too soon. Indeed, you have killed someone outside the realm of battle, and you carry guilt over this act."

Jade gasped when Anbai said this. She glanced at her husband. "Did you tell her?" she cried.

He shook his head. "Of course not. She knows through sensing your inner qi. But Jade, it was an honorable killing. He tried to violate you. Release your guilt."

"Breathe deeply," suggested Anbai. "And put the collective purpose over the personal."

Jade took several deep breaths. Luan patted her back strongly, and it seemed to her that he clapped away clouds of negative energy in her heart. Maybe there was something to this qi energy training after all. She looked again at Anbai, with tears in her eyes.

Luan said, "This kind of energy training is exhausting. It changes you inside, and that is as hard as digging ditches. We will break until after our meal."

He looked surprised when Jade protested, "No! It's fascinating. I want to learn more. I feel quite light of burden now, and clear-minded. May I try it myself?"

"All right," said Luan, seeing Anbai nod. "Try to understand the energy of Anbai."

Jade focused her attention on her friend, then closed her eyes. She was eager to know all she could glean about Anbai. Could she do this? She was about to find out.

Jade breathed deeply. She felt she was trying to breathe in the essence of her friend. Still, she could not discern anything she could put words to. Her friend's spirit seemed like pure fresh air — nothing more. Her own heart throbbed with liking for this woman.

Anbai must be an expert — a true master — at keeping her energy clear, Jade thought. Or else I am just no good at this at all.

"It's understandable if you cannot do it at the beginning," said Luan, as if ready to close the session. "This is your very first lesson with it."

"Wait," said Jade. Then she gasped as insight came to her. "You killed a man outside of battle too! For the same reason I did! You resonate with me because of that!" She gazed in shock at her gentle friend.

Now tears sprang into Anbai's eyes and she nodded at Luan in sorrowful confirmation. The two women unfolded their legs and embraced. They were both sobbing.

"Ah," said Luan. He was obviously trying to hide his astonishment. "Healing has taken place here and now. Excellent work, both of you! You will both be warriors of more clarity after this."

Jade decided she would tuck that compliment into her heart to savor later. Right now, she and Anbai clung to one another, sobbing, and feeling the balm of a forgiving energy wash over deep wounds.

"As penance," Luan said, "Be extra kind to the male warriors in this troop. Serve good men and forgive the bad."

The two women, entangled in one another's arms, hair awry, and faces streaked with tears, nodded.

CHAPTER 36

They trained for several days. The first half of the training was clearing Jade's qi, and the second half was using her new clarity in battle. During one of her meditative sessions with Anbai, Jade heard Wu Lei's voice speaking to her clearly, deep within the layers of her heart and mind.

"I will always be here with you, listening through the silence. When you are in great need, you will hear my voice and know my guidance. I will always protect and love you."

Jade reflected on how wonderful her new life was. She was learning things every day with her new husband—and her first husband was still with her!

One by one, Luan had the warriors of the troop challenge Jade to a fighting match. She knew he started her off with the easier ones, progressing—as she defeated each in turn—to the toughest warriors in the unit. By now Jade was channeling qi energy expertly, incorporating it almost instinctively with her Shaolin style, getting better with each battle. Each day Luan assigned her a warrior superior to the one she had conquered the day before, and each day he appeared astonished at how easily she dispatched him or her.

"You are a fast learner," he complimented her.

When Jade had defeated everyone in the troop except Luan, the warriors gathered to watch the couple fight.

"Don't hold back," she warned Luan.

"I have no intention of doing so."

She assumed the usual tigress stance, but she decided against a fast, frontal attack, for she knew that was what he would expect of her. Qi had taught her that she could take the force of her initial rush and parcel it out throughout a fight, using it effectively in small bursts. She did not think Luan knew she knew this yet.

Luan assumed his stance, and his eyes narrowed, waiting for her initial assault. Surprised that she did not rush him, he appeared to be caught off balance for a moment, but he was too good a warrior not to immediately make up a new plan. Sensing his energy, Jade knew that he would provoke an attack from her.

He delivered a kick to her shin; it was painful, but she had turned enough in time to deflect its main force from her bone. The ball of his foot left a bruise on her calf muscle, but she bent her knee and delivered a kick to his side with her other leg. His arm came down, down on her head, pushing down on her neck, and she would have lost her balance, but she channeled qi to turn herself in a cartwheel, her hands barely touching the dusty ground as her fulcrum. When she rose to face him again, she could see the respect in Luan's eyes.

The battle seemed endless after that. The rustle of their clothing, the spit of the dust at their feet, the solid thunk of punches and their groans and cries seemed to take them into an eternity of fighting. Jade allowed herself to appear to be getting dizzy and tired. She almost was; Luan was a master of energy, and she was running out of it now. She had reserved one last burst for a rush at the end, though, a small store of energy she concealed from him. She smiled inside when she felt more relaxation behind his blows; he was certain he was going to win, wearing her down.

Never relax in front of a tigress, she thought, but she did not let her amusement well up in her, or she knew he would sense it. Instead she projected flagging energy. She let her blows falter a bit at the end of each to apprise him of her growing weakness.

Then, bunching up her haunches, she sprang with her last energy reserve. Almost to her shock, she bowled Luan over, and, with a bit of added luck, his head hit the ground in his fall.

Luan appeared dazed and dizzy on the ground, his head lolling from side to side. She cautiously climbed off him and stood, her knees shaking, her hands formed claws, knowing that if he got up she would not have the strength to fight him another second. She could barely keep her feet now. Her stomach felt as if it had fallen down to her toes. Her head was pounding.

He did not get up. After a few seconds Ching came forward and held out a hand, to help him up. The warriors, shocked, did not applaud. They simply stared, open-mouthed, at Jade. When, at last, Luan stood unsteadily on his feet. Jade could see he was not faking the dazedness and dizziness.

"You have won," he said. "The universe was with you today. Qi was with you today. At last you are ready."

Jade tried to smile, but the effort was too much. She had no energy left; her limbs were like rubber. She felt herself losing consciousness, heard Anbai's cry as if from a great distance. Soon it mingled with the cries of the other warriors as she pitched down into a whirl of dust.

CHAPTER 37

When Jade awakened, she was lying in their tent, and she had been bathed and dressed. Anbai was making her tea. Luan was also in the tent, and he glanced at her almost humorously.

"Humph," said Jade, gratefully sipping the tea and nodding at Anbai. "You certainly seem fine, Luan, for someone who was defeated in battle."

Luan smiled. "I have always been a fast healer."

Anbai said, "I will leave you now, Commander," and she bowed herself out of the tent.

"Why am I dressed like this?" Jade asked, seeing that she was wearing finery.

"One last test. You have learned to use qi in fighting; now you must learn to use it to charm."

"To charm? To charm who—for what?"

"We are going into Beijing. You will return to the blacksmith's shop where you learned some history of the Serpent Shadow dart and charm more information from the store owner. You will go as a lady."

Jade felt excitement rise in her breast. At last—something to do with finding Wu Lei's killer!

"What should I try to find out from him?" she asked.

"Find out more about the Serpent Shadow darts."

Jade pursed her lips and tilted her head. "I do not think he will readily tell me."

"Pass this last test, Jade, and we leave for Nanjing to defeat the Golden Ginkgo Society—the Society which claims the allegiance of your first husband's killer."

Distracted by the mention of Wu Lei, Jade mused, "He must have known something about them. He must have been on their trail. I cannot think of any other reason why they would kill him."

"Now we are on their trail," said Luan. "And we must know enough arts of manner and persuasion that they do not know it. Get ready to depart for Beijing in twenty minutes. I have some business to attend to, and then we will go."

"All right," she said. She was recovered from their fight and her mind was flying ahead to the dusty shop in Beijing. What could she find out there?

Thoughtfully, she went to her stores of items and pulled out the jeweled box Wu Lei's parents had given her. She probed the golden ginkgo leaf in its lining. What story could it tell her?

Deciding to try to her new qi energy skills, she sat down in a lotus position with the box on her lap. She rubbed the ginkgo leaf between her fingertips, and then gently ran her hand along the red silk lining, again and again. Her emotions were calm. She stroked the box, as if gently inquiring into its secrets.

Nothing came to her. She thought that by now ten minutes had gone by and Luan would be back soon to take her to Beijing. She sighed and was about to get up and put the box back, regretfully, among her things. Suddenly an oval appeared in her mind, almost like a mirror. It was full of darkness. Then the edges of the mirror began to glow with the faintest of light. Jade willed herself to keep calm.

The light flickered, lighting the interior of the mirror, and then Wu Lei's face appeared. She wanted to cry out to him, but she was afraid that would break the spell. She forced herself to remain serene, inviting him to tell her what he would. She felt his love for her; she felt her own love for him. That helped to calm her down.

Slowly, Wu Lei raised his hand and drew Chinese characters in red lettering on his side of the mirror. She squinted to read them.

The character for serpent, yes. Wu Lei tapped the glass as if to tell her to think more sharply. He gestured and she saw behind him a viper—a viper with a nest of eggs. A female viper.

A woman is involved, she communicated to him. *A woman who has much power.*

Wu Lei nodded. He drew a dagger on the mirror and filled it in with black. A black dagger!

A female viper and a black dagger! Are those code names? she wondered. Or were the Chinese characters similar to some persons' names? Were these the people behind Wu Lei's murder? What relation had they to the Golden Ginkgo Society?

She asked these things of her vision, but Wu Lei shook his head. She felt that he knew exactly who they were, but could not tell her in so many words.

Who are they? What is their plan? Jade wanted to demand this of Wu Lei. Yet as if she had driven away the spiritual moment, Wu Lei's image began to fade. Soon he was gone, like the flame of a candle extinguished by a wind.

Jade forced herself to calm. She tried to channel serene qi energy by thinking of a bird in flight — a crane — over snow-topped mountains shining with silver streams. Tranquility came back over her, and she communicated a simple goodbye and thank you to Wu Lei. She rose to pack away the jeweled box.

The tent flap snapped and Luan strode in. He seemed busy and preoccupied and in a hurry to leave. In the past Jade would have blurted out her experience to him, unable to keep it to herself. Now she kept it quietly within her, cogitating on it, confident that its value would be revealed.

Luan stopped what he was doing and stared at her.

"Jade," he said. "Standing there, in your peach and pink silk dress embroidered with the whitest of cranes — you look positively regal. And you carry a regal calm as well."

"You have made me better with all your training," she said modestly.

"That was Jingwei's dress," he nodded. "And you look as beautiful in it as she did. I have been fortunate to be blessed with two wonderful wives."

Jade nodded tranquilly. "And I with two wonderful husbands."

"Are you ready to go to Beijing?"

"I am ready," she said. "I feel ready for anything."

"Good." He extended her hand to her, and, treating her as a regal lady, led her from the tent to a waiting palanquin.

CHAPTER 38

With Jade's new calm and exquisite clothes, the proprietor of the dusty little blacksmith shop in Beijing did not recognize her as the harried, grief-stricken woman he had met previously who was so obviously probing for information. He was still cautiously close-mouthed, though. That was the way a businessman should be in imperial Beijing.

"Why do you want to know about such ancient darts?" he asked conversationally.

She had charmed the proprietor into seating her and serving her tea. She sipped her tea slowly, serenely, as if the whole affair were of little moment.

"My husband is a minister in the court of the provincial governor. His master is an avid collector of antiquities—especially weaponry. My husband seeks a higher position and I would like to help him achieve it. I thought that if I could acquire something so rare and historically significant..."

The proprietor nodded. Since her serenity was perfect, and she seemed more interested in sipping her tea and smoothing out the folds of her silken dress, he told her something of the darts' history. They were cast in halves, he told her, and the inside lined with poison that did not spoil over time. The tip of the arrow connected to the inner chamber of poison, and the design of the dart forced the flow of poison once it was triggered by penetration into warm flesh.

"They are ingenious," the proprietor told her. "And extremely rare. In fact, there are no known ones left but for one in the deepest archives of Nanjing, the ancient capital. Indeed, they were considered so dangerous they were outlawed long ago."

Again, Jade showed no emotion. Her eyes did not dance. She did not look bored, but she looked as if gathering the information was merely one of several afternoon errands a lady like her might have to run in Beijing. After a time, she thanked the proprietor and left the shop. Luan, who was waiting across the street for her, nodded to her, and she nodded back, calmly, affirming that she had some information.

* * *

The blacksmith shook his head, watching the woman in the peach robes make her way across the street. He wished he had such an enterprising wife. He might have been the farrier chosen to outfit the imperial cavalry.

As he turned back to his forge, a man in a red hooded tunic slipped into the shop his eyes darting about as he feared he would be seen.

"Well!" the proprietor said. "Why do you steal in here so? It is broad daylight, and this is an honest business."

The man stepped forward. On the hood and sleeves of his red coat were embroidered a series of markings. At first glance, they looked simply like a tailor's design, but upon close examination, it would be seen that they were in the shape of small black daggers.

"I have a mold," he said. "A double-chambered mold into which I would have you pour silver to make me a special dart. I will pay you well."

"Let me see the mold," said the proprietor. "I will see if I can work with it."

When he saw the mold, the proprietor gasped. It was an ancient mold. In fact, it was of the design of the silver Serpent Shadow darts the minister's wife had just inquired about. He was about to cry out loud about how a lovely lady had just been in the shop, asking about the make of such darts, but something stopped him. The stillness and serenity of Jade's face came back to him and moved him, somehow, to want to protect her. He would not discuss her with this stranger.

"Where did you get this mold?" the proprietor asked.

"Are you a student of history?" the red-hooded man asked.

The proprietor dissembled. "No, of course not. I am a blacksmith. I rarely work with silver. This is unusual, that is all, and it looks quite old."

"I found it in a pile of old iron molds in Nanjing, where I am from."

"What will you put in the middle chamber?"

"Nothing at all." A smile appeared from under the shadow of the hood. "It is just for amusement's sake. For … a game."

The proprietor was sure he was lying. "I have not the skill to work with silver," he said.

"I saw a very beautiful lady leave this shop a few minutes ago. I cannot believe she was interested in iron, not silver or gold."

"I sometimes do work in brass. She wanted a mirror in which to preen."

The man the proprietor was beginning to think of as Black Dagger lifted the him of his tunic. He wore a money belt—a long thong threaded with gold and silver coins.

"Would this help you to be able to do such a specialized work as casting my dart? I require only one."

Stunned speechless—for he'd never seen so much money—the proprietor nodded slowly. He would have been afraid to refuse this man even without the offer of such generous payment. He took the mold and set to work.

When the beautiful Serpent dart was forged, soldered together, and cooled, Black Dagger took it into his hands and turned his back on the proprietor, who was too frightened to ask him what he was doing. Then Black Dagger turned and, lifting the hem of his tunic once more, pulled the money belt from his waist and lowered it into the proprietor's hands.

"With this I would buy your silence," said Black Dagger.

"I have no reason to tell people of my customers' preferences," the proprietor shrugged. "Or where they get quaint antique molds."

"Good. But I must make certain." Black Dagger nodded to the coil of silver and gold in the blacksmith's large hands. "Your fortune is made this day."

The proprietor opened his mouth to thank his strange customer, but before he could utter a word, Black Dagger made a flicking gesture and the dart the smith had just made flew at him. His hands full of coins, he could not block it or move to defend himself. It lodged in his throat.

Within seconds, he felt the poison take his heart in a death grip, his blood turning icy within him. The blacksmith watched, his vision slowly fading, as a grinning Black Dagger swept up the silver and gold and returned it to his waist. The smith's last sensation was the plucking of the dart from his jugular.

With a backward glance, Black Dagger pocketed it and left him to let the poison do its work.

CHAPTER 39

Due to its strategic location, Nanjing was known as the "door of the East and West, and the throat of the South and North." The ancient capital of the Southern dynasties, it served as an inland port for the Yangtze River, which connected to the Yellow Sea. The sparkling port city of Shanghai beckoned not far away.

Nanjing stood on uneven terrain and encompassed two peaks of the Ningzhen mountain range within its walls; the Zhong Mountain, curling like a dragon, and the Stone Mountain, crouching like a tiger, lent the city unique character. Long stretches of the Great Wall overshadowed plains and lakes, the extensive city walls taking surprising twists and turns as the followed the asymmetrical terrain.

The palace resembled that of Beijing, with an innermost Forbidden City surrounded by imperial grounds. Similar marble bridges arched gracefully over streams. The drum and bell tower, once used to welcome imperial visitors with a fanfare of percussion, as well as hooting horns of bamboo, were now silent but still stood as a reminder of the city's glory days before Beijing became the capital.

As they approached Nanjing after several week's journey by horseback, Jade tried not to be awe-struck by the classic, imposing city. She and Luan had disguised themselves as knife-peddlers. They wore the clothes of peasants, brought to them secretly within the protective walls of the imperial palace in Beijing. Ching and his wife, Anbai, had been commissioned to procure the clothing in the midnight streets of Beijing, and the couple had successfully done so through a network of their own secret contacts.

Anbai had embraced Jade fondly before drawing away from the smell of the female peasant clothes. Likewise, Ching and Luan had shared a brotherly embrace. The Emperor and Empress, unattended for once in their imperial lives by eunuchs, were in the room, treading softly in silk slippers, their imperial nightclothes rustling and their voices hushed.

"Why have you chosen the guise of a knife peddler?" whispered the Empress to Luan.

"A peddler comes and goes, and is in a position to call upon the high and the low," explained Luan. "From kitchen slaves of the imperial palace to peasants splitting a chicken, everyone requires a sharp knife."

"And," said Jade, drawing a knife as though it were a long sword, which made a ringing sound as it left its scabbard, "bored guards will consent to have their blades sharpened while they are on duty, providing opportunities for conversation—and espionage."

"There is another advantage to being a knife-peddler," said Luan.

He spread his arms wide, his full sleeves falling from his forearms. Flexing his arm muscles, he made the deadly knives hidden in his sleeves glide into in his hands. He closed his palms firmly around their hilts. At the astonishment of the others, he laughed, then tossed the knives into two spinning, shiny metallic arcs in front of him. They clanged once in a mid-air tryst, and then each spun away from the other to settle into the opposite hands from which they had originated.

"A knife-peddler is always armed," he smiled.

The impressed Empress grinned in return. "So I see."

"Where did those knives come from?" asked the Emperor, looking around. "It was almost as if you summoned them out of thin air."

"They were in his sleeves," said Ching.

"Ching knows all," smiled Luan.

"That is why he and Anbai will join you as spies in Nanjing," said the Emperor. "A few days after you leave, we will dispatch our second couple as support for your espionage."

Luan and Jade had journeyed over land by horse and then sold their horses in a small town upriver from Nanjing. In this small town, Luan met and bribed a small boat owner to allow him and

Jade passage to the west side of Nanjing via the Yangtze River. The man was going to unload his catches of carp, shad, eels, and yellow-head catfish on the banks of the city.

Now, as they approached the great city, Jade wished it was not dark; she would have liked to enjoy the views of the verdant lands on either bank of the broad and famous river. Golden monkeys, swallows, and eagles were known to inhabit its shores.

The fisherman bored her with tales of how he had nearly landed a paddlefish the other day, and how it had almost capsized his boat with its weight and its impressive length of over five feet. Regretfully, he said, he'd had to cut it loose or go down trying to land it. He told the story several times, with little variation, as if by repeating the story he could finally interest her. Jade idly trailed a hand in the cool and fresh-feeling water, seeking to distract herself from the man's repetitive words.

Just then a large creature appeared at the side of the boat. Dimly glimpsing its sectioned back in the slow unrolling of the coming dawn, Jade realized it was an alligator. It looked like it weighed a hundred pounds.

She froze, not knowing whether the sudden movement of retracting her hand from the water would attract a strike from the animal. She was angry at herself; boredom was the enemy of a woman like her; it caused her to let her guard down. The rows of ferocious teeth in the dim dawn light gleamed, and then something else flashed, gathering what light there was on its polished, gleaming surface. Luan had brought forth one of his secret knives, and soon its twin made an appearance. He plunged the knives into the water beast again and again, hand over hand in a glinting steel wheel of motion, striking with first and then the other at a spot behind the beast's head. With a cry of terror, the fisherman threw himself on the other side of the boat, away from the alligator.

This had the fortunate effect of balancing Luan's weight as he leaned heavily out of the boat. The huge jaws and teeth of the alligator swayed from side to side, seeking to bite his attacker, while Jade hastily withdrew and also threw her weight on the other side of the boat.

Swinging his jaws, the animal could not reach Luan with his teeth. Then, with tremendous strength backed by the concentrated energy of qi and balanced by the weight of his companions on the other side of the boat, Luan plunged both knives even further into the beast. Blood and bubbles churned; the thrashing beast thumped against the boat in a most terrifying way, and then the mass of the alligator went still. They watched it sink amidst bloody froth and foam, until the river water swallowed it whole and once more turned golden in dawn's light.

Jade threw herself into Luan's arms and heard the knives clatter to the floor of the boat as he clasped his arms and hands around her, enfolding her. He stroked her hair briefly, comfortingly, and let her go.

"This is a tale you must not tell," Luan said to the terrified fisherman.

"I will not tell. Yet a man's heroic rescue of his wife is a story to be recounted."

"You must not," Luan pressed. "We do not wish to draw attention to ourselves. Here is silver for your silence. Is it enough?"

The fisherman weighed the small bag Luan gave him, peeked inside, and smiled with satisfaction.

"Stick to your story of a paddlefish," Luan advised, and the fisherman promised he would. "I will give you more silver still if I hear no rumors of this from the river while I am in Nanjing," said Luan. "At some point, we will want passage to Shanghai, and you shall be our boatman if you keep silent. Can you be ready to leave at short notice?"

"Yes," said the fisherman. "Just hoist a red flag on a tall fishing pole on the riverbank near where we unload. That has ever been my son's signal to me that he needed me to come to shore."

"I will do that," Luan said, "*if* I hear nothing from you between then and now but silence."

The fisherman happily jingled the bag of coins Luan had given him. "They say silence is golden," he quipped. "But my silence shall be silver!"

"Or bought with it, anyway," murmured Jade.

CHAPTER 40

uan and Jade helped the fisherman unload his catch as an excuse to disembark on shore in Nanjing. After thanking him, Luan then began to talk to various fishermen about the knives he had for sale. Since fishermen were always interested in knives, and because Luan had some fine ones, conversation flowed easily and naturally. Jade made their whetstone and leather strop sing, sharpening knives for the fisherman for a small fee.

They mingled with the fisherman on the riverbank for several hours, selling and sharpening knives, making friends as the morning grew stronger. They were invited to share a breakfast of fire-fried fish on shore, and they enjoyed the fresh sustenance. They were traveling lightly and had not brought food stores with them.

The couple worked their way from the city's shore, listening, making conversation, and gleaning all the information they could, mingling easily with the vendors of fish and the citizens coming to the riverbank to purchase. Infiltrating Nanjing had been easier than they had imagined it would be.

They soon learned that, although the Golden Ginkgo Society had taken over the city, not all citizens considered themselves members. Most were indifferent, as long as they were left alone to ply their trades and raise their families. The Society, people told them, so far were no worse than the imperial officials who had formerly run the city. What was more, Golden Ginkgo members were usually poor, so they were easy to bribe. A person could get a Golden Gingko member to look the other way for a far less substantial fee than it had taken to close the eyes of an imperial official. The price of doing business was decreasing, so the citizenry was generally supportive of the Society, although they neither understood nor cared about the its ideals.

"Manchu — Chinese — no matter who rules, all that matters is that we are allowed to go about our lives in relative peace," one fishmonger told them. This seemed to be the general consensus.

"Good," Luan whispered to Jade. "It is not a city filled with ideologues."

"It may be, once Golden Ginkgo has properly consolidated its power and spread more propaganda."

"Yes, we must work to prevent that."

They made their way around the city, attracting little notice, wending their way by silent agreement toward the Forbidden City, where the Society's leader — a man they were told was named Wei-Ling — now reigned as a self-appointed governor. Their peasant clothes protected them, as did their status as peddlers. Peddlers might wander into and about a city at any time. Perhaps because the takeover was recent, security in Society-dominated Nanjing seemed almost non-existent, a fact that could make Luan and Jade's job easier.

Early in the afternoon, Luan suggested they pause to refresh themselves. He pointed to a ginkgo tree planted in a large walled planter, where people could sit on the edges of the wall and enjoy the shade. It was set back somewhat from the public road, affording those who sat beneath it both shade and privacy.

"The ginkgo is the oldest tree on earth," Luan told her conversationally. "It can survive anywhere; it is so hardy. Yet it is beautiful; leafy green in spring and summer, and saffron yellow in autumn. Sometimes it is called 'maidenhair.'"

"Why?"

"I suppose because of its softness and fullness."

"That seems a rather suggestive name to me," said Jade, leaning against the trunk of the ginkgo tree rather than sitting on the wall. She then sank to the ground. "I like to feel the earth beneath my feet," she explained when Luan looked at her quizzically.

"The earth is not merely beneath your feet," he joked.

She picked up a handful of dirt and tossed it at him, but lightly and jokingly.

"There is nothing that could make these garments dirtier than they already are," he observed with good humor, brushing the dirt off.

The fact that he could be light-hearted in this dangerous situation appealed to Jade. She had a taste for danger and risk. She enjoyed the anticipation of it, not knowing what the outcome would be and having to rely on her own muscles and brain to get her through difficulties. Yet with the tension of all that, the value of humor in such situations was not lost on her.

"I am dying of thirst," she said to Luan.

"It is early. Perhaps there is still dew on the ginkgo leaves." He stood on the soil next to her and picked a handful of the fan-shaped, green leaves.

"Here," he said, handing them to her. "Drink the moisture."

The split, fan-like leaves of the ginkgo tree were indeed covered with dew. Jade slaked her thirst with the cool moisture of the dew as it slid down her throat. She sighed with satisfaction.

"Let us make this ginkgo tree our meeting place, should we become separated," Luan suggested. "It has sheltered us now. Perhaps it will shelter us again and give us life."

"Yes. It is good, central location," Jade agreed. "With the shore accessible nearby. The qi is excellent here. Fresh and revitalizing. I wish we could stay here forever."

Luan smiled. "You want to stay with me forever?"

"Ah, yes!" said Jade, joking. She spread her hands as if in declaration. "I will stay with you as long as there is dew on the ginkgo leaves!"

"That will be a long time," said Luan. "I told you, it is a very hardy tree and can survive anything."

Their eyes met for a moment. Although they had been joking, in some ways, Jade felt, this was their real marriage vow — not taken under compulsion before the Emperor, but taken here, voluntarily, in peasant clothes, with danger all around them.

"I—I—" she stuttered, feeling serious and looking down.

"There is no need to speak."

For a moment, it all faded away—Wu Lei's death, the silver Serpent Shadow dart around her neck, the man she had killed in the village, the hasty marriage, the fighting in camp, everything seemed new again and fresh. As fresh as morning dew on the ginkgo leaves.

Could I possibly be in love with Luan? she wondered.

With almost forced impassiveness, Luan said, "It is time to find Wei-Ling, the new Emperor of Nanjing."

Jade nodded, gathered up her parcel of knife-sharpening equipment, and stood before him, ready for the mission.

CHAPTER 41

uan and Jade approached the Donghua Gate to the palace and struck up a friendly conversation with the gatekeeper. This man said he did not know if the imperial kitchen was in need of knives, but he allowed Jade to sharpen his sword for free as he conversed with Luan.

Luan said, "We made a pretty penny on the shore this morning, so many fishermen needed new knives and old knives sharpened. Serving the new regime's kitchen would be an honor for us. I would be happy to pay you for entry through the gate so we can show our wares to the kitchen servants."

"Ah!" said the gatekeeper. "That would cost more silver than a poor peddler has."

"It would be worth much silver to me, though," said Luan. "Besides, we did exceedingly well at the shore today." He handed the gatekeeper a short, but heavy thong threaded with silver coins.

The gatekeeper looked dubious but obligingly took the string of coins and shifted its weight from hand-to-hand.

"Not enough," he said, matter of factly.

"I had heard that Golden Ginkgo officials are not as greedy as the imperial officials who served before them," Jade spoke up. "Am I mistaken? We could have purchased the whole gate with that in the past, not just entry through it."

"Golden Gingko officials take no bribes," said the gatekeeper self-righteously. "We are not like Manchu officials! No amount of silver can buy entry through this gate!"

Luan steered Jade away from the gate by the elbow.

"What do you think we should do?" he asked in an undertone, once he was certain they were out of earshot of the gatekeeper.

"I think if you offer him much more silver, he will no longer believe you are a mere peddler. To have a gatekeeper of the imperial palace think you an impostor would not be a good thing."

"I agree. We could be exposed within minutes. Let me demonstrate some knife skills and see if we can attract some interest and respect."

Luan and Jade found a market street and purchased some meat, vegetables, and a board made of bamboo. Then they returned to the area in front of the gate. The gatekeeper ignored them, turning his face away with his nose in the air, affecting disinterest.

The two knives in Luan's sleeves shot out and he grasped them in his hands. Bringing them forward in front of him, he clanged them together, sharpening their blades together and making them ring out. Jade smiled as people on the street began to glance their way. Luan spread his hands far apart, a knife in each, and tossed the weapons upward, spinning, until each landed perfectly in the opposite palm. Jade smiled again, and seeing her smile, Luan seemed to perform just for her, tossing one knife and then the other high into the air from behind his back before catching it in front of him. Then he did what appeared to be a highly dangerous juggling act with the deadly, spinning blades, his hands a fleshy blur amidst the shining metal. Catching both at once, he spun each knife like a pinwheel as he slowly began to twist from his waist, swinging the knives in a wide arc around him.

By now a crowd had gathered. Luan tossed one spinning knife from behind him and caught it in front, meanwhile rotating the other behind his neck. Ducking his head slightly, he brought the spinning projectile forward, and he did this several times, bringing each spinning knife forward over his head from behind, all without suffering a scratch.

By this time the crowd was clapping and cheering. Luan tossed both spinning knives high into the air, and everyone looked up as he knew they would. It seemed impossible, but they crossed one another's paths in mid-air with a faint clang, as if in greeting, and then returned to his outstretched hands. He smiled as if it were mere child's play, meanwhile spinning the two blades wildly. The bright sunlight glinting on the metal made it look almost like a fireworks exhibition.

Luan had instructed Jade what to do. She came forward, smiling beguilingly, holding the bamboo board in front of her like a tray. Upon it was a large white onion and a green cabbage. Luan whirled around once, and with a cry, spun his knives. In a blur of motion accompanied by the sounds of chopping upon wood, he diced the vegetables until they were almost as fine as sand. The crowd gasped and then burst into applause.

Even though they knew he was now straining to peer through the gate in order to see the exhibition, Luan and Jade ignored the gatekeeper. When the crowd became too thick for him to see anything at all, the gatekeeper climbed up on the gate and shouted.

"Disperse now! Disperse! This talented man and his lovely wife are for the imperial kitchens! Let them through now! No one else may come through the gate but Knife and Wife!"

CHAPTER 42

When "Knife and Wife" were at last inside the gate and the gatekeeper was fussily locking it behind them to keep the crowd out, Luan said to him, "She is my sister, not my wife."

"Excuse me. My mistake," said the gatekeeper with a flush of embarrassment. "This way to the imperial kitchens!"

Jade did not question Luan's judgment in introducing her as his sister. They both knew that the fate of the empire might depend upon her seducing someone who was willing to spill secrets. She would be more attractive to the men in this Forbidden City if they assumed she was unmarried. Her beauty was a weapon they could not afford to lay aside.

As soon as the kitchen staff witnessed Luan's proficiency with his wares, they were certain the new Son of Heaven, Wei-Ling, would welcome him. Messages were sent to the "Heavenly One" at once and he soon summoned Knife and Wife.

"She is my sister," Luan insisted so vehemently that Jade found herself getting annoyed. "Knife and Sister, not Knife and Wife."

They found Wei-Ling seated on a golden throne reminiscent of the great Dragon Throne in Beijing. His seat was a long, golden bench with a filigreed back. Red lacquer pillars topped by carved globes of gold stood sentinel before his throne, partially blocking the cool, marble stairs that led to the imperial platform. A gold backdrop was behind the throne, carved with snakes and dragons and topped by a crown-like cornice. It was impressive and beautiful, and carried the authority of an ancient seat of government. The Emperors of ancient times had sat upon this throne.

Wei-Ling was a very ordinary-looking man. He was also very young, and his skin and hair shone with youth's dew. Jade pondered whether this made him appear pure and innocent — a counter to the corruption of the empire. She decided it only made him look naive and unprepared for august responsibility.

He addressed them without preamble. "Do you see I have no cushions on my throne?" he demanded.

Luan's eyelids flickered indifferently over the throne. He affected a simple-minded look, as if he simply could not comprehend.

"It is because," said Wei-Ling, softening, "I am a man of the people, like you. The Manchu Emperor is only out for himself! I am one of the people! I live for the people! I will take the Dragon Throne and give it back to the people—the Han people, the true inheritors of China!"

Luan and Jade looked at him in a sort of dumb wonderment.

"I've heard you have skills," Wei-Ling said, more calmly, to Luan. "And that your wife can make a blade on a whetstone sing like a Beijing opera singer."

"She is my sister," said Luan humbly. "We have some poor skills, hardly fit to display before a majesty such as yourself."

"Sister?" asked Wei-Ling, instantly turning his attention to Jade. "Woman! Turn your face up to me!"

Jade had never been spoken to in such a manner by the true Emperor, with such a whip-like tone. Still, she turned her face up to Wei-Ling, who then told her to stand up and walk before him, turning around and around.

"My clothing is unsuitable," she said, "to appear so before a king."

"I like peasant clothing," retorted Wei-Ling. "Fancy clothing is the mark of the Manchu empire. All true Chinese are poor."

Luan and Jade looked down to hide their thoughts. Jade was sure Luan was thinking the same thing she was: that Wei-Ling was living very well for a poor man of the people. His clothing was silk, he sat on a throne, and the kitchens were bursting with every possible type of delicacy, spice, vegetable, meat, and fish.

"Demonstrate your skills," Wei-Ling ordered. Then he clapped his hands together like a child at a party in his honor, anticipating fun, treats, and plenty of attention.

By this time Luan and Jade had performed together enough that they were a most entertaining pair. Their movements were synchronized as in a dance, and the sounds of the whetstone and bamboo cutting board serving admirably as percussion. They performed Luan's knife performance and the cutting of the onion and cabbage on Jade's bamboo cutting board skillfully.

"It really is better than a Beijing opera!" Wei-Ling clapped his hands after their performance.

Jade and Luan exchanged glances under their eyelashes. This great leader of the formidable Golden Ginkgo Society seemed almost like a child. This impression was furthered when Wei-Ling pettishly summoned a servant and demanded that the finely chopped onion and cabbage on the bamboo board be saved for his luncheon.

"It must be given to no one else!" he pouted. "No one—only me!"

"Yes, your majesty," said the servant, bowing.

"You!" Wei-Ling pointed an imperious finger at Luan. "Chief chef! You!" he pointed to Jade. "Chief concubine! Go!" He clapped his hands and several servants appeared.

"We will escort you to your new chambers and administer baths and issue appropriate clothing for palace dwellers."

Jade was given a chamber close to the throne room, and, as her brother, Luan was given a chamber just across the hall. She breathed a sigh of relief about the proximity of her room to Luan's. It would certainly make conspiring together easier.

As soon as she was bathed and robed, Jade slipped across the hall and tapped on the door to Luan's chamber. He let her in. Like her he was wearing a scarlet and yellow silk robe.

"I knew it was a possibility, but I cannot bear to be that ridiculous man's concubine!" she hissed, once the door was firmly shut behind her. "It would be like seducing a little boy! He can't be more than eighteen."

"It may be necessary for the mission," Luan said grimly. "However, I do have a plan. It does not seem to me from what we have heard that the people will fight hard for this new Son of

Heaven. Did you see the look of disgust the servant gave him when he asked for the vegetables for his own lunch?"

"They allowed him to take over the city."

"Yes, but they did not know how much of a childish despot he was going to be once his hindquarters hit the Nanjing Dragon Throne. It will take more time, but I believe that if imperial troops came and attacked the city, few would fight to the death. Nanjing can be reclaimed for the real Emperor with just a show of force, I believe." He touched her arm. "Can you forestall Wei-Ling's amorous attentions for one week while still getting close enough to learn more of his heart and mind?"

Jade's eyes lit up. She had hatched a plan in her mind. "Yes. Can you bring me a panful of beef blood each night?"

"I am the chief chef," shrugged Luan. "That should be easily accomplished."

"No one must know. I will tell Wei-Ling that I am having a woman's monthly indisposition, and he must wait a week for me. I will prove it by showing him blood-soaked garments."

Luan frowned for a moment. Then he laughed so hard, he slapped his knee.

"What a clever woman you are!" he said, wiping his eyes.

Was that a note of relief in his voice? Jade hoped so; she would have been glad to know that he would care should she have to give herself sexually to the petulant Wei-Ling.

CHAPTER 43

The keeper of the kitchen, Wang Chaochang, seemed to have been there since the last dynasty. He was extremely rotund, with mountain ranges of fat around his waist, and he was advanced in years. So portly was he that his red face broke out in a sweat if he so much as crossed the room. He did very little of the actual cooking himself, but he clearly ran the kitchen at his own convenience. He was sharp-tongued and quick with his orders to the kitchen staff, who served as his hands and legs.

"Yes, I have been here a long time," Wang Chaochang told Luan when Luan reported for duty the next morning. "I have no political feelings. The Society keeps me on because I am good at what I do—and because I refuse to leave. Can you imagine them trying to dislodge me? If they sworded me, no weapon could penetrate my fat to strike a vital organ. And I would not want to be the one to haul my porcine carcass out!"

Wang Chaochang then suffered a laughing fit that became such a severe coughing fit that Luan wondered if he was going to expire right there, perhaps with his large and heavy head crashing down with a thunk on the wooden table.

Wang Chaochang finally recovered and took out his annoyance on a servant boy.

"You there! You're putting far too much soy sauce into that dish!"

"The Heavenly Son likes soy sauce."

"That's enough to choke a deer. Stop immediately!"

Wang Chaochang threw a copper pan at the boy. This seemed to be his standard means of discipline, for the servant boy adroitly sidestepped the pan, which landed on the floor with a clatter.

"Oh, hang it. Hang him," said Wang Chaochang. "If he chokes on salt and the Emperor takes back Nanjing, what is it to me?" He glanced at Luan. Luan's eyes narrowed somewhat. The obese cook seemed, to him, to be protesting just a little too much.

Now that he was chief chef by Wei-Ling's order, Luan confided to Wang Chaochang that his culinary skills included knife work, but not cooking and seasoning. This seemed to please Wang Chaochang.

"Fine. I will remain as the real chief chef, and you can have the title and all the glory in front of the Heavenly Son. Just do chopping duty."

"I would be happy to tend the fires as well," Luan offered.

"Yes, yes." Wang Chaochang dismissed the matter with a wave of a chubby hand. "Just bring me a plateful of that beef they are cooking."

"It is nearly raw," Luan pointed out, glancing at the bloody red chunk of meat floating on top of a cauldron on the roaring fire.

"I like it that way."

Luan obediently fished the heavy beefsteak out of the steaming pot then used his knife skills to julienne it. A great deal of blood came out as he did so, and he asked Wang Chaochang if he could collect the blood.

"It is supposed to be good for a man to drink," Luan explained. "It gives vitality."

"Take it. Take all you like," said Wang Chaochang, tucking a large white napkin into the neck of his tunic and diving into the julienned raw beef. Luan quietly scooped the blood off the cutting board into a small vessel to take to Jade.

"Your sister is quite beautiful," Wang Chaochang addressed Luan.

Luan sighed. "Yes."

"It's been too long since we've seen a beautiful woman around here. Attractive females have too much to gain in Manchu society.

The Golden Gingko only attracts plain, earnest women. Nothing wrong with that, but it is not so easy on the eyes, unlike your sibling."

Luan schooled his features so that they would not show his emotion. He was not sure even this beef blood ploy would withstand the fire growing in Wei-Ling's eyes when he gazed at Jade.

Luan had heard Wei-Ling's peremptory knock on Jade's door last night, succeeded by her welcoming voice and then more verbal interchanges within the room. When he heard Wei-Ling's scathing words of disappointment and retreating footsteps just moments later, secretly Luan had rejoiced. Jade must have told Wei-Ling she was indisposed by her womanly issue. The beef blood would serve as proof should Wei-Ling's impatience overcome him tonight. He hoped she could stave off Wei-Ling's desire for a week.

Luan's position as cook put him in an excellent position to send smoke signals to watchers who would then transmit the messages to Beijing. Today he would send the messages that the Society's grip on power was tenuous.

Luan reminded himself not to exaggerate the weakness of Wei-Ling's grip on the people in order to gain a hasty yes to his request for troops. He must assess the political situation with complete objectivity. Many lives and the fate of the empire were in his hands; he could not let concern for his wife's virtue skew his judgment. The mission had to come first. He did not allow himself to heave the heavy sigh that built up in him at the thought of Jade and Wei-Ling together in a silken bed.

CHAPTER 44

Luan and Jade were invited to attend one of Wei-Ling's speeches to the household staff and groundskeepers. It was given in the same imperial hall where they had first met Wei-Ling sitting upon the ancient Nanjing Dragon Throne.

The household and outdoor staff gathered — about fifty people — and seated themselves on thin, colorful cushions on the floor before the throne. It was crowded and noisy, and the gossipy household staff talked to one another so much that a cloud of chatter seemed to rise from the gathering. Luan arranged a cushion as comfortably as possible for Jade and helped her to sit down on it. Then Wei-Ling came striding in, seeming not even to glance at the audience. The moment he entered, servants lined up along the walls began to beat drums and blow bamboo horns in greeting.

Luan looked around in a discreet way. Although the expressions on the staff were vaguely receptive, and although there was plenty of noise from the horns and the drums, he did not sense the energy of enthusiasm. He wondered if the staff felt, as Jade had, that for someone who fulminated so much about equality, Wei-Ling was living like an Emperor and seemed indifferent to anything but his own comforts. Luan became more firm in his notion that he could accurately report to the Emperor via smoke signal that the house and grounds staff would not fight to defend Wei-Ling. Luan would have to sound out the guards next to see if they would battle for the presumptuous interloper. If they would not, he would request troops at once.

Jade nudged him out of his busy thoughts.

"Look at that woman standing against the wall over there," she said. "She looks vaguely familiar. Isn't that Willow?"

"How could it be? No, it is just an old crone who resembles her."

"I think it really is her," Jade murmured. "She followed us here!"

Now Wei-Ling was looking directly at Jade, seated on the floor next to Luan, and he immediately demanded that she come up to the front row. Jade ducked her head, rose, and modestly seated herself in front of Wei-Ling. Luan deliberately mastered his facial expression to look impassive. He supposed, as a brother seeking his fortune in a new city, he should look happy that his sister was so favored by the ruler. He stifled a sigh.

Seemingly satisfied at her close attendance, Wei-Ling launched into his speech.

"Officials!" he began, "Officials! Corrupt imperial officials have run this country for centuries. They have been almost uniformly Manchu. The system is rigged. The examinations for officialdom are so rigorous that neither you nor I could ever pass them without the assistance of highly paid tutors. Only the rich can afford such tutors; thus, only the sons of the rich can rise. What is more, there is money exchanged by the doors of the very cells where the examinations are given! People do not rise because of ability. They rise because of money, and money alone! The system is rigged against you! I—I alone—am your champion and savior!"

The household staff, rather dutifully it seemed, burst into applause.

Luan frowned. Of course, it was known that there was corruption in the examination system in some places. At the same time, it was the one avenue for the son of a poor farmer to enter the professional classes. After all, even a poor farm boy could study on his own, and many had risen through the ranks of society through the examination. Luan remembered that the Emperor had told him Wei-Ling himself had failed the examinations three times.

So that is the source of his bitterness, he thought.

When the dutiful applause died down, Wei-Ling went on.

"Our nation runs on bribery and corruption, and this has been true for many, many decades, even hundreds of years. There is no genuine rule of law. Everything is done on the arbitrary whims of the Emperor and Empress. We have been forced to wear the queue or hairstyle of the Manchu! Manchus sit on the throne and appoint

Manchu successors! Manchus think they are better than Chinese, and every official of any significance is Manchu! This oppression by foreigners must cease!"

At this, the applause was a little more sincere. Luan ducked his head. He and Jade were both Manchu, even though they spoke and wrote Chinese perfectly and were able to imitate the distinctive mannerisms of the Chinese. Yet, as a fair-minded man, he had to admit that there was some justice in Wei-Ling's allegations. Manchus were at the top in Chinese society in the Chinese people's own country.

The audience seemed to be warming to the wildly gesticulating young man, who was so passionate he was almost choking on his own words. His face was red, and he strode up and down the stage, making concise, cutting gestures with his hands.

"The Golden Ginkgo Society exists to right all these historic wrongs; to end the superior smugness of the Manchus; to give China back to the Chinese! Chinese first!"

Wei-Ling then drummed on the seat of the golden Dragon Throne, and the servants lining the walls began to drum in rhythm too. Soon all the people in the room were on their feet, stomping and clapping. The noise was thunderous.

"Thank you!" Wei-Ling said, and he strode from the room to the cheerful toots of bamboo horns. "Jade! Follow me!" he called out as he exited the doorway.

The consensus among the servants in the kitchen was that it had been a very good speech. The servants seemed a little heartened, and there was more willingness in their movements as they worked.

"Not bad for a boy," said Wang Chaochang. Wang Chaochang assumed an almost fatherly air in talking about their ruler.

Luan began composing his smoke signal for the day carefully. Wei-Ling still had influence; that much was clear. There was some justice in his positions, and people would respond to that. At the same time, Luan sensed that as long as they kept their positions in the palace, the staff there did not really care who ruled them. The guards were the important ones, he reasoned. He would have to spend some time among the guards.

Yet he could not shake a strange feeling. Wei-Ling's gestures and words had not seemed to be coming from deep within him. There was a parroting, repetitive quality to them; his gestures had resembled those of a marionette. He had relied on catch-phrases and applause lines, as well as the drumming and stomping to make it an impressive speech. The kernels of truth in what he said were just that kernels. The rest was bombast.

Luan quietly sent his signals from the fire. He knew that imperial troops could besiege Nanjing soon, within the week, if Luan's reports convinced them that the Society's grip on power was loose enough.

For some reason, though, the Emperor had fallen silent on one question of major personal importance to Luan. Luan had asked whether, if the situation warranted it, he or Jade should assassinate Wei-Ling. Luan could understand the Emperor's hesitation. Certainly he would not want to make a martyr of Wei-Ling. At the same time, once this weak person was out of the way, Luan sensed the Golden Ginkgo Society, such as it was, might collapse.

Just as he was ruminating on this, Wang Chaochang rose from his place at the kitchen table and waddled close to Luan. Luan threw him a quizzical look.

As if imparting a confidence, Wang Chaochang leaned close to Luan, almost leaning on him, and whispered in his ear, "Your sister will not be able to resist Wei-Ling much longer."

"Why should she?" asked Luan, affecting indifference.

"Ah!" chortled Wang Chaochang. "You are of the old school! If a ruler looks with favor upon a man's sister, the man sees a higher position coming for himself!"

"There is nothing wrong with wanting to get ahead." Luan shrugged.

"Yes. A woman's face and form are still her fortune. I suppose no matter what political party reigns, that will always be the case."

Then, with the air of a man who did not care much about such things, the heavy cook seated himself once more at the kitchen table and began to eat luncheon.

CHAPTER 45

uan felt he should stay in the kitchen to pick up more information from the gossip of the kitchen staff, but he felt strongly drawn to check on Jade. He had seen Wei-Ling gesture for her to approach him after the meeting, and he wondered where they were and what was going on. Of course, it was important that he be always aware of Wei-Ling's movements as well as keep his ears open to his supporters. He decided it would be prudent from the standpoint of the mission to go to Jade's room and see if Wei-Ling was there and what was going on. He convinced himself it was prudent.

He stealthily padded down the hallway toward where the doors of Jade's and his rooms faced one another. There was no need to be quiet, he learned, when he heard loud voices coming from behind Jade's door. He quickened his pace. When he got to the room, two guards were standing outside. He pretended to be having trouble with his door so as to listen a moment longer to the voices that were audible even out here in the hall.

"I tell you, I want a woman who binds her feet!" Wei-Ling was shouting inside Jade's room. "Why are your feet not bound? They should have been bound since girlhood—then they would look like lotuses!"

"Surely you know that a woman's bound feet look nothing like lotuses," Jade was arguing. "They are broken, bent, distorted, and they have to be wrapped so tightly and for so long that when they are unwrapped, the smell of rotten flesh is overpowering. It is unnatural. This is something we Chinese could learn from the Manchus! Manchu women do not bind their feet!"

"Argumentative wench," said Wei-Ling, and for a moment Luan tensed. He was afraid Yin Men was going to strike Jade or, worse, accuse her of treason.

All the young man said, though, was say, "Be ready tonight. I will show you who is the master here. I will send a woman to bind your feet before I deign to visit you in your bedroom."

"I have told you, my lord, I am indisposed."

"I do not believe you!"

"Why would I lie to you, my lord?" asked Jade.

"I have spies everywhere. I know everything. I know your brother asked for blood from the kitchen today."

"For his own strength only, my lord," said Jade disingenuously.

Luan's heart started thumping hard within his chest. Wei-Ling knew about the beef blood—already! How could he?

Luan opened his bedchamber door and went inside, closing it behind him. He was sweating and now breathing hard with this news. He leaned his back against the door and took deep breaths to calm himself.

Wang Chaochang! It had to be Wang Chaochang the fat, seemingly harmless cook who had reported on him! Thinking of the smoke signals he was sending from Wang Chaochang's kitchen, Luan felt something like panic.

Jade's door banged open and then thundered shut. The swish of silken clothing that Luan heard seemed congruent with the stride of a man. He heard a clatter as the two armed guards followed Wei-Ling down the hall. Yes, Wei-Ling must have stormed out of Jade's room. Luan waited until the hall was silent, and then he silently slid over to her red lacquered door. He tapped lightly in a pre-arranged signal, and a frightened-looking Jade let him in.

"I will not be able to stave him off much longer," she confided to him in a whisper once the door was closed. "I have never played the concubine before, and he is like a child—like an importunate child. He is very spoiled for a man of the people, and he apparently does not include women in his ideas of liberation. I do not understand. I do not sense in him the committed heart of a revolutionary—he is almost like a—a—" Jade put her tongue between her lips as if tasting for the appropriate word.

"Puppet?"

"Yes."

They looked at each other, both nodding gravely at the implications of this.

"Who is pulling the strings?" Jade wondered aloud.

"I have more bad news. Wang Chaochang, the cook, is not so harmless as he seems. Apparently he has already reported to Wei-Ling about the beef blood."

Luan watched his wife turn pale.

"That means my ruse is seen through. I do not know if I will be able to fend him off much longer without that."

"What is more my ability to send smoke signals is now compromised. The cook Wang Chaochang said he had no political feelings and was merely a palace fixture. That cannot be true if he is reporting to Wei-Ling about the beef blood. Wang Chaochang is in league with Wei-Ling; loyal to him; even doing spy duties for him. That makes the kitchen a very unsafe place for me. And here I thought we were doing so well!"

Luan felt his wife's worried gaze upon him, searching his face anxiously.

"Well," he said, "We knew it would be dangerous and fraught. We knew we would be second-guessing everyone and how much they know. It is the nature of the work. I must calm myself, so I can sense qi."

"Let us meditate together, here on this bed, and see if we can find some clarity as to how to move forward," Jade urged.

They faced one another in the lotus position, knees touching, and held hands. Then they touched foreheads, still holding hands, breathing deeply, and summoning tranquility. After a few minutes Luan felt calmer, and he noticed Jade's breathing was deeper and more even.

"We were chosen for this mission," he said with new assurance. "We have each other. We will be able to carry it out."

He rose and went to the door to listen. His emergence from Jade's room would need to be secret, of course. Confidence coursed through him. Jade was loyal. They were masters at what they did; they were growing to know and trust one another. They would be triumphant in this journey for the Empire.

He opened the enameled door and peered down the corridor. All clear. He turned to nod to Jade before leaving her room, but the ghastly look on her face stopped him. Her eyes were riveted on the bed where he had been sitting. She had gone white, and her mouth was a line of shock, horror, and dawning realization.

"What is it?" he hissed, closing the door again.

Without a word, Jade moved her hand on the bed, scooped up an object, and held it up for him to see.

It was a silver dart—a Serpent Shadow dart—newly minted but still unmistakable. With a look of grim determination, Jade reached into the bodice of her dress and drew out the red cord on which she kept the dart that had killed her first husband. She held the two darts up to one another, side by side.

But for the shiny newness of the one she found on the bed, the two darts were a perfect match.

CHAPTER 46

J ade's eyes rose slowly to meet Luan's.

"So it was you," she whispered. "You killed my husband. You were the purveyor of the poisoned dart." She touched the tip of the one she had found in the bedding. "I suppose if I pricked my finger with this, I would be poisoned. Is that your intention? Kill me too? Just like you killed Wu Lei? You cheat! You traitor! You monster!"

She held up the shining silver dart. "Did you have this minted in the shop you sent me to in Beijing?"

"Of course not. It is not mine. Don't be ridiculous, Jade. That was planted on me. Wang Chaochang—"

At his words, the tigress sprang with the full onslaught of her fury and pain. Desperately, Luan grasped her wrists and immobilized her. He had not stilled her tongue, however. It dripped with poison to his soul, with words that stung as much as a dart.

"So Wang Chaochang knows who we are?" she asked sarcastically. "He knows who I am? He knows my husband was killed with the ancient twin to your dart? He planted that on you? Then everything is over anyway, isn't it? We are discovered. I might as well kill you now, you murderous coward, before Wei-Ling does."

Luan willed himself to be calm. Everything was falling apart. Yet he knew from his studies of ancient Chinese literature that this was when the real tests came; times such as these called for the steadiest of heads and hearts.

"I swear to you, on the graves of my wife and son, I did not do this," he told her. "Someone is trying to make it look like I did—to divide us—"

Her breathing seemed calmer now. Again, her words dripped with a poisoned calm. "Then the inescapable conclusion is that they know who we are and that we are spies. We are doomed either way."

They stood staring at one another, their world rocking, in the palace of the enemy city, Nanjing. Now they were enemies too. Luan could see the hatred and desire for revenge darkening Jade's eyes.

There was a knock at the door.

"Come in," said Luan without thinking, wondering what he was inviting into the bedchamber.

A servant entered, bowed, and said, "Wei-Ling summons the chief concubine to his royal bedchamber."

"I am coming right away," Jade said, then gave Luan a filthy look. "I will settle with you later. Meanwhile, I hope you squirm, thinking of me with Wei-Ling."

"Jade—"

He could think of nothing to do. Desperately, he wished for counsel. Anbai and Ching must be somewhere in the city by now; the Emperor had sent them soon after Jade's and his departure. They would know through his smoke signals that Jade and he were in the palace, but how would they gain access? Who could he turn to for help now that things were falling apart?

Once again, everything seemed impossible.

Stricken, he decided to seek the clear air on a parapet of the castle, to look out over the mountain, to try to settle his qi so as to figure out what he should do.

Perhaps I will see a crane flying. Perhaps my first wife will come and save me from this despair. Perhaps there is a new smoke signal. Anything! I need help.

Would Jade turn traitor now, convinced that her own new husband, a highly placed noble in the Emperor's court, was a murderer? Would she assume he had acted under the Emperor's orders? Would she truly become Wei-Ling's concubine and thus get herself in a position of influence? Would she become a turncoat, fighting alongside the Golden Ginkgo Society against the empire that had betrayed her?

He had thought they would be in danger on all sides. This was even worse. All sides seemed to be pressing in on him, like a magic, man-sized box, with every wall moving to crush him. Apparently, he and Jade were known and trapped; she was about to be violated by Wei-Ling. God only knew what the cook Wang Chaochang would do to Luan when he appeared in the kitchen to cook dinner, and he had no idea where his friends were or what kind of pressures they might be facing as spies for the empire.

Luan's head ached. As he gazed, immobilized, out the window in the direction of Beijing, he realized there were smoke signals coming from the nearest way station.

He read two words: "Assassination approved."

His spirits lifted within him, his raised his head high, and he felt his heart start beating rapidly with excitement and hope.

Exiting his room, he sped toward Wei-Ling's bedchamber, his loyalty to his Emperor and his desire to help his wife united in his heart. He would save Jade by killing Wei-Ling. That would prove his loyalty to her.

For once, marriage and mission converged. Maybe all was not lost after all.

CHAPTER 47

Jade walked into Wei-Ling's empty bedchamber, where she had been instructed to wait for her lord. She felt empty. Nothing mattered any more. Even her desire for vengeance and her anger were crushed within her, knowing that Luan, whom she had trusted and given herself to, was the murderer of her beloved first husband. All was lost.

She might as well throw herself into the life of a concubine—she no longer cared what happened to her, what happened to the Empire. The Emperor had matched her to her husband's murderer! Had he known it was so? How could he not have? There was no one to be trusted anywhere.

She had heard concubines often became addicted to opium to escape the mental anguish of their lives. Maybe that should be her fate too. She would give anything not to feel this searing emotional pain—the pain that she had been betrayed by Luan and the Emperor, husband and lord. Perhaps she could rise up with Wei-Ling and defeat the Empire through the Golden Ginkgo Society. That would be a richly deserved fate for everyone's perfidy.

Yet she hated Wei-Ling. She had hoped for—she had to admit it to herself now—she had hoped for new love with Luan, fresh as dew on the ginkgo leaves, to wash away the pain of the past. Now she was utterly betrayed and deserted, with the agony of losing Wu Lei couples with the anguish and isolation of Luan's duplicity. There was nowhere to turn but to Wei-Ling.

There was a soft knock on the door and a stooped woman entered the room with a silver-handled box full of live coals. The woman bowed slightly to Jade and proceeded to load the coals into the fire grate and then to warm the sheets with the glowing, empty pan.

"It will be sundown soon, and the air grows chilly," the woman explained.

"Where is Wei-Ling?' Jade asked with some dread.

"He is coming soon enough," said the woman. Then she turned to Jade, removed her head scarf, and revealed her face. It was Anbai!

Jade cried aloud, running to embrace her friend. "I have never been so happy to see anyone in my life! Are you now a servant at the palace?"

"Yes, a charwoman. I undercut the prices of the usual charwomen shamelessly and was easily hired!"

The two embraced again.

Jade said, "All is not well. Everything is ruined, if you want to know the truth. We are undone."

She poured out her heart to her friend about Luan's betrayal, Wei-Ling's pressing her to be his concubine, the cook's perfidy, and how she no longer even believed in the Emperor and Empress for having matched her in marriage to her husband's murderer.

Anbai cried, "All this cannot be! Luan is true to the Empire, and the Empire would have no reason to kill your husband. He was killed by Golden Ginkgo, the enemy of the Empire. It is possible they are just trying to divide the two of you. Someone planted that silver dart on Luan."

"No," said Jade, shaking her head. "No, I do not believe that. But if it is so, the news is even worse. They know exactly who we are here. We are completely exposed."

There was a shuffling sound outside the door. Anbai put her finger to her lips and stepped close to the door.

"Yes?" she asked.

"The chief concubine is here. Let me in."

"I am the chief concubine," said Jade loudly.

With a frown of puzzlement, Anbai opened the door.

Willow stood in the doorway.

"Get out of my way!" she said, pushing past Anbai. "He will be here any minute!"

Jade said, "What are you doing—you will betray us all! Although I think we are already betrayed." She shook her head bemusedly. She no longer knew what to think.

"Yes, Wang Chaochang knows who you are," said Willow. "And Wang Chaochang and Wei-Ling are closer than you think. Wang Chaochang has more power than you know. Like me, he keeps his secrets under wraps."

"Do they know that Luan and I are spies?" Jade demanded to know.

"Yes. But Wei-Ling wants you, and Wang Chaochang gives makes sure Wei-Ling gets whatever he wants whenever he wants it, because the boy is so weak and spoiled he will ruin everything if not constantly appeased. He is a puppet, but a petulant puppet."

"But who pulls the puppet's strings? Who is the real power behind the throne?"

"If you don't know by now, I scarcely want to tell you," chided Willow.

As she was speaking, Willow was disrobing. Jade stared, taken aback. As she had guessed, Willow was much slimmer and more compact than her bulky, mannish clothing revealed. In fact, her body was youthful and lithe as she strode around the room, getting herself ready to receive Wei-Ling. She unwound the tightly coiled braids she always wore, and her black hair fanned out, long and silky. As she bathed her face in a basin, the dirt, smears, and acid expression faded from it. She turned back to them.

Willow was young—and beautiful.

"Chief concubine at your service," she said. She turned her back on Jade and Anbai momentarily as she struggled to don a gossamer gown. They saw a beautiful silver swan tattooed on the small of her back. Jade was astonished at how shapely and beautiful Willow was.

"Now go," said Willow. "I will take care of Wei-Ling."

"But he asked for me," objected Jade.

"Oh, do you want him?" Willow started applying vermilion to her lips and cheeks, and it made the porcelain skin of her face stand out in relief and added depths to her large and lovely eyes. She shook her hair again, and it blossomed around her, thick and luxurious.

"No, but it seems his desire for me is my only protection," said Jade.

Willow turned to them with her arms spread out, her beautiful figure revealed in the gossamer dress, her face shining with the lotion she had applied to it.

"I think I can make him forget all about you," said Willow. "He will take the low-hanging fruit rather than pursue you. I will make up some story that you were ill or —"

"Had my monthly woman's situation," said Jade. "That is what I have been telling him, although he no longer believes me."

"Yes. I will tell him it is really true."

Willow then stretched herself luxuriously across the bed in a sensuous position.

"Now go," she ordered, momentarily sitting up. "Go find your husband. I suggest you all try to escape."

"Luan killed my first husband," said Jade. "I am sure of it. I will not go to him."

"Nonsense," said the Silver Swan so dismissively Jade almost believed her. "Luan did not kill Wu Lei. Things are not what they appear. It has all been an intricate plot on the part of Golden Ginkgo to get to Luan through you because — because of who Luan is."

"Luan is a general, in high regard. That is all."

"Luan is the spare arrow in the Emperor's quiver. That is all I can tell you. Now, go! Escape if you can. I would tell you more, but there is no time. Wei-Ling will be here any moment."

At that thought, Jade and Anbai tore out of the bedchamber and blindly ran down the corridor to they knew not where, leaving the shimmering woman alone in the bed, shining like a silver flame.

CHAPTER 48

They fled down corridor after corridor, not knowing where they were going. Although Jade had it in her mind to escape to the streets of Nanjing somehow, she felt they were going more deeply into the palace.

"Stop!" she said to Anbai. "We must use qi—we must use our heads, not listen to the fear in our hearts. Besides you are not discovered, only I am. Perhaps you should go back."

They both heard a footstep in the corridor they had just left. With a desperate look on her face, Anbai pressed on a heavy wooden door with a thick iron chain across its surface. To their surprise, the door moved inward, and the two slender young women were able to slip beneath the black chain through the narrow opening.

It was a dusty, cavernous chamber. With her finger to her lips, Anbai pushed the heavy wooden door shut, her face contorted in agony to do so without even the clink of the weighty iron chain. She accomplished this with no sound other than the faintest of clicks as the door settled into place.

"If he does not hear us, he will never know we are here," she whispered.

The two women listened intently. They heard the footsteps approach and then continue down the corridor without pausing. The owner of the feet was apparently unsuspecting. Both women let out measured sighs of relief, and Anbai touched her heart as if to indicate that it was palpitating.

They gazed around in the dim light. It was a capacious chamber, apparently used for storage. Enameled and wooden boxes and trunks filled the room, most of them covered with dust. Anbai sneezed.

"You should consider going back," said Jade.

"No, I am discovered too. As is Ching. I am sure of it. We thought it was good luck when we got hired so easily, but now I think, if Wang Chaochang is in league with Wei-Ling, they know who we are, too," said Anbai sadly.

She recounted how readily she and Ching had been accepted by Wang Chaochang, the cook, after they had bribed the guard to get into the palace. Wang Chaochang had been sitting at the kitchen table, surrounded by food, when Anbai and Ching had approached him.

At first, Wang Chaochang had said, "There is no work at the palace. Be on your way. We have just recently hired Knife and Wife." He had grinned.

Luan had been there and had said, "My sister is completely taken up with the Emperor. She will not be able to perform as many duties as we had hoped."

Wang Chaochang had stuffed a cabbage-filled, aromatic dumpling into his gaping mouth. He had finished it, obviously relishing it, then squinted at Luan through the rolls of fat obscuring his small eyes. He wiped his mouth and burped and looked over Anbai and Ching in their poor, dirt-stained clothing.

"Can you work?" asked Wang Chaochang, tearing another cabbage dumpling in half between his teeth.

"Yes. We are experienced. We worked in a great house in Shanghai. Here are our references." Ching handed Wang Chaochang a letter with the official seal of a Shanghai magistrate.

"Hm," said Wang Chaochang. "We cannot pay great house prices."

"We would not expect that of a people's government."

"Ah, you are sympathizers, then?"

"Yes," Ching had said. "Down with the Emperor and the Manchu overlords!"

Anbai had echoed his sentiments.

Wang Chaochang had answered, "You are employed, both of you."

Anbai whispered to Jade, "Upon reflection, I don't think he would have hired us so easily had he not understood that we, too, were spies. I felt almost as if his eyes were twinkling at Luan, as if knowing why he had spoken up for us."

"Yes, the cook knows much," said Jade. "and he is in cahoots with Wei-Ling. He cannot be trusted."

"So I suspect I am in as much danger as you are," said Anbai.

"I expect Wei-Ling will be sending guards to find me once he discovers my escape from his bed," said Jade. "Although I am sure few men would turn down Willow, and that may keep him happy for a time. My goodness, who could have known she harbored such beauty underneath that disguise of an older, petulant, nasty-tempered woman?"

"The empire has many layers," was all Anbai said.

"Too many for me!" said Jade. "And Luan is one of those deep layers."

She told Anbai about the silver darts, their history, and her discovery of a newly minted one on Luan's person.

"That is why I think he killed my husband Wu Lei," she said bitterly. "I imagine he was going to kill me. I think he must be in league with the Golden Ginkgo Society. Why does the Emperor not know?"

Anbai shook her head. "That does not seem possible. Luan is a true man, inside and outside. I could never believe he is a traitor to all we hold dear."

"Why did he have the dart, then?"

"Perhaps someone planted it on him to divide the two of you, just as Willow said. She seems to know a great deal of all that is going on. I' am prone to believe her."

At that moment, they heard footsteps again and, with the instincts of warriors, padded further back into the room and hid themselves in the shadows behind a large trunk, ready to spring out fighting to the death if need be. After a few seconds pause, Jade slipped even further back into the room, timing her movements with the sounds of the approaching boots so as to avoid being heard. Better for them to be found separately, she reasoned, if they were to be discovered. One might be able to escape as the first one found fought off the intruder. Yet once again, the footsteps went past the door, and Jade heard Anbai's audible sigh of relief.

"What is this place, I wonder?" Jade whispered. They seemed to be in some sort of inner sanctum in the very core of the palace. Their eyes now adjusted to the dimness, and they noticed that there were maps on the tables and walls.

"These are not all ancient," said Anbai, touching one. "Even though this appears to be a room of archives. Look. This province bears the new division lines the Emperor decided on last year."

Jade and Anbai pored over the map. It was up-to-date, they decided. Someone was using this room for something more than old storage.

"There is the Yongding River," said Jade. She was startled. "Look!" she said, hardly able to credit her eyes. "It is marked where the small island is."

Two black X marks were etched on the island where she and Luan had stayed together. Her finger traced the route to the warrior troops' hide-out camp in the desert, and sure enough, there were many Xs there. As she gazed across the map of China, she realized that the Xs denoted warrior couples and troops' locations.

"They know about us," she whispered. "They know all about us. Details I could never have guessed." Her heart wrenched and she shuddered. Had there been spies on the island the very night she and Luan had consummated their marriage, thinking and feeling like they were the only man and woman in the world?

Her blood drained from her face and to her feet, leaving her pale and shaken. The tentacles of the Golden Ginkgo Society were long, clever, and entwining. She felt as if they had encircled her very heart and were strangling her from inside.

CHAPTER 49

e could have been killed, she thought. *We were totally vulnerable. Why did they not slaughter us then? It is because Luan is their secret agent? Was it he who told them we were on the island when this map was drawn?*

This fresh evidence of Luan's duplicity left her dizzy.

"Look," said Anbai. She had lifted the lid of a heavy trunk. Inside was an assortment of weapons with the imperial seal. Some were old and some were new. The ancient ones no doubt belonged here in Nanjing's archives, but the newer ones must have been stolen from military supplies.

"We must search this room thoroughly," said Jade. "This seems to be some sort of war room for the Society."

They began to shuffle through the papers left on a large, ornate, hand-carved wooden table. Although the crevices of the table legs' carvings were filled with dust, many of the documents were of recent date. There were several such current letters in a hand that was hard to discern, but after poring over it for some minutes, Jade thought she could make out the words in Chinese: "Kill them all."

All? All of whom? She had a horrible feeling it meant them, the now exposed infiltrators in Nanjing. She supposed they would make an exception for that turncoat Luan, since he was one of them.

Further down the page, it said: "Madam Viper wills it."

Madam Viper! Jade remembered the vision Wu Lei had shown her while she was practicing qi. Who was this Madam Viper? Why was she so powerful in the Golden Ginkgo Society?

Could Madam Viper be Willow? Willow was clearly already masking her true identity from her own unit—she had masked the identity Jade now thought of as "Silver Swan." Could she be a double agent for the Golden Ginkgo?

Jade's terrified gaze swept over the map again. There were four ink blotches on Shanghai. Closer examination showed that the blotches were the obliteration of four Xs drawn on Shanghai—herself, Luan, Anbai, and Ching! She was sure of it. As she leaned in more closely, she saw that there was a trail of broken lines leading to Nanjing, where four Xs were reconstituted in the palace.

They were discovered. This confirmed it. But how to warn Luan and Ching?

Jade chided herself. There was no need to warn Luan. He was right at home here with the murderous Society. He was one of the ones she had to escape from.

Anbai had followed her gaze on the map, and she seemed to understand all that Jade did.

"Our duty is to escape," said Anbai. "With what knowledge we have intact. Even if it means leaving our husbands behind, we must warn the Emperor and Empress how well they know our troops' movements. That is a crucial piece of intelligence."

"I agree," said Jade.

She admired the fact that Anbai, in this moment of horrific discovery, was able to put her mission above sentiment for her husband. Jade too was focused on the mission, but the pain at Luan's duplicity was like a knife wound in her heart. Well, as a warrior, one fought on, even when wounded. She would fight on. Somehow they had to escape from this palace.

In unspoken accord, both women began casting around the room for exit windows or doors. If they could traverse deep, secret corridors of the castle, perhaps they could find a hidden exit. They were so intent on their search that they only belatedly heard heavy boots outside the door. A moment later, a key was thrust into the weighty padlock on the other side. The heavy lock protested with many metallic groans, but at last it gave up. They heard the lock fall, heard the clunk of metal as it was removed and cast aside, and then the ponderous wooden door swung inward and a shaft of light from the hallway silhouetted a tall man in a guard's uniform, a sword in his hand.

It was too late to hide. Anbai and Jade rapidly assumed fighting stances.

CHAPTER 50

The guard raised his sword as if to cleave Jade in half. Then he laughed, as if in recognition.

"Madam, there is no need to fear. You are summoned to Master Wei-Ling's bedchamber. You are wanted. That is all."

"Oh." Jade squinted at him.

"Is that not the new charwoman with you?" he asked.

"Yes. She has been acting as my helper."

"She may come along too. There are several bedchambers in that hallway that need a charwoman's services."

Anbai and Jade glanced at one another. There seemed to be little else to do but to follow the guard. He set a strong pace throughout the corridors until at last they came to Wei-Ling's bedchamber.

Jade hesitated at the doorway. What should she do? She tried to read the guard's face, but it was inscrutable. She wondered why he had not asked her about her presence in the map room, but perhaps he did not feel it was his place as a guard. In any case, he had not arrested her, so Wei-Ling apparently was not infuriated with her.

With a significant look at Jade, Anbai disappeared into one of the empty bedchambers, murmuring something about getting on with her cleaning tasks. Jade swallowed. They both knew that escape was their mission now. She knew that Anbai would do all she could to make her escape from Nanjing, and she had a better chance of it than Jade. Jade envied her as she faced Wei-Ling's bedchamber door, covered with elaborate inlaid enamel and gold scrolling.

She rapped on the door with her knuckles. The door flew open, and a hand reached out from the sleeve of a silver robe and grabbed Jade's wrist roughly.

"My lord!" she protested as she was pulled into the room. The enameled door slammed behind her, leaving the guard outside, and she nearly pitched into Silver Swan, who was the one holding her wrist.

She was clad in silver silk, which was embroidered with white cranes, their legs black and pointed and their beaks a bright Chinese red. Her shapely body was shown off by the silk's drape. Then Jade's mind swam as she noted what appeared to be red watercolor spreading across the belly of the silver silk dress. It appeared to be blood.

"Are you hurt?" she cried.

"I am not," Silver Swan whispered. "But Wei-Ling is dead. He met a merciful end."

"What?"

"I was very quick and effective."

Silver Swan reached over to the bed and swept the voluminous silk bedcover aside. There was Wei-Ling, naked, and curled up in an infant-like position. His body was slight, his mouth was slack, and his eyes were peacefully closed. The wound in his chest—neat and precise—wept bright red blood that Silver Swan bent to swab away with a wet cloth.

"He's nothing more than a dressed-up boy," said Silver Swan sympathetically. She flipped the silk coverlet back over Wei-Ling's body. "Although he found me beautiful, he had no idea what to do with me. Apparently, he had never had a woman before. We spent the whole time with him weeping in my arms, telling me about how his mother bosses him around and doesn't let him be a man. He's a puppet—a puppet of a very powerful couple, his parents. I suspect the mother is even more powerful than the father."

"Who are they?" In Jade's mind, she was seeing images of a Madam Viper—venomous, ugly, and cruel—and Black Dagger, surely a natural-born killer. Yet she had no faces to go with the images. She had no idea who they were.

"Alas, I don't know." Silver Swan sat down on the bed as if she had to rest, oblivious to the lump of silk bedding that covered

Wei-Ling. "They are not of Nanjing, I know that. You see, I had a secret mission in Nanjing, and I know most of the undercurrents here. But their identities I do not know. My late husband was chief magistrate here."

Jade marveled how even Silver Swan's voice was different from Willow's. It was light and silken, not heavy, gruff, and sullen as it had always been in camp.

"The Emperor created my husband's position to serve as attaché. He was frequently called upon to travel for his work, or at least that was what we told people in Nanjing. Those were the times when we went out with the elite warriors When we were not on assignment, we were a Nanjing society couple, wealthy and of high status.

"Nanjing has had the seeds of rebellion in it for a long time. My husband and I, and the aristocracy here, were always bulwarks against a popular uprising. But my husband was killed. Much like yours, he was assassinated, only by a poisoned dagger—this very one with which I killed Wei-Ling."

Silver Swan held up a beautiful silver dagger, intricately engraved and jewel-encrusted. The blade, Jade could tell, was extremely sharp. Silver Swan absent-mindedly patted the heap of silken bedding, as if to tell Wei-Ling to sleep well.

"Without my husband, Nanjing became vulnerable. I am certain he was assassinated by the Golden Ginkgo, but I have never been able to ascertain who the ringleaders are. As I say, Wei-Ling was a puppet. I suppose they needed someone young and fresh to lead a people's revolution—someone who could inspire the idealistic and naive. I sometimes suspect the strings are being pulled from far away, though—maybe even in Beijing."

Jade asked, "There is a Madam Viper whose name keeps cropping up. Does that you give any ideas?"

"No. That is clearly an alias. It bears no relation to a real person or a real name."

Jade's gaze returned to the heap of bedding covering Wei-Ling.

"What shall we do with him? He will be found, and you will be the first to be suspected."

"Actually, you will be the first to be suspected, Jade. No one knows I took your place as chief concubine. You, especially, must escape. Do you know where Luan is?"

Jade's face fell. "No."

"I believe he is on the fifth parapet. I thought I detected smoke signals from there. Of course, with the cook suspecting him, he could no longer send them from the kitchen fire."

Jade's mind snapped back to the business at hand. "How can we escape? They are onto us. They know — you would not believe how much they know, Fragrant — I mean, Silver Swan. They know all about the elite spousal troops and their locations. I believe Luan told them."

Silver Swan shook her head so dismissively, Jade almost believed in Luan again. Silver Swan's porcelain brow was unfurrowed. "The aristocracy is alerted and armed, ready to fight on the side of the imperial troops, which are on their way. Prince Li has been leading them here. Now that Luan has signaled them that your four are found out and that Wei-Ling's rule is weak at the core, they will not only approach; they will attack and try to oust Golden Ginkgo's power structure. That may not destroy the Society — but it will demoralize and scatter it. Then it will be a matter of mopping up operations in its lesser enclaves."

"The imperial army is on its way here?"

"Yes. Yet we cannot be sure that the four of you would not be mistaken for Society members by the imperial troops. There will be great chaos, and you are in the palace. That is why you must flee, and immediately. The troops will be here by dawn. You are in danger from the Society and in danger from the imperial troops.

"I suggest that one of us stay behind. If the fighting is fierce, we must display Wei-Ling's body from the balcony. If we hold his dead body up for the guards in the courtyard to see, and let the news spread that their leader is dead, hopefully that will demoralize those who follow him and embolden those in Nanjing who would throw off his yoke. I will stay."

Jade said, "You are not strong enough to heft Wei-Ling's body onto the balcony for the people to see."

"Am I not? I beat you in combat, don't forget that. And I was hampered by my heavy clothing. Listen, Jade. Nanjing is my city. My sister died because of the Society's false promises. I am ready to die for its defeat should it come to that. Now, there is no time to argue. Dawn will be here all too soon. Luan is on the fifth parapet. Go join him."

When Jade Blossom did not move, Silver Swan cried impatiently, "Do you doubt him still?"

Jade was formulating an answer when there was a peremptory knock on the door.

CHAPTER 51

"I do not like the sound of that," whispered Silver Swan. "Who—" "Shhh!" said Jade. "I am the one who is supposed to be in here. Go. Hide." Jade adjusted the silken coverlet over Wei-Ling's body so that no part of it showed. Out of the corner of her eye, she saw Silver Swan slip behind the silk curtains on the wall-length, rice paper windows that shielded the room from the balcony.

Jade straightened her hair and her clothes and opened the door.

It was the guard. She recognized his eyes, but she did not recognize his garb. He was wearing neat, compact, ninja like clothes rather than the armor and uniform of a palace guard. But his eyes were unforgettable. They were very dark and deepest, yet their gaze was like a stiletto—pointed and sharp like a black dagger.

"Yes?" she said, her eyebrows and voice kiting upward. She fought her fear down to appear calm. "My lover, Wei-Ling sleeps. I have exhausted him with pleasure."

"Indeed."

The guard shouldered his way past her and strode into the room.

"How dare you enter the room when the ruler is with his chief concubine?"

"This is not Manchu territory. We are less formal here."

He plucked the coverlet from Wei-Ling's body.

"Ah, it is as I expected," he said, his mouth a thin line of anger.

"Who are you, presumptuous one?" demanded Jade.

"I have many names," the guard said. "But some call me Black Dagger."

Black Dagger! Wu Lei had warned her about a Black Dagger in her vision! Was this the head of the Golden Ginkgo, the power behind

Wei-Ling's throne, and the partner of Madam Viper, whoever she was? Jade involuntarily took a step back before she summoned up her own courage.

Black Dagger studied Wei-Ling. "Nicely done," he said. "I imagine his end was quick."

"I did not kill him," said Jade. "In fact, I was just about to call you. I found him like this. There is an assassin in the palace."

"Indeed. Then why did you lie to me that you had exhausted him with passion?"

"I was afraid of being accused of his death."

"Ah, you are quick with your lies," Black Dagger said. "One after another after another."

Jade had no answer, and he did not seem to expect one.

"I know who you are," he went on, "and my job, as a loyal palace guard, is to kill you for what you have done. You are an infiltrator and a spy and an assassin. There will be no trial. I carry a great deal of authority, and any legal proceeding would only be a show trial anyway. The Golden Ginkgo is getting rather good at show trials, as we have many enemies yet must keep our pact with the people. But you won't even have that mock courtesy."

Jade moved further back into the room.

"Who are you?" she asked again.

"I am—for you—the devil himself. Jade, you are about to die. There is no hope and no help. The corridors are utterly deserted—I have created a distraction elsewhere. Your friends and husband are all escaping. You are the last one left in Nanjing. And you will be the one to pay for this spy mission, with every ounce of pain I can wring out of your flesh. Who am I?" He advanced toward her. "Why, I am the one who killed your husband, Wu Lei. How beautiful that you are both sent into the life beyond by the same hand—the hand of Black Dagger. Do you know why Wu Lei was killed? It does not matter if I tell you. Your lips will be sealed in cold death within minutes. He knew too much about the Society.

He was too hot on the trail. He had told no one all he knew because he did not want to arouse suspicion. But we knew he was getting closer. You will die with many questions in your heart, but Wu Lei knew, and he knew too much. What better place to murder someone than on a battlefield?"

"Where indeed," echoed Jade faintly. In the back of her mind, it registered that it had not been Luan who had killed Wu Lei after all. Luan was innocent. This thought gave her a certain strength as she listened with horror to Black Dagger's next words.

"It was enjoyable to watch him die in agony and to see his poor, beautiful bride so beside herself with grief. Exquisite pleasure to see such esteemed members of the empire steeped in agony. All pain to the empire and its representatives pleases me. And now I will see you steeped in more agony. Your throat is lovely, dear lady, and meant for love and song, but I think this will look beautiful lodged in its veins, with its slow-acting poison."

It was a Serpent dart. In her rapidly calculating mind, she knew that when she fought him, she would have to avoid being pricked with it at all costs.

She tried to look frightened, cowed. She retreated, as if she could not help herself, and was glad to see him aggressively step forward, closing the distance between them. Her feet fought for leverage; her heart fought for calm.

You are not alone, she heard Wu Lei whisper in her mind. *I will help you take vengeance on my murderer.*

And I, said Jingwei. *I will fight by his side.*

This, and the strength of her new conviction of Luan's innocence, allowed her to think even as the murderer glowered down at her.

Qi. She had to channel qi. She had to breathe deeply, fight down her own impulses to leap, tigress style, into the fray.

Her training with Luan and Anbai sank into her mind. She had to use a power greater than her own against such an enemy.

Guarding her expression, making it one of fear and confusion, she calculated the exact distance she had to traverse. Then, with a graceful movement that seemed to take him by surprise, waiting as he was for the tigress's leap, she swung her leg high, aimed for his wrist, and sent the silver dart flying out of his hand. It clattered on the floor, and she calculated exactly where it was. She would keep him away from there at all costs.

As his eyes followed the silver dart and his mouth opened in surprise and disappointment, Jade rushed him. Now she had to overwhelm him quickly in true tiger style, knocking him off his feet. Qi was with her, as was the element of surprise, and she bowled him over onto his back, her own body atop his. She pulled her upper body weight up with her arms, and before he could rise, hefted her own weight up on her hands and brought a knee up under his chin, giving him a skull-rattling blow to the jaw. Then she catapulted over his head and somersaulted until she had her feet beneath her and could rise and whirl to face him. He slumped to the side, hands to his face, and she kicked him, hard, in the head. Those palace platform shoes were good for something! Still, he was alert and strong enough to grab her foot. He then twisted her foot painfully, making the knee of her standing leg buckle underneath her, and she crashed down on her backside on the hard tile.

CHAPTER 52

Jade struggled to get her bearings, but Black Dagger's foot was on her chest, shoving her down on the tile. The hard floor made her shoulders ache, and his foot and weight were enough to crush her breathing. He laughed at her, his mouth distorted with cruelty. But she wasn't weak, and she wouldn't give up. Her legs rose up in well-executed scissor kicks to his buttocks, but she could not unbalance him. She strove to tiger-claw his vulnerable parts, but she could not reach that high.

Laughing, he moved his foot to press hard on one of her breasts, a critical mistake on his part since the shifting of his weight to one foot gave Jade the chance to roll out from underneath him. Her clothing was still pinned, though, and it hindered her from reaching the silver dart on the floor, for which she was desperately reaching. He moved again, swiftly, releasing her clothing, but grasping her shoulders to drag her away from the dart. He lifted her and slammed her down on the tile so hard, her head cracked against the solid surface. Her vision blurred and darkened at the edges.

There was a sliding, scraping sound, as of metal on stone, and Jade thought he must be trying to retrieve the silver dart. That thought angered her enough to bring blood flooding back into her head and face, pumping life into her. When Black Dagger stood up over her, and lifted his foot to crack her skull, she caught the foot in both hands, channeled qi, and twisted his leg. Black Dagger lost his balance and hit the floor with a satisfying thud. Vengeful satisfaction coursing through her with the knowledge that she had badly hurt her husband's murderer.

She blinked several times, and her vision began to clear. She had but one goal now, and it was to get the dart. She'd thought he had it; she did not see it in his hand, so she crawled to where she had heard it fall, all the while keeping her eyes trained on Black Dagger, who was supine on the floor. She could not find it, grope as she might, with her still compromised vision. She shook her head, trying to clear it, and stood.

Black Dagger, too, staggered to his feet and resumed a shaky fighting stance, obviously dizzy and disoriented. The moment their eyes met, he rushed at her. Though he was weaker than before it was enough to fling her backward. His weight and momentum carried him after her and he crushed her against the wall, his hands gripping her throat, his face inches from hers.

In the blackness that threatened to overwhelm her, she saw the curtain to her right shift and felt someone fumbling for her hand. A moment, and something cold, sleek and metallic slipped between her fingers.

The dart! Silver Swan must have seen where it had fallen and snatched it from concealment.

She lolled her head and slid downward to force him to change his grip, took a quick breath, and plunged the dart into his thigh, the most exposed and vulnerable part of his body. She read the sudden pain in his face, saw the dawn of realization in his eyes. He screamed, and Jade used the moment to thrust him away from her. He fell to the floor, landing on his back, twisting and kicking desperately as both his hands sought to pull out the Serpent dart before it dispensed its full charge of poison into his blood.

Jade, merciless, positioned herself behind him and chopped at his neck with precise blows, making him roar with pain and rage, and distracting him from his weakening attempts to remove the dart. When his hand faltered and fell, Jade straightened and watched as Black Dagger stopped moving and the light of life drained from his eyes. She watched and laughed, a black flood of vengeance flowing through her. She gave in to the darkness, dropping to her knees and pulling Black Dagger's head back by his hair. Her wooden platform shoes had come off in the struggle; one lay just within reach. She snatched it up and raised it above her head, thoughts of Wu Lei and her love for him feeding the dark flood in her heart.

"I will destroy you!" she shrieked, bringing the shoe down on the dead man's face again and again. "I will destroy you!"

She felt hands on her sleeves, tugging at her gently, rousing her from her from the drunkenness of vengeance.

"He is gone," Silver Swan murmured in her ear. "Wu Lei is avenged. You must stop now. You must make your escape. Qi will not flow through you if you keep this up. You must calm down. Justice is served. Enough!"

Jade closed her eyes and remembered her qi training with Luan and Anbai. She felt ashamed, but her heart also danced that her husband's murderer was dead. Silver Swan was right, though. It was time to regain self-possession.

"You will be executed for his murder and Wei-Ling's," she pointed out to Silver Swan. "I cannot escape and let you stay alone."

Silver Swan thought for a moment. "I have no wish to escape from Nanjing. I must rally the aristocracy. I am the leader of an important part of the resistance. No, you must go, Jade. You alone must go. I will barricade the door and keep people from entering."

"They will be surprised Wei-Ling is not appearing anywhere — no, this cannot work!"

"It must. Don't worry. No one will disturb him with a concubine. You have a few hours. Take advantage of them. And dawn will come. Dawn will come — and with it the imperial troops."

Silver Swan gazed toward the window that led to a balcony overlooking a palace courtyard.

"Dawn will come," she repeated softly, strengthening herself with that hope.

The two women searched the body for any clues as to Black Dagger's real identity. Tucked into a hidden pocket in his vest, they found a note. It read: *Beloved Brother. When you have a chance, kill all four. Our Han Chinese lineage will emerge triumphant in the contest for the Dragon Throne.* This was followed by the Chinese character for 'serpent'.

"Madam Viper," said Jade. "If we find out who Black Dagger was, and more about his family, we discover one of the puppeteers pulling Wei-Ling's strings."

Silver Swan shoved a sheaf of papers into Jade's hands. "Here. All the information he was carrying. Sort through it when you are safely out of Nanjing. It may yield more clues. Now go. Go!"

Jade rushed to the door, opened it a crack, and looked up and down the empty corridor. She slipped into the hallway, leaving Silver Swan alone with two dead men in the ornate, silk-strewn bedchamber.

CHAPTER 53

Jade listened at bedchamber doors down the corridor, seeking Anbai. If she heard movement within, she moved on to the next one. She did not think Anbai would be moving around, but would use her charwoman disguise only if someone entered the room she was in.

She stopped in front of one door. It was utterly silent, but the silence had a strange, quivering quality to it, as if someone was behind the door, barely breathing, a presence, but a silent one.

Slowly, she pushed the door open an inch and peered into the room. She started when a dark brown eye topped by a lovely arched eyebrow, peered back at her. Anbai!

"Thank goodness!" Anbai breathed, after she had drawn Jade into the bedchamber. "I have been afraid to stir a muscle."

"Silver Swan said Luan is on the fifth parapet. Let us take a circuitous route there to avoid detection."

"Perhaps it is better to be who we are; then we will not arouse suspicion. Walk slowly and proudly, as chief concubine and her maidservant."

They traversed corridors and wound their way upward. They met no one.

At the opening to the fifth parapet, Anbai said, "If we meet sentries, pretend we are just seeking fresh air. Pretend I was overcome by inhaling ash and you were kind enough to bring me up here."

Jade nodded. The two women emerged onto the parapet, trying to act as normally as possible. It was dark, and they just make out the outlines of sentries.

Anbai spoke. "Oh, milady! Thank you so much for bringing me here. The fresh air is reviving me! You are so kind."

A knot of men was gathered at the edge of the parapet. Two figures disengaged themselves from the group and a match was struck. Jade almost cried aloud with relief to see the features of Luan. A barely audible sigh of relief came from Anbai when the reflected light fell on the features of Ching.

Jade wanted to run to her husband, begging for his forgiveness for doubting him. She steeled herself to behave according to their guise.

"Brother, we are seeking fresh air," she said. "This charwoman was overcome by smoke and nearly fainted while warming the beds."

"Oh," said Luan casually. "Well, there is a lot of fresh air up here."

Ching came forward and expressed measured concern for his wife, as if little was at stake.

All assumed casual postures, as if they were simply having an evening stroll in the fresh air of the parapet. Yet all knew their situation was desperate. All had information they needed to share. All had to escape, before the Golden Ginkgo Society knew that they knew they were discovered.

Luan looked reflectively out over the city, as if musing on its beauty.

"The Golden Ginkgo Society," he said, as if he were simply musing aloud.

Ching and Anbai looked alert. Jade nodded.

"Named after such a beautiful tree." That was all he said, but Jade understood, and the glints under Anbai's and Ching's eyelashes told her they understood too.

After more desultory conversation, Anbai and Ching noted that they had to return to their cleaning duties. After a few more minutes, Jade said that she should attend to Wei-Ling. She, too, left the parapet at a slow pace, without any visible haste. As Luan had hinted, she would meet her comrades again under the ginkgo tree outside the palace walls.

CHAPTER 54

Jade hurried to her bedchamber in order to pick up a few things for her escape from Nanjing. She entered the room, and within seconds heard a scratch at the door. She drew close to the door and heard Luan give a pre-arranged signal. She opened the door and let him in.

"What happened with Wei-Ling?" he asked.

"He did not violate me," she whispered. "He is dead."

Luan was impassive. "Did you kill him?"

"Silver Swan — Willow — did. She took my place in his bed. We were right. He was but a puppet."

She brought him quickly up to date on all she had discovered, as well as telling him about the death of Black Dagger.

"You have done well," he said, impressed. "Assassinated Wei-Ling, assassinated Black Dagger — your husband's murderer — found a clue to the puppeteers' identities, and set up a plan with Silver Swan to rally the aristocracy against Golden Ginkgo while covering the killings. Well done, Jade! I have not accomplished nearly so much. We must send signals about the assassination of Wei-Ling, however, as that is information the oncoming imperial troops will need to know in planning their attack. This is a weakness, now, that they must exploit. I will risk one more smoke signal from the kitchen."

Jade objected. "No! You know Wang Chaochang knows about us. He was in league with Wei-Ling!"

"But Wang Chaochang does not know Wei-Ling is dead. He will keep up the pretense until he can spring his trap. But we will be gone by then." He smiled at her worried face. "Besides, he retires very early in the evenings. I imagine the kitchen is empty by now."

Jade stood tall before him. "Black Dagger killed my husband. I am sorry for ever doubting you. I was wrong to do so. I will prove my loyalty to you by dying by your side if need be."

"I already attributed your mistrust to your emotion over your loss. I forgive you. I must make haste now. The guards no doubt assume Wei-Ling is spending the night with you in his bedchamber. Lie low here for a time. If I do not return for you soon, go to the designated place."

*　　*　　*

Luan went to the kitchen. It was, as he had anticipated, dark and deserted. Wang Chaochang usually retired directly after dinner, and the servants finished up as quickly as they could and went to enjoy the last few shreds of the day on their own.

Luan built up the fire and sent night spark signals that Wei-Ling was dead but that his body had yet to be discovered. He hoped it would hearten imperial troops who were now amassing, he imagined, in the dark mountains and hills just outside the city. He finished the message just as Wang Chaochang waddled into the kitchen.

"Hello," said Wang Chaochang, immediately going to the cupboard to get himself some food.

"Hello," said Luan. He tried to hide a rising sense of panic as his heart began to beat painfully within him.

Wang Chaochang settled down at the table and chewed on a cold duck wing. "Mm, this is good," he said.

For a few moments the kitchen was silent but for the smacking of the heavy man's lips as he demolished the duck wing and licked the grease from this mouth and fingers.

"So did you hear?" he asked at length.

"Hear what?" asked Luan, careful to keep the concern he felt from showing on his face.

Wang Chaochang lowered his voice to a whisper. "It's very hush-hush. They don't want anyone to know yet. Your sister—

that beautiful little minx — stabbed Wei-Ling in her bedroom! He is dead!"

"No!" said Luan, trying to assume an adequate expression of horror.

"Mm," said Wang Chaochang, tearing into a second duck wing. "She is being taken to the dungeon as we speak. You'd better get down there quickly before any of the guards have their way with her. They'll be so busy arguing who gets to go first, she'll still be safe."

Duty compelled Luan to spend a few more seconds of precious time asking, "And Wei-Ling's body?"

"Oh, it's still in the bedroom. The guards were far more interested in Jade, especially since it appears she killed one of them too. I guess he happened in on her, and she thought she had to dispatch him as well."

There was an odd look of sorrow in the pupils of Wang Chaochang's eyes. The cook was always one to be eating, but he pushed food into his mouth with a sort of desperation now, as if trying to comfort an inner wound.

There was no time to speculate as to whether this was a purposeful lie. Luan exploded into action, leaping down the stone stairs to the dungeon-like basement of the castle. Sure enough, the guards were drawing straws as to who would have the first go with Jade, who looked infuriated as she stood behind the bars of the cage-like room they had locked her in. Her face lit up when she saw Luan.

There were four guards, and Luan was so enraged he was certain he would be able to kill them all. He deliberately controlled his emotions, though, and concentrated on calling upon qi to come to him and work to his advantage. He must be cool and methodical.

The guards were armed with lengthy spears and knives of their own, but Luan moved too quickly to allow them to draw their weapons. He whirled, and the knives hidden in his sleeves slapped into his palms. His knives spinning, and with the force of his qi, Luan cut two of the guards' spears in half. The guards, taken by surprise, could only gape at the broken shafts as their spear tips clattered to the floor.

With a sweep of his leg, Luan kicked the broken weapons out of reach. He tossed his knives in a spinning arc, and when they passed at the apex of the arc, with the two men gaping at them, he used his elbows to jab the two disarmed guards, one after another, in the bellies. The men collapsed as he caught his two knives, and turned on the other guards, who shuffled backward.

"Stop, Luan," one of them said, hands raised. "We will not harm your sister."

"You will harm no one, ever again," said Luan. "You have raised your weapons in the name of the Golden Ginkgo, and you will go down with the Golden Ginkgo. Drop your weapons."

The guards stood, as if rooted to the spot, but one of them said, "The Society may go down. But its ideas of justice and fairness will live on. Mark my words, the Society rocked the Dragon Throne, and it may never be steady again."

"Drop your weapons," Luan ordered again. "I will drop mine, too." His weapons clanked to the ground. "Fight me hand to hand. I will prove to you the honor of the empire."

The guards dropped their weapons and circled Luan. They were strong, but brute force worked against them as they charged Luan. Like liquid, he melted away in front of them and let them pass, but he extended his foot and tripped one while he chopped the other across the back with enough qi to make the snap of vertebrae audible. The man screamed in pain, while the other crawled on the floor, begging Luan for mercy.

"I do have mercy," said Luan, "as does the Emperor," and then he rendered each man unconscious with a glancing blow to the neck. Quickly, he searched their pockets for the key to Jade's cell. He found it and opened the door, only to be nearly knocked to the floor as his wife threw herself upon him.

"There, there," he soothed her. "There is no time to talk. Let us go."

"Are we going to the ginkgo tree to rendezvous with Anbai and Ching?"

"Yes, and then to the river bank to hail a boat."

A flicker of light caught Luan's attention. A chink in the basement wall had begun to shine with the morning's first light.

"Dawn!" cried Jade.

Indeed, the noise of Luan's battle with the guards had drowned out the sounds they now heard multiplying and increasing in volume above them. The palace was in chaos. Women screamed and men shouted in the streets, and the percussion of marching men echoed above their heads.

Imperial troops were invading the city.

CHAPTER 55

nakes of fear coiled and twisted in Luan's gut. He had hoped to be on the river by now, escaping from the city. Instead, they were in the palace where they might well be taken for Society members if imperial troops stormed in. There was no hope of making it to the ginkgo tree, much less the riverbank; the city was in chaos.

Both Jade and Luan assumed fighting stances as they heard someone coming down the dank dungeon steps. From the heaviness of the tread, they could tell the newcomer weighed a great deal. It must surely be Wang Chaochang. He paused and breathed heavily on each step. In a moment, Wang Chaochang hove into view like a huge ship coming into a harbor. His clothes were dripping like sails in a storm, so badly was he sweating.

"Wait," he puffed, putting his hand on his chest and taking deep breaths. "Wait. I can help you."

"Why would you help us?" asked Jade sharply.

"I have information."

"That explains how, not why," Luan pointed out.

"I knew about the smoke signals and I did not tell; I allowed your fellow spies employment. I told you about your sister in the dungeon. Protect me now, Luan! Testify of my aid to the Emperor's sons! Three of them are leading the charge on Nanjing. Prince Li is already ensconced in the old drum and bell tower as his headquarters. I can get you there. I know a secret route."

"Prince Li knows us by sight," said Jade to Luan. "Perhaps we should go there."

"You will betray us to Golden Ginkgo," Luan accused Wang Chaochang. "You will lead us into a trap. How do we know Prince Li is in the drum and bell tower?"

Wang Chaochang tried to meet Luan's eyes, but soon the plump man's eyes began to water, and then he broke down a wept. His bulk shook and his small, piggish eyes completely disappeared in the swelling rolls of fat around them. He was a pitiable sight, and there was no mistaking that he was feeling deep sorrow. It took Wang Chaochang several minutes to be able to speak.

"The Society is fighting everywhere in the city," he said in a broken voice. "Many of them are being rounded up by imperial troops. They will storm the palace last. They know of the death of Wei-Ling." At this he choked up again. "There is no one to betray you to. We ourselves are betrayed. We will be defeated. We are no match for a direct attack by the Emperor's army. It is over. My only hope is that you will testify to my helping you and that you will sue for mercy for me."

Luan looked at the cook skeptically. Yet there was no mistaking the waves of sorrow and loss that roiled his qi. While Luan did not trust Wang Chaochang or like him at all, he could not deny that the man was shaken to his core. The cook might be useful in getting them through the city. That was better than being trapped in the palace. There was no leverage for escape or credibility if they stayed pinned within its walls.

"Let us go to the drum and bell tower then," Luan said at last, sheathing his knives in his sleeves. "I promise you I will not forget any favors to us." He looked at Jade, who nodded grimly.

On the far end of the dungeon was a stone door. It was nearly invisible in the dimness. Wang Chaochang threw his bulk against it, Luan helped, and it gave inward, revealing a dark passageway. Jade and Luan glanced at one another as they followed Wang Chaochang in. It could very well be a trap. They wished they had better choices.

The tunnel smelled of mold and mildew, and they heard the trickle of water that seemed to be coming from behind the earthen walls. The ground beneath their feet was damp; wet gravel crunched beneath Luan's shoes, which were soon soaked through. His feet grew sore walking on the uneven stones; the air in the tunnel grew more and more fetid and the journey laborious. What was more, Wang Chaochang had to pause every so often to take deep breaths and to wipe the sweat and tears from his eyes.

Luan took the opportunity to walk ahead of him, drawing Jade into a whispered consultation.

"Why do you suppose he weeps so?" Jade asked.

"Perhaps he believed strongly in the Society. Perhaps he was loyal to the leader Wei-Ling."

"Do you think he is really taking us to the drum and bell tower?"

Luan sighed deeply. "I do not know. I hope so. I also hope it is true that Prince Li is there. We've only Wang Chaochang's word to rely on. But for his tears, I would not believe anything he says. He seems a broken man; as if he has nothing else to lose and is ready to surrender."

"I agree," said Jade, but her lips pursed with suspicion too.

"It is soon; it is soon," the cook huffed, coming up behind them and assisting himself by pressing a hand against the slimy tunnel walls. "The last part is the hardest, though; the tunnel inclines toward the street."

True to Wang Chaochang's word, the pebbled tunnel did not merely wend upward; the incline was straight, short, and steep. The cook had to pause every few steps. Finally, he waved them onward.

"Go. Find Prince Li. I will follow. Tell them to arrest me in the tunnel, but please put in a good word for me."

"We will," said Luan. "If indeed Prince Li occupies the drum and bell tower, and if this path leads there."

"I am telling the truth," said the cook, wilting against the wall, apparently in a mixture of physical exhaustion and sorrow.

"We will soon know," said Jade. "If you have lied to us, your blood will answer for it."

They had to bend forward from their waists to traverse the last few feet of the tunnel, and it was a relief when Luan lifted a door on the low ceiling and they could stand at full height in the opening. What they saw struck them with awe.

253

CHAPTER 56

unlight glinted off the famous twenty-four stone pillars that marched the perimeter of the ancient tower. The building was so fabled, they instantly knew they beheld the ancient drum and bell tower of imperial Nanjing. They had surfaced toward the rear of the building. When a guard on patrol marched into sight, they slipped back down into the tunnel, holding the trap door with their fingertips, settling it into its frame soundlessly. A moment later, Luan lifted the door an inch or two and watched as the guard strode around a corner, out of sight.

"Go!" Luan said to Jade, who bestirred herself to run toward a dark archway.

She melted into its shadows and stood stock still in the darkness as the guard approached again. Luan sent out a calming wave of qi toward the guard, who thoughtfully went on his way, his marching steps a little less sharp as they struck the paving stones. Luan pushed himself to his full height, lifting the door with his hands and putting it aside. He scrambled out from the tunnel and lowered the door into its frame. It was invisible from the street; its surface was painted and mottled to resemble street stones.

Luan reflected that Wang Chaochang would have to lift the door himself to exit the tunnel; judging by the man's seemingly waning strength, the tunnel was a good temporary prison for him. He joined Jade in the shadows. The archway opened to a door, and to their joy, the bolt was not shot inside. They slipped into the building.

Immediately, a cry went up from troops inside the tower and they were rushed upon, seized by the arms, and pushed and pulled roughly into the interior of the building. More soldiers brought chains to bind their wrists.

"Prince Li said he would like to see some Golden Ginkgo members up close," one of them growled, pulling painfully on the chains that bound their hands. "You'll do."

Another said, "I had heard Society women were plain and earnest. This one's earnest enough, but plain? Hello, sweetheart, are you really a Golden Ginkgo?"

Luan burned with anger at the way the guard's eyes slipped over Jade's face and figure, as if she were a treat designed for his pleasure.

"Indeed, she is not Golden Ginkgo. Nor am I. Take us to Prince Li if you would know who we are. He is well-acquainted with us," growled Luan, putting the force of his qi behind the words.

The guards, exchanged glances, then moved to obey him, hauling Jade and Luan into the next chamber and wrenching their chains so as to make them fall to the floor.

"Make obeisance to the prince," the head guard snarled at them.

Bruised and angry, they began to kowtow on the cold stone floor, but they tried hard to show their faces to Prince Li as they did so. Daylight from one of the tower windows fell upon Jade's fair face, lighting it up.

"Oh, oh, yes, yes, they are with us," said Prince Li almost absent-mindedly. "Yes, these are my father's people. They are covert agents here in Nanjing. Rise, General Luan Luan. My brothers will be glad to see you. Your espionage has been excellent. We received your messages and have come in confidence. The Golden Ginkgo Society is folding before us. The city is all but ours. My father and mother will be pleased."

Prince Li, a man in his early twenties, looked very proud of himself. Luan and Jade tried not to let their expressions show their thoughts. Prince Li and the other two sons had been fighting one another and living lives of decadence since their teenage years. Their father and mother had rarely been pleased with them. Some had whispered that once the Society crisis was resolved, the Emperor and Empress would face a succession crisis.

An imperial soldier from another division rushed in; he did not even make obeisances before choking out, "Prince Lon and Prince Shi are dead! An assassin infiltrated this building and struck them with poisoned darts!"

Prince Li and Luan turned ashen.

"No!" Prince Li shouted.

"We have apprehended the assassin," the troops said, as if this might comfort the prince.

"Bring him in!" thundered Prince Li. "I will kill him with my own hands."

"No, no," whispered Jade under her breath as Wang Chaochang appeared, pulled by two sweating guards who looked at the prince as if imploring him for mercy. The fat cook was refusing to walk on his own accord, and his feet dragged against the stone floor as the guards wrestled to steer his bulk toward the prince. They deposited him in front of the prince, where he huddled on the stone floor.

Prince Li grabbed a spear from one of the guards and stuck Wang Chaochang in his padded hindquarters, prodding him viciously. Wang Chaochang cried out in pain.

"Are you sure this is the man?" asked Luan. "Are you certain? In all fairness, this is the one who led Jade and me away from the palace and to this tower."

"On your knees!" Prince Li thundered at Wang Chaochang.

Wang Chaochang scrambled to his knees and nearly toppled over under his own weight. Prince Li ordered one of the guards to bring him a sword. The man hurriedly obeyed.

"Not sharp enough!" said the prince, feeling the edge of the blade and throwing the sword away with a clatter on the stone floor. "Bring me another!"

Prince Li tested the next sword's edge with his fingers, bringing up a bright red droplet of blood. He smeared the blood on Wang Chaochang's face.

"That is royal blood. That is as close as you will ever get to the lineal Dragon Throne of the Son of Heaven."

Luan interjected, "In all fairness, Wang Chaochang helped us find the drum and bell tower."

Prince Li raised the sword high above his own head.

Wang Chaochang screamed out, "Do you think I care whether I die or not now that my son is dead? But I will tell you this: you can kill me. You can kill my son. You can kill every member of the Golden Ginkgo, but our ideas will never die. Truth and justice live on!"

"Does murder live on in your scheme of justice?" queried Prince Li.

He pulled Wang Chaochang's head back by the long, greasy hair and made a neat, jugular-severing cut across the throat. When the corpulent body crumpled, Prince Li sawed at the neck with the sword and then held up the severed head by the hair.

"Thus die all traitors," he said. "Search his pockets to see if there is a copper's piece of value in his entire existence."

CHAPTER 57

Luan glanced at Jade. She looked pale and shocked at the events that were unfolding. Prince Li said, "Agents, search his pockets." Luan and Jade bent over the headless dead man and searched his pockets, ignoring the blood flowing from the severed stump of his neck.

"Many short orders from a Madam Viper," commented Luan, perusing a sheaf of letters from Wang Chaochang's pocket. "It seems they are in league. The orders seem to come from afar; she speaks as if she is not in the city."

"I have found signed notes from one using the Serpent symbol," said Jade. "Giving short orders as well."

"This man was very high up in the Society," said Luan. "It appears that he and Madam Viper were controlling Wei-Ling. I would say they are the highest in command of the organization."

"A woman?" said Prince Li with contempt. "So this man, this murderer of my brothers, was the co-chief of the Golden Ginkgo Society?"

"So it would appear," said Luan, scanning the pages in his hands. "He seems second only to Madam Viper as far as authority goes. Prince Li, here is a letter that asks permission from Madam Viper for Wei-Ling to insert lines about the official examination into his speeches. Wang Chaochang recommends such rhetoric."

"That permission was granted," nodded Jade. "We heard such a speech from Wei-Ling."

Prince Li ordered the body removed and burned, and asked Luan and Jade to accompany him to a more private chamber. They followed him to a smaller adjoining room, part of the inner tower, that had no windows. When the stone slab door was slammed shut, they were sealed in.

"Do you have any other information to impart?" asked Prince Li.

"It appears to me," said Luan slowly, "that Wang Chaochang was Wei-Ling's father. He controlled him from behind the scenes, posing as a mere servant. It also appears that Madam Viper and Wang Chaochang were husband and wife. Thus, Madam Viper is the mother of Wei-Ling."

"Hm," said Prince Li. "Father told me that Wei-Ling's birth origins are mysterious, and the Golden Ginkgo preferred to keep it that way to give him some mystique. Yet you say that Wei-Ling was a blind, a figurehead. He was a figurehead for his evil parents. Well, one down; one to go," added Prince Li, his face hardening. "We will find out who Madam Viper is. And now I, and I alone, am the heir to the Dragon Throne. Agents, you are to join the house to house canvass of the city, taking it back from the Society."

Such soldierly work was not usually given to spies or to the elite spousal teams, but Luan and Jade obeyed their prince. The city was entirely reclaimed for the Dragon Throne within a few days, and Luan and Jade were ordered back to the Nanjing palace.

The palace was alive with imperial soldiers, many now doing palace duty. Prince Li received Jade and Luan in the same imperial hall Wei-Ling had received them such a short time ago.

Luan and Jade made obeisance.

"You did your mission well," the prince told them when they had risen. "I have heard of everything you did during your espionage mission and you have been excellent warriors on behalf of my father, the Son of Heaven, these past few days. You will be richly rewarded in Beijing. Please go and prepare for immediate journey there. You deserve long baths, much food, and much rest after all your labors. My father is delighted that the city is regained, although he mourns my older brothers. He has declared them heroes, and is comforted to have raised such brave sons."

"Any man would be," murmured Luan politely.

After making more obeisances, the couple retired to Luan's room in the palace to prepare for their trip back to Beijing.

"I am worried about Silver Swan," said Jade to Luan. "She simply disappeared!"

"There are rumors that a woman dressed all in silver hoisted Wei-Ling's body on the balcony of his room and called out to the palace guards. She cried out in Chinese and then in Manchu: 'Your leader is dead! Surrender to the imperial troops who represent the true Son of Heaven!' She held a light up to his face and the troops were so distracted and full of despair at the sight that the imperial army had an easy time of breaking into the palace. The imperial officers were grateful to her and would have liked to thank her, but they could not find her. Perhaps she made her escape in the melee. I would not put anything beyond her capacities."

"Then you knew," said Jade. "You knew Willow was Silver Swan? Did the Emperor and Empress know?"

"Of course they did. They pretended not to, but we three have known of Willow's mission and her disguise since the death of her husband. That is why I never questioned her loyalty. I knew who she really was and what dangers and intrigues she had already participated in."

"I hope she is safe," said Jade. "She was ready to sacrifice her life for me. Urging me to escape while she stayed with the bodies of Wei-Ling and Black Dagger."

"She would have done that gladly if it was good for the empire."

"To think I have hated her so," said Jade regretfully. "I hope she is alive, and I have a chance to do her a good turn."

"Perhaps we will meet her in Beijing," said Luan. "Now make haste, please. We have a journey before us."

CHAPTER 58

In spite of the re-taking of Nanjing for the empire, the atmosphere in Beijing was not celebratory. Jade noticed it immediately as soon as they arrived in the Forbidden City. There was a solemnity about and fear.

"Something is wrong," she told Luan.

"Yes, I feel it too," said Luan. "I almost smell blood in the air."

"Because of the deaths of the princes, perhaps?"

"I doubt it. I think the Emperor is happy that they at last lived up to their royal blood and acted heroically on the empire's behalf. Better that than the wastrel lives they were leading. Of course, there will be ceremonial mourning, but this qi is different."

"I agree," said Jade.

The closer they approached the inner rooms of the Celestial Palace, the more oppressive the atmosphere became. There seemed to be suspicion everywhere. At last they entered the Inner Court of the Hall of Heavenly Harmony.

The Son of Heaven and his wife the Empress were dressed in white, the color of mourning, and were seated on the large, round, yellow silken chair upon the dais. The two man-high, matching Ming vases seemed to frown down upon everyone from their sentinel positions at either side of their majesties.

Liu Huimin, smooth-faced, solemn, stood behind the Empress, who was clearly grieving her sons. Liu Huimin was holding a papyrus roll. Jade and Luan entered the room, made obeisances, and took places among the small crowd of warriors and nobles gathered there.

"Wong Lung," intoned Liu Huimin, reading a name from the papyrus roll, and a man was brought forward by imperial palace guards.

"You are Wong Lung?" asked Liu Huimin.

"Yes."

"Wong Lung, refugee from Nanjing, convicted of treason against their majesties via membership in the Golden Ginkgo Society. Do your duty, swordsman," Liu Huimin said.

Wong Lung was forced to kneel. A palace swordsman came forward and struck the man's head from his shoulders.

"Executions in the Inner Court of the Hall of Heavenly Harmony!" whispered Jade. "Indeed, something is terribly awry!"

Liu Huimin calmly crossed off the name from her list. Servants came forward and removed the bloodied torso and head and mopped up the blood. Fresh cloth was lain for the next unfortunate on the list.

"Willow, otherwise known as Silver Swan," called out Liu Huimin. "Refugee from Nanjing, convicted of treason as a double agent for the Golden Ginkgo Society. Do your duty, swordsman."

Silver Swan came forward. She shook her shimmering arms, glad in white silk with silver threads, until they were free of the guards who would hold her. She looked at Liu Huimin with contempt, and, with a graceful and elaborate bow, positioned herself to be beheaded. It was almost as if she were doing an elaborate dance. Her black hair shone with health and jeweled ornaments that glittered as much as her eyes.

"No!" Jade shouted. "Your majesties! This woman saved my life!"

The Emperor seemed to awaken from a somnolent state of sorrow. He stared at Jade as if he did not recognize her, but his eyes livened at the sight of Luan.

"General Luan," he said, almost brokenly. "Control your wife."

"Yes, your majesty," said Luan. "Jade, mind yourself."

Jade went up on tiptoe to whisper in his ear.

"The atmosphere is thick with lies, intrigues and obfuscations! You can feel it as well as I." There was fear in her voice. "No one is safe in this atmosphere. Speak up, please! They will listen to you."

"I will try," he whispered back as Liu Huimin shook her scroll, cleared her throat, and was about to read the indictment again.

"Your majesties!" cried Luan. "I beg for your ears for just a moment's time. Silver Swan executed Wei-Ling and one known as Black Dagger. Both were very high up in the Golden Ginkgo Society. As you know Wei-Ling was the movement's young face, and Black Dagger was an assassin and enforcer. Silver Swan is a patriot, not a double agent."

Liu Huimin's face tightened in annoyance and then relaxed into her usual smooth calm. "Then why does she has two names and two identities—one for among us and one for Nanjing?"

"Their majesties have long known of Silver Swan's espionage and activities. She is a well-known double agent for our side. There is no evidence that she has turned traitor. I ask permission for my wife to recount Silver Swan's noble actions."

Jade spoke out boldly. She recounted how Wei-Ling had appointed her chief concubine, and how Silver Swan had saved her from violation by Wei-Ling and had also killed him after beguiling from him much knowledge about the Society.

"Because of Silver Swan, we learned that Wei-Ling was a puppet, being manipulated by his parents. Because of Silver Swan, we know that his parents are the real powers behind the Golden Ginkgo, like a shadow Emperor and Empress. We do not know who they are, but we can trace some lineage. Black Dagger was the brother of Madam Viper, whom we suspect was Wei-Ling's mother and the shadow Empress of the Society. We know Wang Chaochang, who posed as a cook, was Wei-Ling's father and the second-in-command of the GGS. Because of Silver Swan, the palace troops were demoralized when she displayed Wei-Ling's dead body on the balcony of his room, calling on them to surrender to the imperial army. She is a heroine of great courage!" Jade stopped, out of breath.

Silver Swan glanced at her, and Jade knew she had repaid her debt to the woman who had saved her life.

"Release Silver Swan," the Emperor ordered, and even though Liu Huimin's mouth pursed in disapproval, and she moved reluctantly, she nodded to the guards to do so.

The Empress said, "Enough of these depressing executions! Clearly these cases must be investigated further before more injustice is done that rightly enflames the hearts of the people against the Dragon Throne."

"Your majesty is wise," said Luan, and the Emperor seemed to rouse up further.

"Liu Huimin, give those scrolls to my legal scholars to investigate. The people may be put under house arrest, nothing further."

Instantly, golden light seemed to burst in through the windows and the thrall and smell of death retreated. Silver Swan hurried to Jade and Luan and clasped hands with them.

Liu Huimin, her eyes flickering beneath their lids, merely looked from them to the royal couple and back.

She approached them and said, "There was nothing personal about this, of course. I was given the roll of names by others."

"Of course," said Jade. She looked closely at Liu Huimin's eyes, which were bleak with sorrow and suffering. "It is clear you do not enjoy this duty. You have been crying not long ago."

"I mourn the dead princes," said Liu Huimin. "That is the source of my sorrow."

Jade was surprised, as the princes were not highly regarded in the Forbidden City, where their excesses were well known. She worried for Huimin, a woman who had shown her much help, advice, and concern. What was really wrong with Huimin that she grieved from a sorrow that seemed as deep as her bones?

CHAPTER 59

I've nothing to wear," complained Jade. "Ah! How often a husband hears those words," said Luan, a small smile twitching his lips as if amused that she would express so feminine and ordinary a concern.

They were in the bedchamber they had shared on their wedding night, getting ready for a banquet called to celebrate the return of Nanjing to imperial power. There was a faint knock at the door, and Luan called out that the visitor should come in. It was Ching and Anbai. Jade and Anbai cried out excitedly to see one another.

"It's a joyful day after all!" said Jade. "In spite of all our losses."

"It is so good to be back in Beijing with all our friends!" cried Anbai. "It is a joyful day indeed!"

The women could not stop hugging one another, while Ching and Luan began an animated discussion about the political situation of the former Golden Ginkgo Society members who had been captured — what they thought should be done with them, and what reforms the Dragon Throne would need to undertake to address the Society's legitimate concerns.

"I do not think summary executions will win lukewarm Society supporters back," said Luan. "And if we don't win them back, the Golden Ginkgo or some society like it will rise again."

"The Dragon Throne is weakened," agreed Ching frankly. "And there is but one male heir, and he is of uneven temperament and untried by real hardship."

"Yes," said Luan. "All has not been resolved by the re-taking of Nanjing."

"Look," said Anbai to Jade, showing her a small satchel she carried. "Silver Swan gave this to me today."

She opened the satchel and drew out a beautiful dress of silver silk, flowing like a moonlit waterfall down in delicate folds. Embroidered along the hem were tone-on-tone silver swans.

"Oh, that is exquisite," murmured Jade. "You will look very nice in it."

"It is for you. Silver Swan asked me to give it to you as a token of her gratitude for how you defended her before the royals and saved her life."

"She saved my life too; she owes me nothing."

"She wanted you to have it."

Anbai turned to Ching. "I think we should go. Jade and Luan must dress."

"But Luan was just telling me about how the prince decapitated old Wang Chaochang," protested Ching.

"We need to go," urged Anbai, smiling.

"We will talk more at the banquet," Luan promised Ching, and Ching and Anbai left the couple alone in the room.

Luan turned to Jade. Letting the shimmering silver silk play over her hands, she was very thoughtful. Peace filled her. She rose to change, but Luan stopped her.

"We have not made love since the island," he told her. "I would enjoy a feast of love with you before the feast of the banquet before us."

Jade remembered how she had suspected and accused Luan of killing her first husband. She had been so unfair to him. His was truly a noble heart. She felt sorry to have doubted him, and grateful for all the adventures they had successfully shared.

Luan gently took the silver dress and tossed it aside, while Jade, smilingly, held out her arms to him.

*   *   *

Luan gasped when saw his wife wearing the silver dress, which draped beautifully over the curves of her slender body, he gasped. Her hair, brushed and oiled, was piled on top of her head and threaded with pearls. She was stunningly beautiful, and he was proud she was his. Their lovemaking was like a happy secret between them as they regally walked to the banquet hall.

"You look like an Empress," he told her. "I cannot imagine that any woman could so intrigue, frustrate, satisfy, and comfort a man in grief for another woman so well as you have done. I already love you, and everything seems new."

"Let us sit next to Anbai and Ching in the hall so you can talk to Ching and I can be with my dear friend and fellow wife Anbai," smiled Jade. "By the way, in your yellow and red silk robes, you look like an Emperor. Indeed, you are the Emperor of my heart."

He paused to bow to her. "I would wish no greater title."

When the impressive young couple entered the banquet hall, even Prince Li rose. They were embarrassed by the applause bestowed upon them and gracefully bowed and made their obeisance to their majesties, who were applauding like everyone else. They made their way to their banquet seats near Ching and Anbai, both with high color in their cheeks from all the warmth, attention, and excitement. Then they quietly found one another's hands under the banquet table and held on all throughout the meal, with small smiles playing across both of their faces as their newfound love for one another throbbed in their hearts.

Yet as Jade finished her silver bowl of hot rice with seven fruits — a rice used on celebratory occasions — she saw a small, folded up piece of paper in the bottom of it.

"No," she whispered. "No." She nudged Luan then, eyes darting to and fro, she brought the note down near their laps so that both she and Luan could read it.

The note said: *They killed my husband and my son. I will have vengeance. In ninety days, the empire will fall.* It carried Madam Viper's signature mark.

"The Society is not defeated," said Luan ruefully. "One of its principals--the main one--remains alive and active. Our work is not finished yet."

Jade's eyes sought Luan's, but his were already flickering over the banquet hall, checking person after person, looking for hints and sensing qi, searching for clues as to the source of the note.

"Do you notice anything amiss?" Jade asked him.

"Only that Liu Huimin is not in her usual place by the Empress's side. I do not see her here. That is unusual."

"Liu Huimin's loyalty is not in question," said Jade huffishly, sipping wine. "She has the Empress's complete confidence. She could not be Madam Viper."

Luan sighed. "Probably not. Yet there are always intrigues, threats, and dangers, and many of them are very close to the Dragon Throne. But do not worry. We will find and identify Madam Viper once and for all and uncover and defeat her plots. I believe in you--I believe in myself--and I believe in us."

They clicked their silver goblets, their eyes meeting in trust and love, united in heart, purpose, and loyalty to the Dragon Throne.

SPECIAL OFFER FOR READERS

Register now to receive Special Offers as well as the Exclusive Sneak Peek of the Todd's upcoming novel, *The Emperor's Last Arrow* (Book 2 of the Dew on Ginkgo Leaves series) when it arrives early 2018. Join fellow fans at <u>www.dewonginkgoleaves.com</u>

About the Author

270

Todd L. Shuler is an internationally known management consultant, bestselling author and speaker. Todd is the author of *Dew on Ginkgo Leaves: The Tigress and The General, The Tiger Tamer: Managing and Transforming Your Business Without Getting Eaten Alive, The Well-Watered Life and One Month of the Well-Watered Life Devotional*. This is his fourth book.

For previews of his upcoming books and more information about Todd Shuler, please visit him at <u>www.toddshuler.com</u> or follow him on social media - Facebook, Twitter (@toddlshuler) and Instagram (toddlshuler).

271